"Funny, bruta̶̶̶̶̶̶̶̶̶̶̶̶̶̶̶̶̶̶̶̶̶̶̶̶̶̶̶̶̶̶̶̶̶̶̶̶ly

"Gough is one of the most inventively reliable bloodsmiths in the trade. His plots and characters are strong and convincing, his mordant humour never forced, the action violent but believable."
— *The Times* (London)

"Gough's pacing never slows . . . his light-hearted yet straightforward, carefully plotted procedurals stand up well against the best in the business."
— *Lansing State Journal*

"Gough's greatest gift is his ability to produce some of the sleaziest bad guys in the business."
— *Halifax Chronicle-Herald*

"Gough is a real find. . . . For anyone into hardboiled American fiction, try heading north of the border for a treat."
— *Vox*

"Gough's characters come to life with his wry humour."
— *Calgary Herald*

"Gough's work is laced with acid humour and tight-as-a-chokehold prose. If he lived in the U.S., he'd already be a superstar."
— *Daily Post* (Liverpool, England)

"Gough is one of the best crime writers in the country. . . . His murder mysteries are of the hardboiled variety, but with a wickedly twisted brand of black comedy. . . . Wild and wingy rollercoaster rides."
— *Toronto Sun*

"[Gough] routinely serves up sharp, tightly written novels. . . ."
— *Gazette* (Montreal)

"For those who like the genre, it is no easier to put down a Gough crime novel than it is to step off a swiftly moving train."
— *Whig-Standard* (Kingston)

ALSO BY LAURENCE GOUGH

FUNNY MONEY

LAURENCE GOUGH

M&S

Cloth edition published in 2000
First paperback edition published in 2002

National Library of Canada Cataloguing in Publication Data

Gough, Laurence
Funny money

(A Willows and Parker mystery)
ISBN 0-7710-3544-6

I. Title. II. Series: Gough, Laurence. Willows and Parker mystery.

PS8563.O8393F86 2002   C813.'54   C2001-903279-X
PR9199.3.G652F86 2002

We acknowledge the financial support of the Government of Canada through the Book Publishing Industry Development Program for our publishing activities. We further acknowledge the support of the Canada Council for the Arts and the Ontario Arts Council for our publishing program.

Cover photograph: Renzo Cattoni
Typeset in Minion by M&S, Toronto
Printed and bound in Canada

McClelland & Stewart Ltd.
The Canadian Publishers
481 University Avenue
Toronto, Ontario
M5G 2E9
www.mcclelland.com

1 2 3 4 5   06 05 04 03 02

Thanks to my editor, Pat Kennedy, are long overdue. Pat's boundless energy, tact, keen perception, and unflagging good humour are largely responsible for whatever success this series has achieved.

"Send in the clowns"
  – Stephen Sondheim, as sung by Sarah Vaughan

"Every game has its rules."
  – Humbert Humbert, in *Lolita* by Vladimir Nabokov

1

Detective Claire Parker turned the shower's nozzle so the spray of water beat against the tiled wall. She pushed back the frosted glass door, snatched a towel off the rack and stepped onto the oval bath carpet. Quickly towelling herself off, she went to the open door and called out to her fellow detective and lover, Jack Willows, who was in the bedroom, just down the hall.

"I'm out of the shower, Jack."

She waited a moment and then called out again.

"Jack, you there?"

Apparently not. She slipped into her terrycloth robe. She'd forgotten to turn on the ceiling fan, and the bathroom was like a sauna. She flipped the switch, and the air began to clear. Where was Jack? She continued to towel dry her hair as she left the bathroom. She'd expected to find him in bed, but the duvet was turned aside and he wasn't there. She went to the top of the stairs.

"Jack, where are you?"

Willows was in the main-floor den, watching the nightly half-hour sports round-up on Global and nursing a nip of Cutty on the rocks. He started guiltily as he heard Claire calling him.

Fifteen minutes earlier he'd felt sexy as hell. When Claire had said she was going to take a shower, he'd offered to wash her back, and been turned down. She didn't like sharing the shower and he didn't blame her because, somehow, without meaning to, he always ended up between her and the water. A shower could be a cold and lonely place. Rejected, he'd stayed downstairs, poured himself a small drink and flopped down in front of the TV. A tactical error, because the instant he stretched out on the couch, a week full of too-long days came crashing heavily down on him, and it was all he could do to keep his eyes open.

Claire called out to him again. He fumbled for the remote, killed the television, and sat up. He drained his glass. When a man dozed off in the middle of the first drink of the evening, the poor guy was getting old. He turned off the light and walked down the hall to the foot of the stairs.

"Be right there, honey."

Claire smiled down at him. "Fell asleep, didn't you?"

"No, but I was doing some awfully deep thinking. I'll be up in a minute. I'm just going to check the locks."

Willows prowled around the house. Tripod, their three-legged marmalade cat, was balanced precariously on the outside sill of the kitchen window. He went to the back door and let him in, and shut the door and shot the deadbolt. Walking back down the hall, he noticed that Sean's light was on, and tapped lightly.

"Who is it?"

"Dad."

"Come on in."

Willows pushed open the door. Sean was in bed, lying on his side, reading and making notes. A high-school dropout, Sean had spent several years in the minimum-wage wilderness. His dead-end career as a convenience-store clerk ended when he was shot and seriously wounded during a robbery. This traumatic event turned his life around. To everyone's surprise he applied for admittance to Simon Fraser University as a mature student. He was in his second semester, had a 3.8 grade-point average and had never been happier in his life. Gone, probably forever, was his tattered Kiss poster. Which was okay. What bothered Willows, a lot, was that Sean was a criminology major and wanted to become a police officer.

Willows said, "Hitting the books?"

"Got a quiz tomorrow."

"Don't forget to get a good night's sleep. There's no point in studying all night and sleeping through the exam."

Sean rolled his eyes. "Right, Dad. Thanks for reminding me."

Willows' daughter Annie's bedroom door was shut. He had stopped looking in on her about a year ago, at her request. His children kept getting older, and it seemed that hardly a day passed when they didn't find another small but significant and inevitably wounding way to separate from him. Against all his expectations, being a parent just kept getting harder and harder. His role kept changing, diminishing. But at the same time there seemed no end to it. With luck, he'd keep on worrying about Annie and Sean until the day he died.

The front door was locked but he gave it a rattle anyway, out of habit. He started up the stairs, and saw that Claire was still standing by the railing. She was the most beautiful woman he'd ever seen. His pace quickened. Suddenly he wasn't so tired after all.

2

Carlos was driving. Why not, since it was his van, paid for with cash involuntarily provided by a mid-level drug dealer who was now nourishing the rose gardens in Stanley Park. Carlos braked hard for a red light. Where did *that* came from? Rubber skidded on rain-slick asphalt.

Hector mimed abject terror. "Take it easy! *Tap* the brake, don't stomp on it."

Carlos gave his partner a hard look. "Got a driver's licence, Hector? No, you don't. You barely got a licence to be a moron. When your mom got herself under control she told me you were twenty years old before you learned to walk." The van straddled the white lines of a crosswalk. Carlos shifted into reverse and backed up. "That better? Are you happy now?"

"No, I'm not happy. Take a look around. Who d'you see? Cops? Flattened pedestrians?"

Carlos glanced suspiciously around. "I don't see nobody."

"That's right, you don't. Know why? Dumb luck. Just because you got a licence, don't mean you can drive. Anybody can buy a licence. Don't think for a minute that you are in any small way superior to me. You aren't. In fact, chances are excellent that because you actually have a licence you are a far worse driver than I could hope to ever be."

"Oh yeah?"

"Yeah."

Carlos turned to the girl sitting between them, squatting down low in the gap between the bucket seats. He ruffled her damp, stringy hair. "What's your name again, baby?"

"Chantal."

"Got a driver's licence, baby?"

She gave him a fleeting, worried smile. "No, I don't."

"But you will if I want you to, right?" Carlos slapped his thigh, signifying high good humour.

Hector said, "Leave her alone. She's just a kid."

"Right. Little Miss Innocent. How old you gotta be to get a driver's licence, sixteen? How old are you?"

"Old enough."

Carlos laughed. "Ain't that the truth."

The light for cross traffic turned yellow. Carlos gunned it through the last of the red. He made a pistol of his fist and pointed it at Hector. "Don't say a word. Not a word. It takes no brains at all to move on a green light. People do it all the time, it's a no-brainer. Keeping your eyes open, seeing that the light's gonna change, *anticipation*, that's what separates people like you from people like me."

"Suddenly I feel so much wiser," said Hector.

Carlos pulled the van tight against the curb. The front bumper nicked a fire hydrant, causing the vehicle to rock on its springs. "Who put that there?" Carlos turned to Hector. "Pay the bitch." He put the van in park and got out, slammed the door and walked away.

Hector gave Chantal a twitchy, patently insincere smile. "What do I owe you?"

She shrugged. "For everything, or just you?"

"Both of us."

"What did I quote you, was it a hundred?"

Hector frowned. "Yeah, I think that's right."

"But that was, you know . . . I mean, when I said a hundred, that was for, like . . . What time is it?"

The dashboard clock was broken, the glass dial smashed a few days earlier by Carlos' angry fist. Hector shot the sleeve of his black leather jacket, and tilted his wrist to the flickering light of a red and blue neon sign. "Just past eleven." Another twisted smile. "Time flies, huh?"

"How about, would two-fifty be okay?"

"Ouch!"

"Tell me about it." She touched her bruised cheek and then put her hand on his knee. "Two and a half's reasonable. You know it is. I mean, if I broke it down, charged the both of you a separate amount for everything, it'd cost you at least three hundred."

"*Each?*"

"No, for both of you. What I'm saying, you get what you pay for, and you got a lot." She mustered a smile. "You're a nice guy, Hector. Unlike your buddy. If you'd like to see me again sometime, that would be real nice. But right now, it's time for me to move on. I don't get home pretty quick, my boyfriend's going to have a fucking seizure."

"You got a boyfriend? What's his name?"

"I can't tell you that."

"Why not?"

"I just can't."

Hector rubbed his chin. He leaned back in the seat, turned his brain into a metronome and counted off the strokes of the windshield wipers. Carlos had them on medium speed, about forty beats per minute. The glass was speckled with rain, and then it was clean, and then it was speckled with rain again. It was kind of restful, though he wasn't sure why.

He said, "Boyfriend. You call him a boyfriend, but he isn't your boyfriend. He's a scum-of-the-earth pimp."

"No he isn't. He loves me."

Hector snorted derisively. He and Carlos had picked Chantal up on Richards, a downtown street noted for its club life and broad range of hookers of both sexes, and more. Chantal was slim, bordering on emaciated. Her dyed blond hair was cut short, and streaked with fiery red. She wore heavy black boots, torn jeans, and a fake leopardskin jacket that was several sizes too large for her. The overall look was rough-trade waifish, calculated to appeal to middle-aged pervos whose daughters had finally fled their unhappy homes. Something about her had immediately appealed to Hector. Her stance, the perky look in her eyes . . . A lot of girls refused to get in a van. A lot of girls would turn down a ride with Carlos if he were behind the wheel of a Rolls-Royce.

Hector said, "You may not realize it, Chantal, but your pimp boyfriend is nothing but a bloodsucking parasite."

"No, you're wrong. He loves me, but he can't get a job. What're we supposed to do, starve to death?"

Hector popped open the glove compartment. He poked around in the darkness until he found what he was looking for, an army-surplus World War II–era bayonet. "Hold still a minute, don't move." The long blade came within inches of her throat as he eased past her into the van's cargo space. He grunted as he stabbed the knife into a cardboard box. He waved the knife at her. "What're you looking at? Turn around!"

Hector was back in less than a minute, his fist crammed with crisp new American twenties.

"One, two, three, four, five, six . . ." He lost patience, and separated a quarter-inch-thick wad of bills from the mass. "Here you go, this oughta do it."

Chantal reflexively began to count the money, but quickly realized it would be wiser to let it go. She glanced anxiously around, through the windshield and side windows, into the van's rain-streaked side mirrors. No Carlos, but that didn't mean he wasn't just around the corner. There was something about Carlos that wasn't quite right, even by her low standards. She doubted he was married. No woman, no matter how desperate, would marry a creep like him. Carlos was mean-spirited, with an angry, shrivelled heart. You had to watch out for guys like him, keep them under control and not let them get emotional, because once they got started, they couldn't stop, and things could turn bad so quick you couldn't even believe it.

Chantal had become very good at reading people, and Carlos was definitely the scariest trick she'd ever met. The kind of cold-hearted sonofabitch who could slice a girl open, smoke a cigarette while he watched her bleed to death, then roll her up in a carpet and toss her in a dumpster, go home and laugh his head off watching a "Seinfeld" rerun. She'd talked to some of the other girls about creeps like Carlos. Everybody knew they were out there, but at the same time they were kind of an urban legend, because nobody had ever actually run into anybody like that. Or at least lived to tell about it.

She had to crawl across Hector to get out of the van. When he grabbed her and pulled her close, she couldn't stop herself from uttering a pipsqueak scream. He immediately let go of her. The light was dim, but he looked offended.

"Hey, I'm not like that. I wouldn't hurt a cute kid like you!" He pushed open the door. "Beat it, sweetheart."

Chantal crawled awkwardly across his lap. He managed to score one last grope before she could get out of the van. She shrugged into her leopardskin coat as she hurried across Robson Street towards the bright lights of a McDonald's. Behind her, the van door slammed shut.

Hector watched her until she'd vanished into the restaurant. A ragged group of street kids huddled under an awning just up the street. One of the kids had waved at Chantal, but she'd ignored him. Hector decided that, if he ever had a daughter, he hoped she grew up just like her. Not a hooker, but somebody who was pretty, and had guts.

He leaned forward and turned up the volume of the police scanner on the dashboard. There'd been a collision on the Cambie Street bridge, two road-rage drones fighting for the same lane, duelling wannabe Nascar types. Pretty dull stuff, but not as bad as the tow-truck or fire-hall channels. He reached across and adjusted the speed of the windshield wipers. Now they were really moving, frantically slapping back and forth across glass, tossing sheets of water off to the side. Hector was studying his watch, timing the cycle, when Carlos got back into the van.

Hector shied away from him. "Man, you're soaked! Where'd you go, to get some smokes?"

"Had to make a call."

"Whyn't you say so? You coulda used my cell. Assuming you got a quarter."

Carlos patted himself down, found his cigarettes, shook one free of the pack and lit up with his disposable lighter. "No, Jake told me I got to use a land line, a pay phone. He says cellphones ain't safe, 'cause anybody can listen in. Like with the scanner, that easy. Jake told me, without security, all you got is insecurity."

"So, what'd he say?"

Carlos jerked his thumb at the cardboard boxes in the back of the van. "Nothin'. I talked to Marty. He said Jake couldn't come to the phone. He's sick, got some kind of problem with his heart."

"Like it's been missing forever and nobody can find it."

Carlos flicked ash onto the floor. "You never said that, and I never heard it." He took a moment to compose himself. "What happened, Jake had a stroke. They took him away in an ambulance. He might live, but then again he might not. Nobody knows except God, and he ain't talking."

"Not to you, anyway."

Carlos nodded. No point in arguing that one.

Hector said, "What're we supposed to do with the money?"

"Marty's the man, for now. He says we gotta hold on to it until he figures out what to do."

Hector didn't like that one little bit. He and Carlos were unbonded short-haul couriers. They'd been freelancing for drug kingpin Jake Cappalletti for about six months, had started out carting rolls of quarters to Jake's illegal slot machines, worked their way up the ladder rung by rung. The cardboard boxes in the back of the van held ten million in bogus U.S. twenties, fifties and hundreds. The money was destined for the ravenous, wonderfully unsophisticated Russian market, where it would fetch as much as fifty cents on the dollar.

Hector and Carlos, short-haul couriers with short-haul attention spans, were ideally suited to their job. But now, the way Hector saw it, Marty had plunked them down in a unique and scary situation.

He said, "This ain't right."

"What're you talking about?"

"Ten million bucks. How long we supposed to hold on to all that cash? You don't know, because Marty didn't say. Which means we got to hang around until he gives us a call. How many guys know about the money? I don't know and neither do you. But what I do know is that we both know plenty of guys would gladly whack us for the ten, never mind all them zeros."

Carlos turned up the scanner's volume, but Hector wasn't finished, and he turned the volume back down again.

"We were hired to move a quantity of money over a specific distance during a given time. We agreed to perform this task for a reasonable remuneration. But now we're gettin' screwed, and I don't like it."

Carlos slapped Hector on the shoulder. "Look, what we got here is a once-in-a-lifetime opportunity. I agree: if we screw up, we're Alpo. But we ain't gonna screw up. Somebody tries to rob us, we'll blast 'em. Also, Jake's a pretty ruthless guy, but he's fair-minded. He pays top dollar, and he'll stand up for you if something happens and it ain't your fault. You need bail, you got bail. Also, I heard he's got a dental plan."

Carlos took a hard pull on his cigarette, drew back his lips and forcefully expelled smoke from the many gaps between his teeth. He powered down his window and flicked the cigarette butt into the rain. "I'm tired of bein' an independent criminal. Jake's stroke gave us a chance at a full-time job. Be happy."

Hector was not much short of astounded. His brain felt as if it had been twisted like a pretzel. There were few constants in his life, but in the simple yet sometimes complex symbiotic relationship that was Hector and Carlos, he'd always thought of his buddy as the homicidal muscle, and himself as the brains of the outfit. Now here was Carlos with a light bulb suspended over his head, the idea man. It took some getting used to.

Hector considered the situation. Jake was a plenty smart dude. Chances were excellent that he and Marty were the only guys who knew about the ten million. Except, of course, for the guys who'd printed the stuff. But they were too smart to mess with Jake, or anybody working for him, so they were no threat. So, boiling it down, all he and Carlos had to worry about was cops, and if the cops weren't onto them by now, it wasn't going to happen.

"Okay, you're right. All we got to do is sit tight, wait for Marty's call, and then hand over the cash like the honest and dependable crooks we are, at the same time letting Marty know we're looking to get on the payroll."

"Now you're talking!" said Carlos jovially. Identical presences, dark, sharp-toothed and feral, scuttled across his close-set eyes and vanished in perfect synchronization down the black holes of his pupils.

Hector intuitively realized that his partner in crime had done a little math and decided that Hector was worth something less than ten million dollars. No, wait. That was paranoia rearing its ugly head. If Carlos bumped him and scrammed with the cash, who'd watch his back when Marty came a-calling?

Carlos wasn't going to kill him, at least not until he'd talked him into squibbing Marty. With Marty gone, and Jake on his deathbed, Jake's carefully constructed empire would collapse. Drugs, prostitution, gambling . . . the whole damn city would be ripe for the taking. There'd be a bloodbath, as over-ambitious hoods and punks jostled for position. The Vietnamese and Russian and South American gangs would slaughter each other. Who'd care about a few boxes of funny money that got lost in the confusion? Nobody.

At least so Hector reasoned.

3

The minimum-wage kid cleaning the glass door skipped nimbly aside as Chantal forcibly pushed by him. The McDonald's on Main Street was always crowded, no matter how late the hour. There were a lot of Asian families in the neighbourhood, and a nearby SkyTrain station fed the restaurant an unpredictable mix of ordinary people and drug dealers and laterally mobile thieves.

Chantal saw that there were only two cash registers open. Both had long lineups. She leaned over the counter and caught the roving eye of a boy working a deep fryer. She crooked a finger, showed him a crumpled five. He glanced warily around, looking for the manager, gave his stainless-steel rack a brisk shake, put it down, and sauntered over.

"Yeah, what's up?"

Chantal slipped him the five. "Gimme something to drink."

"Thirsty, huh?" He gave her a knowing look. "What d'you want?"

"I don't know . . . an orange pop. C'mon, hurry up, let's go!"

The kid, money in hand, let her see he didn't like being pushed. Stuffing the bill into his pocket, he wandered over to the soft-drink machine. Turning, he gave her the third and probably last look in his limited repertoire – sly and sexy. "What size you want?"

"Small, so you can handle it."

Oops, four looks. Scowling and blushing, the kid poured the drink, expertly and mindlessly secured the plastic lid, and slammed the waxed paper cup down on the counter.

Chantal walked rapidly towards the washrooms. She knew she wouldn't have to ask for a key to the washroom because, even at this late hour, there were a lot of little kids running around. When a kid needed to take a leak, there was no time to go and get a key. Better by far to risk a junkie in the washrooms than a puddle of urine on the floor. She pushed open the door. The washroom was empty. She went over to the sink and splashed water on her face. In the bright glare of the fluorescent lights her skin was pale and grainy, her mouth too red, her eyes too large and far too dark, bruised and vulnerable, the windows of a visibly tattered soul. She yanked the top off the soft-drink container, rinsed out her mouth and forcibly spat a mouthful of orange pop at the mirror. She rinsed and spat again and again, splattering the mirror and walls and sink and her hair and face with bright orange. Two women entered the washroom, chattering animatedly. One look, and they were gone. Chantal sluiced out her mouth again, went into a cubicle and locked it.

She pulled the wad of money Hector had given her out of her pocket. During her time working the street she had learned that the customer was always wrong, and could never be trusted. The rules were simple. When negotiating, never take less than the going rate. No cheques! Payment in advance of services. Count the money, and then count it again. She'd broken the rule with Hector and Carlos, but that was because she hadn't realized there were two men in the van. She'd worked out a mutually acceptable rate with Carlos, and climbed into the van and slammed the door. She'd noticed that the dome light hadn't come on, but that didn't trigger any alarms, because a lot of guys screwed with their lights. Carlos told her to buckle up so the cops wouldn't have a reason to pull them over. As he drove away Chantal snapped her fingers and told him pay up or pull over. That was when Hector came out from behind a cardboard box in the back of the van. He'd seen the look in her eyes and given her a friendly smile, told her to relax and promised her this was her lucky day.

As she counted her hard-earned cash, a quarter-inch-thick stack of American twenties, Chantal was surprised to discover that Hector had not lied. She'd asked him for two hundred and fifty dollars, an outrageous amount, given the neighbourhood she worked in. Hector had paid her almost a thousand dollars. Amazing. She counted the money again, and double-checked her math. Nine hundred and sixty bucks. Talk about easy money. What was an American twenty worth? A least thirty bucks. If she gave Nick half the money and went to a bank tomorrow and exchanged the rest of it for Canadian currency, she could take a couple of nights off and he'd never know about it.

A fist pounded on the cubicle door. "Open up! Come out of there, or I'll call the police!" Chantal sucked in her stomach and stuffed the twenties inside her panties, then stood up and unlocked the door. The washroom was filled with self-righteous McDonald's employees, led by a pint-sized manager who took his dead-end job far too seriously.

She held up her hands in mock surrender. "Okay, I give up, you got me."

"Look at the mess you've made! What's that matter with you? Get out now or I'll have you arrested!"

"All right, I'm leaving." He tried to take her arm and she grabbed his skinny wrist and put his hand to her breast. He pulled away as if she'd tried to brand him. Smiling, she said, "There, now you have something to dream about tonight."

Outside, rain hammered the pavement. There was a pay phone at the far end of the parking lot. If she called a cab, she could be home in twenty minutes.

Hunching her shoulders against a sudden gust of wind, she zipped up her faux leopardskin jacket and started walking.

4

Parker, wearing dark-blue silk pyjamas, opened the mirrored door of the clothes closet. There was only one bathroom in the house and the mornings were always hectic, so she'd gotten into the habit of choosing the next day's clothes before going to bed. Her three black VPD uniforms hung in plastic bags at the far end of the rack. Rank had its privileges. Foremost among those privileges, from Parker's point of view, was that she was hardly ever required to wear a uniform.

It was mid-October, and the Channel 11 weatherman had forecast cloudy skies and temperatures in the mid-teens Celsius. After some deliberation, Parker chose a cream-coloured blouse, chocolate-brown slacks, and a burgundy cashmere boat-neck sweater that Jack had given her for Christmas a few years earlier. She hung the clothes from a hook on the door, then shut the door and examined herself in the mirror. Her hair and lipstick looked fine. She unfastened the top button of her pyjamas. A little cleavage was a good thing. She unfastened another button. There, much better.

She plumped up the pillows and got into bed and settled the duvet around her. There was a half-read novel on the night table, but she was in no mood for reading. She turned on the Victorian lamp with its frosted glass shade shaped like a crescent moon. The lamp was equipped with a ten-watt bulb. She and Willows had bought it in an antique store in Seattle during a weekend vacation the previous spring. The drumming of the shower stopped. She leaped out of bed, hurried across the room, turned off the ceiling light and got back into bed.

In the bathroom, Willows stepped onto the scale and watched the numbers spin around, then slide back and steady. He'd gained five pounds in the past three months. He'd read somewhere that men tended to try to eat away their worries. If it was true, it explained everything, because he was worried as hell about Annie. She'd always been an enthusiastic, hardworking student. All through high school, she'd never missed the honour roll. Now she was in her first year at UBC, the University of British Columbia. Overnight, she'd changed from an ideal student to a rebellious party animal. Willows smiled. The phrase "rebellious party animal" was ludicrous, but devastatingly accurate. He'd actually shouted it accusingly at her during a particularly heated argument. She'd laughed in his face and stormed out of the house, trailing a slipstream of abuse. Though she was only eighteen, she'd come home drunk on several occasions. More than once her clothes had smelled richly of marijuana smoke. She got phone calls at all hours of the day and night from people he didn't know, who were loath to identify themselves.

Annie had just finished writing her mid-terms. She'd always been so eager to discuss her exams, but now she refused to talk about them. She often slept in and missed classes. Her work ethic had deteriorated to the point where Willows was concerned about her failing and dropping out. He'd suffered through years of turmoil with Sean, but he had straightened himself out. Now Annie had gone off the deep end. It was as if she'd been waiting her turn.

The worst part of it was that Willows knew exactly what was bothering her, and he couldn't do anything about it. Years ago, his ex-wife, Sheila, had moved to a tiny coastal town in Mexico to be with her new boyfriend. The terms of the divorce dictated an equal split of their assets. Willows had to remortgage the house his parents had left him. If Parker hadn't stepped in and co-signed the loan, he'd have been forced to sell the house.

In the interim, Sheila had phoned on numerous occasions, demanding money. Sometimes she sounded drunk; she always sounded desperate. Willows had sent her various amounts, depending on his circumstances. It had never been enough. One call followed another, endlessly.

The day after he and Claire had remortgaged the house, Sheila phoned and told him to courier her a certified cheque, in U.S. funds, for the full amount he owed her. Willows contacted her Vancouver lawyer and discovered he'd been fired. Willows didn't know much about Sheila's boyfriend, but what he did know wasn't good. He was concerned for her safety, but there was nothing he could do about it. Sheila hired another lawyer. Under threat of legal action, he was eventually forced to turn over the money. Parker moved in six months later. Sean hardly noticed she was there. Annie, characteristically generous to a fault, welcomed her with open arms and an open heart.

In the years that followed, Sheila had never failed to write to Sean and Annie on their birthdays and at Christmas. But this year she'd skipped Sean's birthday, and then, just a few weeks before school started, Annie's. Willows had written her, and faxed her care of the local post office. Sheila had not responded. He'd recently learned that she and her boyfriend had moved out of their rented house, leaving no forwarding address. He dreaded giving the news to Annie.

Parker called out, "Jack, are you okay?"

Startled, Willows mentally teleported himself back from Mexico. He was still five pounds overweight, and he was cold. He stepped off the scales, and finished towelling himself dry. He was still worrying about Annie when he entered the bedroom.

Parker lay on her side, facing him. She smiled as he drew near the bed.

"Nice towel." She flipped aside the duvet, and moved over a little, making room for him. Eyeing him boldly, she said, "Want a hand getting that off?"

"No, that's . . ."

Parker reached out and gave the towel a yank, pulled it loose. "Well, just look at you!"

Willows slapped his belly. "I'm going to start working out, maybe jog a little . . ." He slipped into bed.

Parker said, "That's not what I was talking about, Jack."

"You weren't?"

"*This* is what I was talking about," said Parker, taking the subject of interest firmly in hand.

Willows reached for the lamp.

"Leave it on." said Parker.

5

Hector had noticed that one of the many advantages of a fleeting, cash-based love fest in the back of a speedily moving vehicle was that he was less inclined to take a nap afterwards.

Lucky thing, because Carlos was in a mood to party.

"What d'you say, Hector? Wanna hit the bars, maybe drive over to the Austin, listen to some music? Or we could drop in to the Cecil, check out the strippers . . ."

"No way." Hector tapped the face of his trusty Timex. "It's almost eleven-thirty, and we're outta groceries."

"What's your point?"

"The Safeway closes at midnight; the bars are open all night long."

"Not really." Across the border, everything was open twenty-four hours a day, minimum. But this was Canada, home of the fifty-cent dollar and roll-up sidewalk. Carlos had often thought that, if he moved to America, he'd only have to spend half as much time thieving to make pretty much the same amount of money. In America, life was sweet. But there was also a tendency to shoot first and ask questions at the inquest . . .

Something else, however. If he moved across the border, it would give him an opportunity to hunt around for a new partner. He and Hector had been together almost a year now, and Hector was slowly driving him nuts. The guy was a whiner, always finding something to complain about. He'd been genetically cursed with an ugly, unremittingly negative attitude about the whole wide world and everything – animal, mineral or vegetable – in it. Plus, he had a hatful of totally weird ideas about money, believed that in a perfect world the working man would give 100 per cent of his income to the government, and that it would be redistributed by faceless bureaucrats, guaranteeing everyone a roof over his head, clothes on his back and three square meals a day. Utopia, he called it. Carlos had wondered aloud if there'd be a 7-series BMW in every garage, and was told in an infuriatingly superior voice that he was missing the point. Yeah, sure he was.

He made a left and headed for the West End. There was a Safeway down by the liquor store at the foot of Robson, half a mile or so from the strip of glittering brand-name shops. He'd drive down Robson for the pleasure of watching Hector flip out. Nothing turned poor Hector's crank like mindless consumption, the average guy's burning need to get rid of his cash, find something else to stuff in his closet . . .

Carlos lit a cigarette. He swerved to avoid a moron on a bicycle. There was a certain kind of person who, when you stuck them on two wheels, somehow immediately decided they were immortal. Maybe their stupid helmets were too tight, cut off the circulation to their brains. Or maybe it was the little flashing red lights they wore that gave them a false sense of security. He cut in front of the cyclist, timing it perfectly, missing him by inches. A cry of rage and fear cut through the muted thunder of the rain, the wet slap of the wipers.

Hector frowned. "What'd he say?"

"Asked me to stop and beat him to a pulp, or shoot him, if I can spare a bullet." They were crawling along, Carlos' eyes on his rearview mirror. He waited until the cyclist was about to overtake him, then slammed on the brakes. The bike wobbled, veered sharply towards the sidewalk, and vanished.

Hector stared glumly out the window. "Where we going?"

"Don't worry about it."

Hector did his best. After a few minutes, he said, "D'you own an umbrella?"

"No, because I like to keep both hands free, like any sensible person would. Though I gotta admit sometimes the idea of a yard-long piece of wood with a sharp metal point on it makes a lot of sense."

"The problem with an umbrella," said Hector, "is that it might keep your head dry, but that's about it. Unless you get a really big one, like those red or blue-and-white striped umbrellas you sometimes see. But they take up so much space."

"That's a bad thing?"

"Think about it. Crowded sidewalks, people in a hurry, everybody carrying big umbrellas: it's a recipe for disaster."

"I can see it now," said Carlos.

"See what?"

"The movie, *Umbrella*." Carlos made that hyena sound that drove Hector nuts. "Maybe it'll star that Leonardo kid. *Titanic*, watch out!"

"Go ahead, make fun. Will you learn anything, being a smartass? No, but that doesn't bother you, and you don't even know why."

Carlos thought about it for a moment. Against all the odds, Hector was right. He said, "Don't tell me you've come up with a better idea."

"Yeah, I did. It works on the same basic principle as a helicopter, but it's battery-powered, and the rotor blades are made of soft plastic."

"Rotor blades?"

"See, the idea is that the propeller blades whirl away the rain. I'm gonna call it the *Whirlaway*.

"Brilliant. But aren't you worried about people turning on their umbrellas and flying away like so many scraps of paper in a hurricane? Sounds kind of like something Inspector Gadget might think twice about, you ask me."

"I'm not saying the idea doesn't need work. I just started thinking about it this morning. But, face it, the common umbrella has been stuck in neutral ever since the spring-loaded automatic. It's time for a change, Carlos. You can be part of the solution, or part of the problem. It's your choice, but those are the only choices you've got."

"Problem," said Carlos. "All my life, I've *always* wanted to be part of the problem."

The brilliantly lit retail strip was behind them now. They were on the downhill slope, in a nondescript area of motor hotels and apartment blocks and big turn-of-the-century houses that had been converted to a warren of cramped but affordable, sometimes charming, apartments.

A few blocks farther on, the landscape changed again, to a retail strip of modest restaurants and retail shops. Carlos tapped the brakes as he drove past the liquor store. A couple of beat cops were busy with a down-and-outer and the shopping cart he'd converted into a mobile dumpster. Carlos turned in to the Safeway parking lot. The cops, in their bright-yellow plastic rain slickers, looked like a couple of large, extremely bad-tempered bathtub ducks. Carlos parked so that the van was straddling a white line. Two parking spots were better than one, because a life fully lived was a life lived to excess. He killed the engine and turned to Hector.

"How much stuff you getting? Do we need a cart?"

"Yeah, we need a cart." Hector arched his back so he could get at his pockets.

"Lose something?"

"No, I'm looking for a quarter."

"I got it." Carlos levered himself out of his seat and rooted around in the back of the van until he found what he was looking for: a large pair of bolt-cutters.

Hector said, "What would you come up with if I said I was looking for fifty cents, a chainsaw?"

Bolt-cutters in hand, Carlos climbed out of the van. When Hector had joined him, he pointed his remote. The locks clicked. The alarm chirped.

Hector had known within five minutes of first meeting Carlos that he was not a particularly well-adjusted personality. No doubt that was why they got along so well together. One of Carlos' many faults was his tendency to exaggerate problems. Substituting a pair of bolt-cutters for a quarter was typical. Hector trailed along behind as Carlos strode towards a train of chained-together shopping carts. The cops had their backs to him but, being cops, they were likely to turn around without notice. How would they react if they turned around and saw Carlos sauntering across the parking lot, great big Carlos with his long, aimless stride, mindless death stare, filthy shoulder-length hair, black jeans and biker boots, and yard-long bolt-cutters with the Home Hardware price tag, for which he surely could not produce a receipt? Hector didn't even want to think about it.

Carlos closed in on the shopping carts. He lifted the bolt-cutters and worked the handles. *Clack! Clack!*

Carlos snapped the blades together speedily and forcibly. *Clack! Clack clack clack!* People were looking at him. Looking at Hector, too, trying to figure out if he was with the freak. Nope, not me. Definitely not.

Clack clack clack!

Hector worked out an escape route. He decided that, if the cops turned around, he'd sprint for the low retaining wall at the back of the parking lot, jump the iron-rail fence, and run down the alley. Ducking down behind the sturdy if stylistically bland bulk of a Volvo station wagon, he loosened his sneaker laces and retied them extra tight.

Clack clack clack! Clack clack clack clack!

6

Willows lay on his back with Parker nestled in his arms. Her head rested comfortably on his naked chest. Parker was warm and cozy, content to lie quietly, listening to the rattle of rain against the window, and the slow, steady beating of Willows's heart. After they'd made love, he'd held her in his arms and stroked her hair and shoulder for a long time, but now his hand had fallen still.

Parker lifted her head. "Jack?"

Willows' breathing faltered. He made a garbled, vaguely interrogative sound, and abruptly rolled over on his side.

Parker was short on sleep. By all rights she should have been exhausted, but she was wide awake and full of energy. She lifted herself up on her elbow and studied Willows' face. They had known each other a long time, more than thirteen years, through Parker's early twenties and into her mid-thirties. Their relationship had progressed by halting, imperceptible degrees, from a coolly distant professional partnership to a passionate love affair and then something akin to routine domestic bliss.

She lowered her head onto the pillow. Willows' divorce had been finalized well over a year ago. A few months after the papers were signed he'd bought her an engagement ring and asked her to marry him. She'd accepted with alacrity, but had made it clear that she wanted to have children. Willows hadn't objected. But on the other hand, he hadn't been wildly enthusiastic either. At the time, his lack of enthusiasm hadn't rung any alarm bells, but lately she'd been worried about it.

Willows was forty-six years old.

Sean was twenty, Annie eighteen. Both children were on the cusp of adulthood. Sean would be leaving home soon and Annie wouldn't be far behind. Why would Jack, at his advanced age, want to start a family all over again?

Parker counted off the months. If she gave birth in mid-June, Jack would be sixty-five by the time their child was Annie's age. And she would be . . . fifty-three.

Sixty-five was getting up there. No wonder Jack was passively reluctant to have more children. From what Parker understood, children began the final rebellion against their parents in their early teens, but usually settled down by the time they were nineteen or twenty. Twenty seemed old. Even so, having to cope with a hulking, hormone-fuelled teenager probably wasn't in anybody's top-ten list of how to spend your sixth decade. How could she have been so wilfully blind to the reality of the situation?

Parker moved over to her own side of the bed. She felt miserable, and then angry, and then unbearably sad, and then angry all over again.

She stretched out her arm and turned off the light. Six weeks earlier, when she was at the most fertile stage of her cycle, she'd teased Willows to a peak of sexual desire and then made sure he didn't use a contraceptive.

Two weeks later, she'd faked her period. How would Jack react if she told him she was pregnant? Would shock turn to dismayed resignation, or even strident demands that she get an abortion? That wasn't going to happen, no matter what. But how much longer could she keep her pregnancy a secret? Parker's mind raced. Money was always tight. They'd gone out to a movie a few nights ago, and it was the first time they'd been out together for longer than she could remember. How could they possibly afford to raise a child? A lonely tear trickled down her cheek. She hoped that, when she told Jack she was pregnant, he would be overjoyed, dizzy with pride.

But if he was unable to handle the situation, to hell with him.

Would he resent her, accuse her of manipulating him, or was she being incredibly unfair to him?

Parker needed to relax. She eased out of bed, tiptoed out of the room and down the hall to the bathroom, shut the door and began to fill the tub. She wanted more than anything to have this baby that was growing inside her. The more she allowed herself to think about it, the more strongly she felt. She sat down on the lip of the tub and trailed her fingers into the water.

What if Jack . . . ?

Parker burst into tears.

7

Nick's hair was so short it was hardly more than a rust-coloured haze hovering over his scalp. His pale-green eyes were unusually large, and wide-spaced. A scattering of freckles lay across his cheeks. His lips were spoiled-looking, pouty.

Nick was good-looking, in a careless, blurred sort of way. Naive women, especially older women, found him attractive because he was a little bit scary. He liked to tell them he was a male model. From time to time he imagined himself smirking and preening for Calvin Klein.

Nick was nineteen years old. His twentieth birthday was two weeks into his future, but he never gave it a moment's thought. A birthday was just another day in his life of days.

He lay sprawled out on his hotel-room bed, flat on his back with his legs together and his arms folded across his chest. His eyes were shut. He'd fallen asleep in this exact position an hour ago and hadn't moved an inch.

The clang of a heavy metal dumpster lid violently yanked him awake. He lifted his head, then let it drop back onto the soiled sheets. The rancid orange light leaking through the tattered curtain hurt his eyes. He yawned, and lit a cigarette. His dog, an even-tempered and undemanding Rottweiler-cross named Tripper, opened her eyes and made a low grumbling sound. She watched Nick closely, because he sometimes blew smoke in her eyes. When he did that, she always jumped off the bed and lay down by the door, her nose to the draft from the hall.

Nick sucked smoke into his lungs. He exhaled a smoke ring, and then another. He concentrated on blowing increasingly small rings, fitting each successive ring into the one preceding it. He blew seven rings, and then missed. He climbed off the bed, unzipped as he plodded towards the bathroom.

He emptied his bladder in short bursts, making as much noise as possible. Finished, he gave himself a shake and tucked himself away, then leaned back and kicked the little chrome lever protruding from the toilet's water tank. The toilet groaned deeply. A rush of water swirled into the bowl and down and away, flooding into an unimaginable network of pipes. Nick took a last pull on his cigarette. He flicked the butt into the toilet and wandered out of the bathroom. He moved listlessly and without purpose, as if he had no idea where he was or what to do next.

He shifted aside the orange curtain and peered down at the alley. Below him, a stooped man wheeled a bicycle loaded with clear plastic garbage bags full of pop and beer cans. Each of the pop cans was worth a nickel. The beer cans were worth a dime apiece. The man climbed into the dumpster, poked around for a few minutes, and climbed out again, empty-handed. He mounted the bike and got it rolling. A bottle shattered on the asphalt. The scavenger stopped the bike, got off, and leaned it against the dumpster. He kicked every last scrap of glass aside, and then climbed back on the bike and started off again.

Nick watched the man until he'd turned the corner at the end of the alley and disappeared from view.

He unlocked the window and pushed it up. The wood was damp and swollen, so he had to push hard. Flakes of dull red paint fell away from the frame, were caught in an updraft, and skittered away. A previous occupant had nailed a rectangle of plywood to the window ledge and made an open-air cage by nailing a balloon of chicken wire to the outside edge of the plywood and to the window frame. The wire kept the pigeons out, and the rats, if there were any. There was enough room to store a quart of milk and six-pack of beer, a fat length of sausage, a loaf of bread, a plastic bag of pre-made salad and a bottle of Paul Newman salad dressing.

Nick cut an inch off the sausage. He stuffed the spicy chunk of meat into his mouth, chewed and swallowed. Still hungry, he cut another, larger, piece of sausage. He sliced the sausage lengthwise several times, and flopped the meat down on a slice of bread. He put a second slice of bread on top of the meat and hammered it with the side of his fist to make everything stick together.

As he lifted the sandwich to his mouth, he suddenly had an almost overpowering urge for mustard. Funny how he always wanted what he didn't have and was too lazy to go out and get. He grabbed a bottle of beer, unscrewed the metal cap and tried to toss it through the chicken wire. The holes were too small. He twisted the wire until he'd made a larger hole. The cap hit the alley. It sounded exactly like a dropped coin, but nobody came running. Nick felt let down. He shut the window against the thrum of rain on the dumpster, and the irritating cooing of the resident pigeons.

He ambled over to the bed and lay down, beer and sandwich in hand. Tripper eyed him, equal parts hungry and wary. Nick ignored her. He took a bite out of the sandwich, rinsed his mouth with a slug of beer. The beer was fairly cold. Not as cold as if it had been in a fridge, but cold enough. He finished the sandwich, and got a second bottle of beer from the window ledge. This time he tried to flip the cap into the toilet through the open bathroom door, and missed by a mile.

He lay back down on the bed and lit another cigarette. Smokes were impossible to steal because they were always behind the counter where you couldn't get at them, and there was nothing in the world that was half as suspicious as a convenience-store clerk.

Nick blew a large smoke ring and then a smaller ring that shot through the first. Alcohol was hard to steal, but you could do it, if you were careful. Food was easy. You had to know where the staff were, and you couldn't hesitate or look around, had to just reach out and grab what you wanted. Well, that was life in a nutshell, wasn't it?

Nick was watching TV when Chantal finally got home. He heard the key in the lock, and then the door swung wide and she walked into the room. He stood up, weaving a little, fifth or sixth beer in hand. She said hello, but he ignored her, went over to the rabbit ears and tried to bring in a better picture, clear the snow out of Humphrey Bogart's eyes.

Chantal said, "Hi, Nick."

"Yeah, hi." Nick had never been a travelling man. The two-hour drive from Abbotsford to Vancouver was the longest trip he'd ever made, by far. But he knew it never snowed in Casablanca.

Tripper rushed past him, happy to see her mistress. Tripper was trained not to bark, but couldn't help uttering a low huffing sound that was welcoming, and full of joy. Chantal scratched her behind the ears, but didn't put much into it.

Nick stood there in his Jockeys, beer in hand, his body swaying like a sapling in a fitful wind.

Chantal said, "Don't you ever get dressed?"

Nick's laugh was high-pitched, frantic, a childish tittering. If he had time to get set, he was able to conjure up a masculine, dignified chuckle. But when he laughed spontaneously, he sounded like a chipmunk full of helium. There was nothing he could do about it, just as there wasn't much he could do about everything else in his life.

Chantal shut and locked the door. She walked past him, into the bathroom. Tripper followed her with her dark-brown eyes, tail wagging hopefully. The hotel room was lit only by the small black-and-white TV. Even so, Nick noticed Chantal's swollen cheek, the smear of blood on her upper lip.

"Jeez, what the fuck happened to you?"

She turned on him. "What d'you think happened, Nick?"

"Beats me. That's why I asked."

Chantal unzipped her jeans and sat down on the toilet. She glared at him through the open door. "What're you looking at?"

"You've got great legs, baby."

"And you are such an asshole." She flushed and stood up, leaned towards the mirror over the sink, splashed cold water on her face, rinsed her mouth. Clots of blood swirled down the drain. She patted herself dry with the end of a worn towel.

Nick checked his watch. "I'm sorry you got roughed up. You okay?"

"Fine."

"You taking a break, or . . . ?"

"No, I'm through for the night."

Nick tapped his watch. "It ain't even midnight."

He plucked a cigarette butt from the ashtray and tossed it at her. The butt hit her on the arm and fell to the floor.

"Tired?" Nick's voice was drenched with sarcasm, and sexual jealousy.

He tossed another butt at her. She batted it away. This wasn't the first time she'd come home with scrapes or bruises. Before, she'd always been very angry, but tonight she was sad and vulnerable. Nick didn't know how to handle it. He fiddled with the rabbit ears.

Chantal said, "Tell me something, Nick. What'd you do tonight?"

Shrug.

"Drink beer, watch TV. What else? Snort a little coke, drink a little more beer?"

He spread his arms wide, as if inviting her to frisk him. "I'm a drug-free zone, baby. Why? Because we're fucking broke."

"Want to know what *I* did tonight?"

"Forget to duck?"

She rushed him, but he was ready. He grabbed her wrists, spun her around and gave her a measured push. She fell face down on the bed. A spring creaked.

Nick sat down beside her. He stroked her calf. "Want an Aspirin?"

"Fuck you!"

"Tylenol?"

Chantal lay quietly for a few moments, and then rolled over and unbuckled her belt and reached down into her panties for the wad of American twenties.

Nick smiled. His teeth were still pretty good. He offered her his beer, and she took the bottle from him and drank deeply. Tripper, sensing a change in the weather, jumped up on the bed and lay down beside them.

She tossed the money in the air. The bills stayed together, so Nick was able to catch them without spilling any. He spread the bills on the blanket and counted them very slowly, his lips moving.

"Six hundred bucks!" He smiled dangerously. "Whatever you did, you must've been pretty damn good at it."

Chantal sat up. "Fuck you," she said without heat.

Nick nodded agreeably. He took the bottle away from her and dropped it on the uncarpeted floor.

8

Tripod came meowing into the room and hopped up on the bed. The cat was about as light on its three feet as an anvil. Purring furiously, he nuzzled Parker's neck. She drowsily reached out and patted him. Tripod was in a playful mood. He raked at her fingers with his sharp claws, raced to the foot of the bed and back again, and chased Parker's retreating hand under the covers. Confident that he'd wakened her, he jumped off the bed and thumped noisily down the stairs.

Parker lay quietly for a few minutes, willing herself to drift off again. She was wasting her time. She had an eerie feeling that, if she tried to count sheep, the sheep would turn into babies.

She squeezed her eyes shut and there they were, an endless succession of identical infants in diapers, leaping cheerfully over a rail fence. No, they weren't identical. Every second baby had Jack's adult face, and the ones in between looked exactly like her.

She pushed aside the covers and got out of bed, found her slippers and robe and padded silently downstairs to the kitchen. She wanted a small Scotch, but she'd stopped drinking the night Jack had made unprotected love to her. Something else he'd failed to notice, she thought resentfully.

She definitely wanted to have a baby. Three or four of them, as a matter of fact. She got the milk from the fridge and poured a

33

mugful into a pot and put the pot down on the stove. She turned the gas burner on low.

She had to tell Jack she was pregnant. The longer she waited, the harder it was going to be to talk to him. But it was already impossible, so how much harder could it be?

She leaned against the kitchen counter. The fridge hummed and the electric clock over the back door made a small, shuddering sound with each second that twitched by. She'd lived in the house for several years, but in all that time she'd never been aware that the clock wasn't perfectly, utterly silent.

What would Annie say, if she knew? How would Sean react if he found out she was pregnant? Willows' children meant so much to her, as much as if they were her own. No, that wasn't quite true. Or maybe it was. She wanted it to be true and she hoped it was true – wasn't that enough?

She stirred the milk with a spoon and turned up the gas. Jack was a decent man, and she loved him. What had come over her to make her trick him like that? She wanted so very much to have a child, but not like this, as a treachery and deceit. Parenthood should be the result of a mutual decision, made calmly and rationally. But she'd never felt so passionate, so needy. She'd been out of control. What was wrong with that? The second hand shuddered around the dial. It was just past midnight, and she was wide awake. When the milk was hot, she poured it into the mug and turned off the stove. As she crept down the hall, she noticed a crack of light under Annie's door. Six months ago she'd have knocked and said hello. Not now, because she was in no mood for a fight, and with Annie, nowadays, even the simplest discussion seemed to deteriorate into an argument.

Tripod was curled up on the sofa. Parker resisted an urge to give him a sharp poke in the ribs. She sat down in an overstuffed chair and sipped her warm milk. The city might be seething with crime, but the house was wonderfully quiet. Her horrid neighbours often let their horrid little cockapoo out about midnight, to do its business wherever it chose – usually on the boulevard in front of the house or in Parker's small, carefully tended garden. A few nights ago a late-night excursion had been cut short by a pack of coyotes. The yappy little thing had escaped, but both it and its enormously inconsiderate owners had been traumatized. A fence was in the works. In the meantime the dog was let out only on a leash, and even then it was encouraged to empty its bladder and bowels with dispatch. Parker liked dogs in general, but she wished the coyotes had been a little bit quicker. Thinking about the cockapoo's close call made her feel better, though she didn't know why. She finished her milk, stood up, and started towards the stairs. Tripod watched her but made no move to follow. Lucky for him. Parker yawned. The milk had made her drowsy, and she was eager to get back into bed.

9

Nick counted the money over and over again. He counted it slowly, and then he counted it quickly, shuffling the bills from hand to hand. He counted six hundred dollars three times and six hundred and twenty dollars once and five hundred and eighty dollars once. Frustrated, he counted the money again, painfully slowly. Six hundred even.

He was sweating heavily. He wiped his face with the back of his hand and started over again. Two of the bills must have been stuck together, because this time he got six-twenty a second time.

He counted it one last time, to make sure. No doubt about it, he was holding six hundred and twenty dollars in crisp new American twenties. It was an unbelievable windfall. Just absolutely fucking amazing. He danced around Chantal, clutching the cash.

"C'mon, let's get something to eat."

"I'm too tired."

"Bullshit."

He noticed at last that her tight-fitting white cotton T-shirt was torn and spotted with orange. What was that all about? He wasn't going to ask. Whatever had happened, there was nothing he could do about it, because nobody could go backwards in time. He said, "You're tired because you're hungry. Your energy levels are low. You'll feel better if you fuel up, get something to drink, grab a bite."

Chantal cocked a hip. She was angry: not play-acting, but really, really angry. Pissed, and she let it show. "You can't wait to spend it, can you?"

Nick mimed amazement. "Didn't anybody ever explain that's what it's for?"

"I got hurt, Nick."

He checked her out. She looked okay. Her face was clean. A little swelling, but no more blood.

She said, "Tell me something, have you ever met a great big asshole named Carlos?"

Fool that he was, Nick thought about it. A memory dimly stirred. "The guy who wrote that book?"

"I'm talking about a trick, not a writer. Long stringy hair, a big, muscular face . . ."

Nick shrugged. The guy could've been a dozen people he knew, or nobody he'd ever met.

"He punched me, Nick. Punched me for no good reason, punched me just because he felt like it. He cut me inside my mouth. It hurts. I can taste blood. When was the last time you tasted your own blood, Nick?"

He lit a cigarette. The last time he'd tasted blood. Let's see now . . . that would be the day before he met Chantal. He'd gotten into a tussle with a punk over . . . something. The punk whacked him a few times, kneed him in the balls and then swung from his ankles and hit him flush on the nose, so hard he'd thought for sure it was broken. He flagged a cab, told the driver to take him to St. Paul's. The guy took a quick look at him, told him he was bleeding, shoved him out of the car. Prick. Nick tried to stop thinking about that night, because what's past is past, but that worm of blood was leaking out of his nose again, across his lip and into his mouth, the memory of it salty and warm. How long ago was that? He tried to pin it down, but the days and weeks were a blur. Thinking about the past was an even bigger waste of time than contemplating the future.

He pulled on a pair of pants and a shirt and a sweater and his boots. He saw that Chantal's leopardskin jacket was stained with dark smears of blood. He tossed her his leather jacket. "Get changed, put that on, let's get the fuck out of here." She shed the leopardskin and he grabbed her by the arm and hustled her towards the door, eager to leave that cramped little room that stank of seduction and betrayal. Chantal pulled back, resisting. Tripper raced around in circles, making sounds like a big furball steam train.

Nick turned on the charm. He pointed out that the dog could use some exercise. What was the point of working so hard if they didn't have a little fun with the money?

His strategy backfired.

"You fucking prick! D'you remember why I started hustling, Nick? Because we were broke, and cold, and hungry, and tired of living in fucking doorways, getting hassled by cops and fucking psychos. Because you were sick, and I was worried you were going to get fucking pneumonia and die."

Nick raised a hand to ward off her anger. "I know, I know . . ."

"It was supposed to be temporary, a way of getting by until you got a fucking job!"

Nick yanked open the door. It banged against the wall and rebounded towards him. He kicked it, hard. The shock of impact travelled up his leg as far as his knee. Fuck! He kicked the door again, relishing the pain. He didn't want to eat any more, all he cared about was sliding out from under Chantal's growing rage, the fire in her eyes and her hard words. Why was she talking to him like that? So abusively. She came in the door and there he was, waiting for her. What did she want?

She wanted to humiliate him, because now she was shouting at him, her voice shrill, spittle flying. He edged out of the room. Doors were opening all along the hallway. Disembodied heads turned towards him, an uneven row of mocking, toothless grins.

Chantal followed him into the hallway. "I hate hooking! You

don't know what it's like, you have no fucking idea how horrible and degrading it is, just no . . . fucking idea!"

"I thought you liked sex." Nick knew or at least suspected that this remark would enrage her, but everybody was watching him and he had to defend himself. Didn't he? He rushed towards a door and it slammed shut. He ran at another door. *Bang!* Tripper barked furiously and hurled herself in the air. Now all the doors were shut. Nick yelled at Tripper to shut up. He kicked at the dog and then turned on Chantal. She wasn't afraid of him and she wasn't done with him.

"What happened to you? You used to love me. You told me you loved me. Now I come home, I've been hit and I'm bleeding, and all you want to do is count the fucking money. You don't love me. You don't even care about me. All you want to do is hang out with your creepy fucking drug-addict friends!"

Most of this was true. Maybe all of it. It was good that Chantal walked her ass out on the street, brought home so much money. But at the same time, Nick had to admit he was sort of disgusted with her. He'd rather die than go out there on the street and sell himself to some fucking pervert. Why didn't she feel the same way? Also, come to think of it, he wasn't the only one who had a weakness for drugs. When it came to snorting up a line, Chantal had always been pretty damn quick to get her nose into the trough.

If there was one thing Nick couldn't stand, it was hypocrisy. He looked her straight in the eye. "Don't lie to me. You love your job and you know it."

Chantal's face crumpled. She burst into tears. Fucking great, that's exactly what he needed.

He waved the money in her face. "You think this is all I care about? Watch!"

Nick crumpled a bill and threw it over the staircase railing. Their room was on the top floor, five storeys up. The twenty fluttered down and down until it was caught by an updraft, warm air from the lobby. Eerily, it stopped falling, hung motionless for an instant and then lifted up a few slow feet before drifting across the breadth of the stairwell and resuming its fall.

Nick couldn't believe what he was doing, even as he continued to do it. He peeled another bill off the roll, pinched it between his thumb and index finger and dangled it over the railing. As he did this he wondered what Chantal had done to earn all that money. What special convoluted tricks had she performed? It made him sick to think about it but he couldn't help thinking about it, just couldn't stop himself from wondering.

His imagination ran laps around his brain. He hated her and he almost hated himself for hating her. He wanted to drag her back into the hotel room and throw her down on the bed and make her *show* him what she did. Make her do it to him. Everything. He wanted to hit her. Furious, he crumpled the second twenty and let it drop.

"Fuck off, stop it, cut that out!"

Chantal rushed him. One hundred and four pounds of out-raged fury. Nick was six-foot-one. Thin, but muscular. He fended her off easily, using his hard-earned street knowledge of leverage and stance. She kept at him, flailing away. Her sharp nails raked his cheek, burnt him but failed to draw blood. The high-pitched, manic squiggle of his laugh infuriated them both. He pushed her away and turned his back on her.

Nick balled up another twenty and flipped it negligently over the railing.

That's three. Sixty dollars. Cash enough to buy a bag of weed or keep them in this fleabag hotel through the weekend. Nick experienced an adrenalin rush. It was weird, but throwing away money was a real fun thing to do. Now he understood why people bothered to drop a few coins in a panhandler's cup. It's the ultimate form of conspicuous consumption, spending money without actually buying anything. He laughed, but the look of rage on Chantal's face made him clamp his mouth shut so hard his teeth hurt.

He crumpled another bill. Couldn't stop himself. The need to defy and hurt her was like a sickness, an addiction. He crushed the twenty into a ball, tossed it into the air and hit it with his fist, sent it flying over the railing.

Chantal was still crying. Her eyes were red, puffy with tears. He crumpled another bill in his fist.

She rushed him again and he slyly retreated, his back to the railing. He taunted her with the bill, waved it over the empty stairwell, pretended to let it go. Tripper was barking loudly, excited and confused.

From far below them came a hoarse shout. Pinky, the night clerk. His booze-addled voice demanded to know what was going on up there.

Nick leaned over the railing and peered down. One of the bills was on the stairs, the rest lay on the ancient white-and-black tiled floor.

Tripper wouldn't stop barking. The fucking dog was going to get their asses kicked out of the hotel.

Where was the third twenty?

Nick had forgotten about Chantal. She lunged at him, snatched at the wad of bills.

He jerked away, lost his balance and went over the railing so easily that he might have rehearsed the move a hundred times. He fell twelve feet and then his arm hit the railing. He and Chantal and Pinky all clearly heard the bone snap. Nick's hand fell open. The crisp new bills trailed after him like the tattered fragments of a green parachute.

Two levels down he hit the railing again. The blow numbed him and violently disrupted his flight pattern, but hardly slowed him at all.

He dropped sixty-two vertical feet in just over two seconds, screaming all the way down, into a heavy thump and heavier silence.

Myron "Pinky" Koblansky stared at Nick for a moment or two and then looked up. The bills floated down. He'd been reading a paperback he'd bought used from a nearby bookstore. When Chantal and Nick started yelling at each other, he'd marked his page and put the book down on the counter in front of him. He was still at his desk when – *splat!*

The book's jacket was a minimalist black-on-white photograph, now speckled with shiny droplets of red. Pinky rubbed the ball of his thumb across the cover, right to left. The red dots were warm and sticky. His thumb made a red smear.

"Holy fuck!"

Pinky shied away from the book as if it had suddenly burst into flames. His chair fell over. He'd been smoking an El Cheapo and working on a mickey of vodka, but he was so terrified that he forgot all about the bottle at a time when he needed it most.

He told himself to get the money, unlocked the door behind him and hurried out of his chicken-wire cage and down a short hallway and into the lobby through a service entrance. The corpse slowed him. He saw everything at once, and it was too much for him to handle. His mind backed off. He picked at details, critically compared what he saw to similar circumstances he'd viewed on TV cop shows.

A few years back, maybe on a recycled "Hill Street Blues" episode, a tenement kid had fallen off a fire escape. The kid had witnessed a crime . . .

Pinky recognized Nick's black leather boots, which he coveted. His eye took in Nick's buzzcut. What a waste to have all that hair and cut it so short. Enjoy it while you got it was his motto.

Nick lay face up on the tiles. Pinky guessed that Nick's head must've cracked open, because there was an awful lot of blood. He followed the trail of blood that led from Nick's shattered skull to . . . nowhere. Despite the building's age, the floor was flat as a pool table. Now he had to go back to Nick, because he was unable to think where else to look. Nick's face was white. It occurred to Pinky that the white face floating in the middle of the shiny red puddle looked like a poached egg. Pinky never thought like that, never compared one thing to another. It really bothered him that he was thinking like that now.

The last bill floated down.

Pinky chewed on his cigar. Crooked lines of blood radiated out from the red puddle in several directions, following the zigzag pattern of grout that ran between the octagonal tiles. The blood was still moving, in erratic fits and starts, so it looked like a spider-web under construction. Pinky's brain was getting away from him again. He was very careful not to step in the blood as he circled the corpse and snatched up the money.

Nick's hand twitched. He made a fist. His fingers curled into his palm, dug into his flesh with so much force that, when the pathologist conducted the autopsy, he would log three small cuts he briefly considered might be defensive wounds.

Nick's knuckles drummed on the tiles. He leaked a little more blood. His hand fell open, and he was still.

Pinky bent to pick up a twenty. A length of ash tumbled from his cigar and he blew it carefully away, his hot breath making the ash scoot across the tiles.

Chantal had stopped screaming. Where was she? He climbed the stairs all the way to the top floor, finding three more bills along the way. The dog was in their room, barking furiously, the door shut and locked.

Winded, gasping, Pinky hurried back to the lobby, took a last quick look around and found Nick staring up at him.

By the time the cops arrived he'd seeded the floor around the corpse with a handful of small change, and sincerely believed he had an answer for every question the city's finest could think to ask him.

10

Carlos' bolt-cutters crunched through the chain. He stared fixedly at the gleaming, rain-speckled row of stainless-steel carts and then said, "The way they shove these things together, it's real sexy, like they're all humping each other."

Hector watched the cops walk around to the front of the liquor store and vanish. Like they'd never existed. He yanked free the emasculated cart. The two short ends of the chain waved goodbye to each other. Fucking Carlos. What a stupe. If his IQ was one point lower, he'd be a cabbage. Hector flinched as Carlos tossed the bolt-cutters into the cart. The two men walked side by side towards the bright lights of the Safeway. Pink and blue neon spilled across the rain-spattered asphalt. Where was Gene Kelly when you needed him? The cart was new, and had a nice, smooth ride. Hector decided that, if he was in the market for a cart, he would definitely give this particular model serious consideration. He wondered if homeless people had a favourite brand of cart, or just took whatever was available. What was the gross vehicle weight of a shopping cart? Hmmm. If you took the cart's basic platform, added hinged pieces of plywood at either end and a wraparound tarp to cover the sides and top and both ends, you'd have a compact but livable mobile home.

Hector pointed this out to Carlos, whose response was entirely predictable.

"Mobile homes made outta shopping carts? Are you outta your fucking mind?"

"Hey, don't be so quick to judge. There's hundreds of people spend their lives huddled in doorways. The mayor's real worried about it. I'm pretty sure he said so on TV last week."

"Sure he did. I bet he's so worried about homeless people that he has an awful time getting to sleep at night in his fucking Shaughnessy mansion."

"People freeze to death every winter."

"Not in Vancouver, they don't. It's too balmy. Your problem, the only book you ever read was *The Little Engine That Could*, and you took it way too serious."

"I try to be a positive force in the world, if that's what you're accusing me of."

"My partner, the world's littlest beam of sunlight."

Peeved, Hector got a foot up on the cart and pushed hard, turning the thing into a kind of low-tech skateboard. He pushed again, hoping to symbolically crash the shopping cart into the autocratic ruling class's automatic door.

The door was too quick for him.

Hector had made a mental list of things they needed. Both men liked to eat a lot of red meat. They hit the frozen-foods section first. Carlos had a weakness for TV dinners. For reasons he'd never understood, those tasty little suckers were only about fifty calories apiece, so Carlos knocked them off an ovenful at a time. He was also a big fan of Hungry Man soups. Liked to take the top off and stick 'em in the microwave and watch the sparks fly . . .

Hector tossed a double handful of frozen dinners into the cart.

Carlos told him to settle down. Mocking Hector, he said, "Just 'cause they're frozen doesn't mean they don't have *feelings*." Reverting to his normal grating tone, he asked, "How we doing for french fries?"

"Gone. You ate the whole kilo watching that 'Jerry Springer' marathon."

Carlos spied his reflection in a glass door and whipped out his rat-tail comb. Hector had never seen anybody preen the way Carlos did, with such fearsome concentration that you could dump a load of cinder blocks on him and he'd probably hardly even notice.

"Superfries or Curlies?"

Big question, worthy of serious thought. Carlos finished with his hair, examined the comb's teeth for cooties or whatever and slipped it back into his pocket. He said, "There a law against gettin' both kinds at once? 'Cause if there is, let's break it."

"Should I get the one-kilo packages?"

Carlos frowned. "How big are the small ones?"

Hector crouched down for a better look inside the freezer. It was mighty cold in there. If a guy was shopping with his wife and she made a smart remark, he could pop her a good one and shove her in there, way back on the bottom shelf behind the french fries, and nobody'd know the difference. For a while, anyway.

Carlos said, "Get the big ones. Bigger's better, right?"

Hector refused to be baited. The plastic bags had a greasy feel to them. As a consumer, he resented the proliferation of brands and choices within brands. The Crest toothpaste people had lost his business when they introduced all those different gels and pastes. A clerk had told him it was all about shelf space. Fuck that. He'd finally wised up when he had about eight different kinds of the wrong toothpaste cluttering up the bathroom, and Carlos bitching endlessly about the mess. Losing patience, Hector had switched to a different, possibly inferior brand. Or at least he would when he got around to it.

He'd never noticed how many kinds of french fries were available. Straight and curly, crinkled, nacho-style, spicy . . . His brain throbbed. He backed out of the freezer with a kilo package of whatever in each fist. "We'll never get all this stuff in the freezer. There ain't gonna be enough room."

"Then we'll make room." Carlos snatched the bags out of his hands, and tossed them unceremoniously into the cart. Hector felt demeaned. He turned his back on Carlos and wheeled the cart down the aisle at suicidal speeds. Any second now, Carlos would start calling him Little Miss Housewife. He just hated it when he did that – not so much the sarcasm, but the stupid, mocking tone of voice he used. He glanced behind him. Carlos had forgotten all about him, was digging his brutal fingers into a two-litre container of chocolate ice cream. He lifted his fingers to his mouth, saw that Hector was watching, and gave him a sly wink.

Hector took a corner so fast the cart rose up on two wheels. Carlos was big on hamburgers, but very particular about what kind of meat he used. Regular hamburger only, because he was a regular guy. Hector tossed several shrink-wrapped packages of extra-lean into the cart and then hurried over to the bakery and grabbed a dozen hamburger buns. With sesame seeds, because Carlos got an ulcer worrying about the glue they used to stick the seeds onto the buns.

Carlos, his arms overflowing with Häagen-Dazs products, caught up with Hector in the Asian-foods section. He dumped the ice cream into the cart, crushing the hamburger buns. Was this an accident? Maybe. There was no way of telling, but for sure Carlos had quick eyes and a ruthless soul. Hector turned his back on the carnage and resumed hauling Cup-a-Soups off the shelves.

"How can you eat that stuff?" spat Carlos derisively. "Tell me something: What *is* a noodle? I mean, what the hell is it?"

"It's like pasta," explained Hector.

"Well, duh!"

Hector gave up. There was no point in engaging in a dialogue with Carlos when he was feeling peevish. It was like trying to discuss the finer points of base-stealing with a fractious newborn.

It was five minutes to twelve. The store closed at midnight. Only three checkout stands were open, and all of them had depressingly long lineups. Using a complex mathematical formula that was based partly on the sheer quantity of food ahead of him, but largely on the age and presumed infirmities of the shoppers, Hector determined that checkout number five was his best bet.

Number two looked promising at first glance, but there was a long-term pensioner in the lineup, and Hector somehow knew she didn't expect to pay for her food. It was amazing how slowly some of them moved, like they were caught inside an invisible bottle of pancake syrup.

Carlos said, "That other lineup's moving faster." He pointed, giving the game away. "Over there, number four."

"Yeah, but that's the express checkout. You gotta have ten items or less."

"Or what happens?" Carlos wrested the cart away from Hector and bulled his way to the express lane. The response from their fellow shoppers was predictable; the deeply repressed national psyche asserted itself in downcast glances and a billowing cloud of unspoken resentment. Carlos snapped his fingers. "Gimme some money."

"I can't, I left my wallet in my other pants."

"You bought a second pair of pants?" Carlos glanced around, seeking eye contact, wanting to share his little joke.

The checkout clerk, a woman in her early twenties, saw what was up. She caught Carlos's dark eye, and held it. "Sir, this is an express lane. You'll have to take your groceries to number five, or number two."

"Fuck that!" whispered Carlos. He gave her the same eyeball curse he'd used to such devastating effect on his mother on the lightning-bristled night he'd sold her sewing machine to a local fence and run like hell, never to return.

The woman turned on him. "Excuse me, what did you say?"

"He said, 'Bad *luck*,'" offered Hector.

Too late. The checkout clerk had endured more foul-tempered customers than most city bus drivers encountered in a lifetime of bad driving, but this was too much. Carlos' casual rudeness was more than she could stand. A lifetime of accumulated bile spewed out of her in an ugly torrent. She gave Carlos the finger. "Fuck you, asshole!"

The crowd fell back. Hector was more surprised than anyone when Carlos made a quick U-turn and pushed his cart past the coffee grinder and out of sight down aisle thirteen. By the time Hector caught up with him, he'd stuffed all the Häagen-Dazs ice cream and most of the meat behind several towering rows of toilet paper.

Hector said, "That stuff's going to go bad if you leave it there, Carlos."

"No kidding."

"Tell me something, how does wasting ten pounds of grade-A hamburger benefit anybody?"

Benefit anybody? Carlos's mouth twisted into a grade-A sneer. He tossed shrink-wrapped packets of meat into the narrow space between two eight-roll packs of toilet paper, and closed the gap. "I drop by a couple of times a week, play hide-and-seek with a cart full of groceries, a whole bunch of rats are gonna benefit real good."

Carlos overturned the cart, spilling the rest of the food across the linoleum floor. He snatched up the bolt-cutters, and a large bottle of Paul Newman salad dressing. "What's this? You know I hate Italian."

"Maybe I got it for myself."

Carlos unscrewed the cap, and poured the contents onto the floor. *Glug, glug, glug.*

11

Parker sat bolt upright, her heart pounding, alert to all possibilities. An unidentified, barely audible sound had disturbed her light sleep and awakened her instantly. She eased out of bed and crept to the bedroom door, which was ajar. She heard the sharp click of the front-door latch. She opened her door wider and went to the top of the stairs.

"Annie, is that you?"

"It's okay, go back to sleep." Annie had been drinking, or smoking dope. Her voice was slurred. Parker briefly considered getting her dressing gown and going downstairs to talk to her. But what was the point? She'd learned the hard way that, when Annie had been drinking, her naturally sweet personality took a decided turn for the worse. If she went downstairs now, she'd be looking for trouble. Annie would start an argument, accuse her of invading her privacy, get herself worked into a lather. She'd wake Jack, and he'd come downstairs in a foul mood and join the fray. Annie would eventually run out of steam and go to bed and fall asleep in minutes. Parker, on the other hand, wouldn't be able to get back to sleep and would fret for hours, to the unmusical accompaniment of Jack's snoring.

She went back to bed, lay down and pulled the blankets up to her chin. The thunder of rain on the roof was a constant, subdued rumble. The city was on the edge of a rain forest. The fact that about 90 per cent of that rain forest had been clear-cut didn't seem to have much effect on the weather, except it seemed to keep getting warmer, season by season. Parker didn't want to think about that, not even for a minute. Too scary. Like Orcas full of PCBs washing up on the beach, polluted to death. She listened to the rain, concentrating on the musical sound of it.

Downstairs, the toilet flushed and a door was slammed. Parker glanced at the luminous red numbers of the alarm clock. She gave Annie ten more minutes to get herself settled, and then eased out of bed and crept downstairs, stealthy as a burglar, and shot the front-door deadbolt. Tripod rubbed up against her ankle, startling her. Parker pulled her foot away, and Tripod lost his balance, staggered, and meowed plaintively. The three-legged cat had adopted them a few years earlier when it had jumped into their unmarked car and hissed and clawed at Willows when he tried to shoo it away. Sean had named him Tripod. He'd given the cat a tiny wooden leg and a black eyepatch the following Christmas. Parker hadn't thought it was funny at the time, but she did now. Tripod rushed down the hall towards the kitchen, stopped and looked back, and meowed again. Parker knew that, if she didn't go straight back upstairs and fall into bed, she was going to have a hard time getting to sleep. But if she didn't feed Tripod, her conscience would nag at her. She stood there, half-asleep and dithering. Tripod meowed again, forcefully. From behind her closed bedroom door, Annie yelled at the cat to please shut up.

Parker hurried into the kitchen and turned on the light over the sink. The cat's stainless-steel bowl was empty. The fifteen-pound bag of dry cat food was in the laundry room, which was connected to the back porch. Parker crouched and picked up the bowl. Tripod wound around her ankles, apparently doing his perverse best to trip her up and break her neck. She filled the bowl and put it down on the floor. Tripod, purring like a freight train, nudged her hand aside and tucked in. How did cats manage to purr and eat at the same time? It was an impossible trick, like whistling while drinking a glass of water.

Parker had just started up the stairs when the phones in the kitchen and living room and den all started ringing at once. The phone in the upstairs bedroom was ringing too, and then the ringing stopped. As Parker climbed the stairs she heard Jack's voice, blurred by sleep but calm and unflustered. "The Lux. Yeah, I know where it is."

So did Parker. The Lux was a fleabag Hastings Street hotel, a favourite of hookers and hypes, and of street kids who'd been lucky enough to scrape up the cost of a bad night's sleep. A month earlier, a quartet of addicts had overdosed in one of the Lux's rooms. The night clerk had unlocked their door a few minutes after midnight, when they didn't respond to his knock. The television was on, but the sound was turned down so low the clerk couldn't hear it above the sound of traffic and his own wildly beating heart. The quartet of fully dressed addicts was stretched out on the queen-size bed. Their eyes were wide open, but all four were, as he put it, "totally dead." The clerk telephoned a radio station that offered a small cash reward for news items, and then he phoned a crime-beat reporter with whom he had a casual business relationship. The reporter told him dead addicts were about as newsworthy as bad weather, and advised him to dial 911. Willows and Parker had taken the call.

As they dressed, Parker said, "What've we got? Not more dead junkies, I hope."

Parker had a deathly fear of needle-stick, the attendant risk of AIDS. Willows didn't blame her. He dreaded frisking addicts, dead or alive.

He said, "No, a kid fell down the stairwell. He and his hooker girlfriend had been staying in a top-floor room for the past few weeks." Willows tucked in his shirt and buckled his belt. "The night clerk heard shouting just before the kid took the fall."

"They were arguing?"

Willows shrugged. "The girlfriend's missing. Nobody knows where she is."

The night clerk, Pinky Koblansky. Parker remembered him because of his porcine complexion, bloodshot eyes, and the ruby ring he wore on the little finger of his pudgy right hand.

Willows glanced around, looking for his brogues. They'd sneaked under the bed. He retrieved them and, as he put on his left shoe, noticed that his sock was inside out. Too late now. He took extra care with his laces because the Lux was situated in a tough neighbourhood. At this time of night the bars were closing, and the chances were fairly good that he might have to subdue a drunk with a swift kick to the fragiles. He glanced up at Parker, afraid that she could read his mind. Not this time. His badge case was in the pocket of his leather jacket, which he hoped was hanging from the brass hook by the door.

He pushed aside the clothes on the left side of the closet, unlocked the gun safe and got his Glock and Parker's. The loaded clips were in a separate locked steel box that Willows kept in the bottom drawer of his bureau. He unlocked that box and tossed Parker her clip and loaded his own pistol. Regulations required a round in the chamber at all times. Willows had never gone along with that, and never would, because he'd once had a nightmare about being shot and killed with his own weapon. No, it wasn't just a nightmare; the experience had been much more substantial than that. Call it a premonition. The clamshell holster had a spring clip. He fastened it to his belt, so it rode high on his hip, as far forward as he could carry it and not have it show when his jacket was open.

Parker was ready. Willows pushed the clothes back so they hid the gun safe again, and followed her out of the room. There was no way of knowing how long they'd be gone, but neither was there any need to leave a note. Sean and Annie had experienced his sudden, sometimes lengthy absences all their lives.

The Lux was lit up like a movie set by the bright lights of CBC, VTV, and Global television crews, the flashing lights of ambulances and patrol cars, and the multiple reflections of all those lights on nearby windows and the wet, black streets.

There was a large and vociferous crowd. Somebody had a boom box. Polka music – the godfather of all oxymorons – echoed off the walls of the surrounding buildings. There hadn't been a Lawrence Welk sighting in decades, but that didn't mean his spirit wasn't still out there somewhere, giving bad ties a good name.

One of the ambulances drove slowly away. There was nothing quite so sweet as a warm parking spot. Willows pulled up to the curb and killed the engine. He and Parker got out of the car and locked up. Willows pocketed the keys. Somewhere behind him a thrown bottle disintegrated against a scabrous brick wall. The uniformed cop at the hotel door recognized Parker and briskly stepped aside to let her and Willows past. Willows advised him to call for a backup unit. The cop, warily eyeing the increasingly boisterous crowd, said he'd get right on it.

A short but steep flight of narrow enclosed stairs led to a battered metal-clad door that had been propped open with a wooden wedge. The door opened on the lobby, which was unusually large but lacked furniture. The original front desk, made of oak and marble, had been torn out years ago, for salvage. The replacement desk was made of plywood and Formica, and was surrounded by a chicken-wire cage to protect hotel staff from thieves and hypes and angry drunks. Pinky Koblansky put down his bottle and waved hello to Parker from behind his metal safety net.

Willows glanced at the body. The victim was a white male in his late teens or early twenties.

A couple of paramedics engaged in a heated discussion with a uniformed officer quieted down as Willows and Parker approached them. The taller of the two said, "We lost him."

"But not until he hit," cracked his partner. Laughing at their little set piece, the two men gathered up their equipment and walked away.

To the cop, Parker said, "Were you first on the scene?"

The cop nodded. He looked so young that, had she met him in a bar, Parker would have demanded picture ID. He was a rookie, the number plate on his uniform identifying him as a recent graduate of the academy.

Parker said, "What's your name?"

"Broadhead."

"Yeah, I can see that. I meant, what's your given name?"

"Kenneth." The cop almost blushed. "Ken."

"Tell us whatever you can tell us, Ken."

"Uh . . . Me and my partner took the call, got here at twenty past twelve. The body was right there, as you see it. The desk clerk was behind the wire, refused to come out." Broadhead shifted his gaze to Willows and then quickly back to Parker. "The kid was dead when I arrived."

"You checked his vitals?" said Willows.

"Yeah, right away." The victim's skull was split wide open, but Broadhead decided not to mention it to the detectives. Let them find out for themselves. He said, "The night clerk said he heard shooting, that the victim had a room on the top floor . . ."

"Shooting?" said Willows.

"Shouting. Did I say . . . ?" Broadhead reddened. "He was staying in room 517, with his girlfriend. I went up there, didn't see anybody. The door to the room was shut."

"Locked?"

"Yeah, it was locked."

Willows was careful of the jagged lines of blood as he closed in on the corpse. A rear pocket bulged. Willows fished out a black wallet made of a coarse, woven synthetic fabric. The wallet had Velcro closures. Willows hated Velcro, because the sound of it made him think of a Band-Aid being ripped off a painful wound. He opened the wallet as slowly as he could, but all that accomplished was to extend his agony. The victim had died poor. Broke, in fact. Willows found a taped razor blade in one of the credit-card slots. The kid had provincial ID, and a social-insurance card.

His name was Nicholas Partridge. He was a local boy, born on January 2, 1981.

Parker crouched down beside Willows. "Got anything?"

"Not really." Willows showed her the picture ID. "Could that be him?"

"Yeah, that's him. Look at the eyes."

Willows nodded his agreement. A line of blood radiating away from Partridge's downside ear was smudged. The splash pattern was classic – elongated teardrops of blood fanning out in a stadium shape from his shattered skull. Close in, the drops were smeared. Willows pointed out the disturbed blood to Parker.

She said, "Think he's been moved?"

"Looks like it. Or he could've spasmed." Willows wanted to move the body but had to wait until it had been sketched and photographed. He glanced at his watch.

Parker, reading his mind, said, "Mel Dutton's on the way over. He should be here any minute."

Willows nodded. At first glance Nicholas Partridge's injuries were entirely consistent with a sixty-foot vertical drop onto a tiled floor. But had he fallen, or had he been pushed? Willows wondered if the blood work would indicate the ingestion of drugs or alcohol. Partridge wore a sweater and long-sleeved shirt, so Willows couldn't check for needle marks. Too bad the girlfriend hadn't stuck around. If she was a junkie, she'd have a natural aversion to cops, and he could understand her vacating the scene. From her point of view, where was the attraction in meeting a whole bunch of pushy, overly inquisitive people in black uniforms?

Willows stood up. His knees creaked. He glanced over at the front desk. "Pinky looks kind of left out and lonely, don't you think?"

Parker nodded. "Maybe we should have a talk with him."

"Good idea."

Pinky saw them coming. He fitted a smile onto his face as if it were a painfully tight shoe.

Parker said, "Pinky . . ."

"Yeah, that's me."

"Is there a way out of there, or do they toss your meals over the wire?"

Pinky jerked a fat thumb at the heavily barred, steel-clad door behind him.

"Come on out," said Willows.

"I'd prefer not to, actually."

Parker said, "Pinky, we're not going to bite. So do all three of us a favour and come on out."

"I got a bad cold." Pinky conjured up a sneeze. "Ah-choo!" He wiped his hand on his pants. "Believe me, it's much better for you if I stay right where I am."

Willows smiled. He said, "You hiding something in there, Pinky? A bottle, or a couple of joints, or a line or two, to help ease you through the long, dark night? We don't care. But we're not going to talk to you through the wire. If you don't haul your ass out of there, you're going to end up with something a lot worse than a head cold."

Pinky's bulging eyes swivelled towards Parker. "Is your friend *threatening* me?"

"Absolutely not."

Pinky chewed nervously on his pendulous lower lip. He risked another quick glance at Willows. Man, the guy looked hot enough to *melt*. He sat up a little straighter on his stool. "No way I'm unlocking that door. You don't like it, maybe you should talk to my lawyer."

"Have you got a lawyer, Pinky?"

"Well, no."

Bolt-cutters. Willows reminded himself to never leave home without them.

12

Jake had a private room in St. Paul's. For most of the city's sick but knowledgeable citizens, St. Paul's might not have been the first destination of choice, but Jake's thugs gave it a five-star rating. If his time to die had come, it seemed like the right place to get the job done. Anyway, Marty had arranged for a private room, and seen to it that Jake had his own nurse, and his down-filled comforter and cozy flannel sheet sets and pillows et cetera had been brought to him straight from his opulent Point Grey mini-mansion.

Jake took great comfort in these familiar things. A hospital was a hospital was a hospital, so it was nice to be able to enjoy a few of the creature comforts. Marty had even thought to provide him with a DVD player that played shiny little discs. He had sent a couple of punks down to A&B Sound to pick up some inspirational music, and a couple of dozen movies, including the complete *Godfather* series and a movie called *Heat*, which Jake had incorrectly assumed was a prequel or maybe a sequel to one of his all-time favourites, an old Cagney film called *White Heat*. Turned out to be a completely different story line, but he enjoyed it anyway, his fevered mind sometimes superimposing Cagney's bulky face and memorized lines over Al Pacino's excellent performance, with predictably confusing results.

Jake was passively watching the film's lengthy shootout when the action suddenly froze. A cop grimaced as he clutched his bloody chest. Flame spouted from the muzzles of assault rifles. An unbound chain of ejected cartridges looped through the air. Shattered glass hung suspended above a corpse-strewn sidewalk.

The sudden way it happened, all that violent, wonderfully choreographed action coming to an instant halt, against all the laws of nature, at the exact moment the noisy soundtrack plunged into a void of silence, made Jake think . . .

Jake thought the silence and freeze-frame effect meant that his time on earth had come to a grinding halt, and that the Great Creator had pulled the plug on him, preparatory to a big escalator opening up in the floor. A *down* escalator, naturally, that would convey him straight to Hell.

Something touched his shoulder. He was too weak to move his ancient head, but he could still get shifty-eyed with the best of them. Peering down and to the side, he spied a quartet of long, thick fingers and a thumb. He strained to rotate his eyeballs another degree or two. The diamond pinky ring he'd given Marty on his first double-digit birthday came slowly into focus.

"Mahty . . . dat you . . . kid?"

Marty said, "Yeah, it's me." As if there was another human being on the planet who'd dare risk uninvited physical contact with Jake. "How's the movie?"

"Not . . . ta . . . shabby."

Marty stepped back, so Jake could see him more easily. He said, "I hate to bother you, but we got a problem I thought you should know about."

"Aside . . . from . . . da fack . . . I'm . . . pullin' . . . back . . . my . . . leg . . . ta . . . kick . . . da . . . can?"

Marty said, "Cut it out, you're gonna be fine." His voice broke. He took a moment to collect himself, and then said, "Think about this, Jake. If the good die young, aren't you bound to live forever?"

Jake lifted a finger, acknowledging the logic. He made a kind of low-pitched wheezy sound that might have signified high good humour. It took a lot out of him. When he'd regained a modicum of strength he said, "So . . . wha's . . . up?"

Marty snapped his fingers. The blonde in the skintight parody of a nurse's uniform stopped crossing and uncrossing her fishnet legs and glanced up from her copy of *Playgirl*. She gave Marty a sultry and enquiring look, shifted her wad of spearmint aside and said, "Yeah, what?"

"Take a short hike, babe."

"The name is Tiffany."

"Take her with you," said Marty politely. He added, "Shut the door behind you, please."

Tiffany nodded and stood up, or rather, uncoiled. Marty hadn't ogled a pair of legs that long since New Orleans, and it had turned out the girl was wearing a pair of stilts.

Jake waited until the door was shut and then said, "Now . . . there's . . . a . . . dish . . . that'd . . . be . . . best . . . tasted . . . *hot*."

Marty smiled. Jake's appetite for women was limitless, and legendary. Up until the last few months, his enthusiasm for sex had made Hugh Hefner look like a low-energy eunuch. He claimed to have fornicated his way through the entire alphabet, first names and last, from A to Z and back again two complete times before his nineteenth birthday. Maybe it was a pack of lies, but Marty doubted it. How far poor Jake had fallen, in such an infernally short time! Tears welled up in his gangster's eyes.

Jake had informally adopted Marty at the tender age of eight, shortly after his father, Martin, who'd also been Jake's right-hand thug, had been felled by a lethal aneurysm. Well, that was what Jake in his wisdom had told him at the time. Only a year or so ago, Marty learned that his father had been riddled by Marty's jealous mother, Isobel, who'd discovered that her husband had a cheatin' heart, not to mention at least one other recklessly wandering organ. She'd emptied Martin's revolver into his back, then attempted to take her own life, but failed due to a lack of ammunition. She had fled the country, but Marty never learned her ultimate fate. Just as well.

Jake's right arm trembled, and then rose up and fell on his chest. His palsied fingers wormed towards his nose. He fumbled weakly with the clear plastic lines through which oxygen flowed into his hairy nostrils and thence to his lungs and brain.

Marty itched to help, but Jake's watery eyes told him to keep his distance. Marty couldn't seem to find the strength to take his eyes off Jake's fumbling, clumsy fingers. Those five rheumatism-riddled digits seemed completely at odds with each other, like the venal, bottomlessly ambitious characters Marty remembered from a dark piece of work by a guy named Shakespeare. Jake was still at it, his discombobulated digits poking and prodding ineffectually at his purplish, grossly swollen nose. It was kind of like watching a baby chick try to peck its exhausted way out of the shell. *Just get it over with!*

Finally Jake had the plastic lifelines adjusted to suit him. He glanced up at Marty and said, "So . . . wha's . . . da . . . pro'lem?"

Marty glanced cautiously towards the door. Take no chances, take no prisoners. He said, "We got a shipment coming in from Paul Mulhouse."

Jake tried to nod. His wattles trembled.

"We're talking ten million in U.S. currency," whispered Marty, so low he had to strain to hear himself. The cash was destined for Moscow and environs. There was peripheral CIA involvement, in return for a favour owed that Jake didn't need to know or worry about. The spooks were interested in further destabilizing the Russian economy. Marty had asked his contact why, and the agent had given himself a hernia and a three-day migraine in his futile attempt to come up with a half-plausible reason.

Jake said, "Da . . . point . . . ya's . . . gettin' at . . . is?"

"I don't know if you remember, but the money was on its way to the house last night when you took sick, Jake. The local cops swarmed the neighbourhood as soon as word got out that you were here, in St. Paul's. Probably they figured the Italians and Russians would move in, try to rearrange the pecking order."

Marty blushed red as a fire truck. Jake took note and idly wondered why.

Marty said, "I think you know the guys we hired to move the money, a couple of freelance slumps named Carlos and Hector."

"We . . . used . . ."

"'Em before? Yeah, two or three times. Never when this much cash was on the line, though. But like I said, I couldn't let them near the house, because the cops were crawling all over the place."

"Yeah, I . . ." Jake's eyes rolled up in their sockets and then came down again. "I . . . heard . . . ya . . . da foist . . . time."

"Sorry," said Marty, genuinely contrite.

Jake made a dismissive snuffling sound.

Marty sat down carefully on the side of the bed and took Jake's palsied hand in his. For the first time in years, he let another human being see the love that was inside him. He said, "I really want you to get better, Jake. Not just for yourself, but for me." Jake's hand was hot and dry, his skin brittle and scaly. Marty held on so tightly that he might have hoped their flesh would merge. He said, "You been a father to me ever since Mom popped the original. I was a helpless little kid, and you took care of me, showed me the ropes. You gotta know I love you like you were my own father, except even more so, 'cause he was so fucked up."

Jake smiled. He shut his rheumy eyes so poor deluded Marty couldn't see what he was thinking. Not that Marty's love was unrequited. But, *jeez*, there were certain things real men didn't talk about. Especially if one of them was dying. Hell, *especially* if one of them was dying. Jake gathered himself. He said, "Da . . . fuckin' . . . point!"

"Yeah, well . . ." Marty wiped his eyes with the back of his hand, sluicing away the grief. He took a deep breath, inhaling more oxygen at a single gulp than Jake had pulled in all night long. "What I was wondering, should I let Carlos and Hector hold on to the money until we get ourselves organized, and the cops back off? Or should we take delivery of it now?"

Jake frowned. He hoped his inability to hold a train of thought was due to all the pharmaceuticals they were pouring into him. Man, he was, uh . . .

Marty said, "Jake?" He waited and waited.

Finally Jake said, "Kill 'em."

Marty was so shocked he almost let it show. Had he heard Jake correctly? What rhymed with "Kill 'em"? "Spill 'em"? In the parlance of the trade, that was basically the same thing. How about "Grill 'em"? Yeah, that must be it. Jake wanted him to question Carlos and Hector. But about what?

He said, "Jake, did I hear you right?" He made a gun of his fist, and then drew his trigger finger across his throat. "You want me to kill Carlos and Hector?"

"Yeah . . . sure. Why . . . not?"

"Bump them off," said Marty. "Squib 'em. Put 'em down, snuff or waste 'em. Is that what you want?"

Jake's liver-spotted hands curled into a pair of pistols. His rheumy eyes sparkled. "Ka-pow!" he shouted. "Ka-pow! Ka-pow!" He showed the whites of his eyes. His head snapped from side to side. An alarm sounded.

Marty dropped to his knees and prayed to a God he desperately wished he believed in.

13

Willows turned to Parker. "Call the fire department. Get a hook-and-ladder over here."

Pinky Koblansky lunged forward. His pudgy tobacco-stained fingers gripped the wire mesh. "What'n hell ya callin' the fire department for?"

"They have two pieces of equipment we need, Pinky. One, a fire hose. Two, a big pair of bolt-cutters."

Pinky's eyes bulged. "What ya gonna do with a fire hose?"

"Clean the wax out of your ears," said Willows. "Why don't you ask me what I'm going to do with the bolt-cutters?"

"Never mind, I'm coming out." He turned and unlocked the steel-clad door behind him.

Parker said, "Don't even think about making a run for it, Pinky."

"You kiddin'? Take a look at me. I couldn't outrun a asthmatic tortoise. A couple nights ago, I'm limping to the bus stop, I pass under a streetlight and notice I can't even keep up with my own shadow." He opened the door, stepped through it and shut the door behind him.

Willows said, "Our witness just vanished."

"Bolt-cutters and a fire hose?" said Parker. "If he skipped, I don't blame him."

A door that had "STORAGE CLOSET" sloppily painted on it in pale-green letters swung open, and out stepped Pinky. "Okay, what can I do for you guys?"

"Tell us what you saw and heard, Pinky," said Willows.

"No problem."

"*Just* what you saw and heard," said Parker.

"No hallucinations, is that what you're saying? Lemme think a minute." Pinky assumed the pose. The seconds dribbled past. He pointed over Parker's shoulder. "Who's that?"

Parker glanced behind her. Dutton. He kept getting quieter and quieter. Spooky. She said, "That's Mel Dutton."

"He's a cop?"

"Yeah, Pinky, he's a cop."

"And that's what he does, takes pictures of dead people?" Pinky uttered a long, low whistle. "Nice job."

Parker said, "Okay, so you were sitting at the desk . . ."

"Huh? Oh, yeah. Right. I was sitting at the desk, and I hear shouting, and then I heard this tinkling. Not like somebody's taking a whiz, but louder. A metallic kind of sound. I look up, but I can't see nothing. I get out of my chair, lean against the wire. There's a bunch of coins falling down the stairwell and hitting the marble floor."

"We didn't see any coins," said Parker.

"Of course not, 'cause I picked 'em up for you." Pinky offered Parker a Styrofoam cup containing a handful of bloody coins. He said, "I already know what you're gonna tell me, that I shouldn't of touched nothing. But if I didn't take the money, somebody else would have stolen it. For sure, I guarantee it, and there woulda been nothin' I could do about it. So, like, I was *pre-servin'* the situation, kind of." He paused to take a deep breath. "Anyways, all of a sudden there's this scream, and a real heavy silence. Then the phone rings. I gotta take the call, 'cause if it's Uncle Morty, and I don't answer right away, he'll kick my ass. So I grab the phone and just as I pick it up . . . *splat!*"

Pinky paused to collect himself. He took a pair of wire-rim glasses out of his pants pocket, wiped the lenses with the tail of his T-shirt, and put the glasses back in his pocket.

"At that point, I dialled 911. I mean, it's Nick, and he's stayin' on the top floor. Gotta be a sixty-foot drop. Onto marble tiles laid on concrete. There's a reason they don't make pillows outta marble, right? The operator asks me do I want the cops or an ambulance, and I said what happened and she said I could expect both of them. Tells me I gotta stay on the line until somebody gets there."

Parker said, "Did you stay on the line, Pinky?"

"Bet your ass I did."

"You heard yelling," said Willows. "How many people would you say were up there?"

"I don't know, maybe two or three."

"Men, women . . . ?"

"One of each, I guess."

"Did you recognize the voices?"

"Yeah, sure. It was that kid over there, Nick, and his girlfriend. And Tripper."

"Tripper?" said Parker.

"Their mutt. It was mostly Nick's girlfriend's, but Nick took care of it when she was off working."

Parker said, "What's her name?"

Pinky was confused. "I already told you, her name's Tripper."

"No, I mean Nick's girlfriend."

"Chantal."

"Is that her first name or her last name?"

"First, I guess. Both, maybe. I never thought to ask, tell you the truth."

"How long had they been staying here?"

"A couple weeks. He paid in advance. They were due to check out at noon tomorrow, but Nick told me they'd be staying another week, maybe longer. He dropped by the desk . . ." Pinky frowned. "I mean, he came by last night, asked me if there was a monthly rate."

"You let dogs stay in the hotel?"

"If you're asking me is it against the rules, I'd have to say yes. But Chantal's a real nice girl, and I could see the dog meant a lot to her. More than Nick, probably. So I said as long as the animal was quiet, and they kept a low profile, it'd be okay."

"She slip you a few extra bucks?"

"No, absolutely not."

Willows said, "Pinky."

"What?"

"How much did Chantal and Nick pay you not to notice Tripper?"

Pinky glanced haphazardly around, looking for an exit that didn't exist. "Twenty a week. I shoulda said no? Uncle Morty pays minimum wage. We're talkin' wrong side of the poverty line, and I *still* gotta pay taxes! And the politicians think that's okay. So now you tell me who's hallucinating!"

Willows said, "What happened after Nick hit the tiles?"

"What d'you mean?"

"I mean, what happened? Did you hear Chantal say anything?"

"Like what?"

"You tell me, Pinky."

"Like, did she scream for help or yell that she didn't mean to push him, it was an accident? No, she didn't. I never heard a peep out of her, one way or the other."

"Okay, let's go back a minute."

"Backwards in time?" Pinky liked the idea. He did a slow reverse shuffle. Willows held his temper in check. Pinky was starting to get to him. Maybe it was the time of night, lack of sleep. More likely it was just plain Pinky. Willows jammed his clenched fists into his coat pockets.

Parker said, "Before Nick fell, when he and Chantal were yelling at each other, what did they say?"

"I dunno . . . not much. It was just a whole lot of noise, like animals growling at each other. Then, bingo. Touchdown!"

"You said you recognized Chantal's voice."

"Correct."

"But you never saw her, is that right?"

"No, that's wrong. She came running down the stairs after he fell. I could hear her all the way, she was making a lot of noise, huffing and puffing, crying." Pinky pointed. "She stopped right there, about six steps up. I saw her legs, and then she bent from the waist and I could see her head, except it was upside down. She stared at Nick for a couple seconds, and then she looked at me, and then she just . . . took off."

"Back upstairs?"

"No, across the lobby and out the door."

Parker said, "She has an argument with her boyfriend, the guy she lives with, and he takes a fall and splits his skull wide open. *Dies.* C'mon, Pinky. She must have said *something.*"

"Well, she didn't. Not a single word."

"Okay, tell us about the expression on her face."

"Blank."

"She didn't look angry, or happy as a clam, or vengeful, or racked with guilt . . . ?"

"No, none of them. Though I gotta admit I'm not sure what I'd be looking for." Pinky folded his arms across his flabby chest. The weight of his thoughts seemed to pull his face down into his chin. He said, "I dunno, for sure I'm no expert, but I'd say she was in shock."

Willows said, "Were there any other witnesses to the fall?"

Pinky's smile was sly. "Just the mutt."

Other mutt, thought Willows uncharitably.

Parker said, "Describe her for us, Pinky."

"Chantal?"

Parker nodded.

"Uh . . . she's about your height, maybe a couple of inches shorter." Pinky rearranged his arms. His hand, palm down, hovered on a level with Parker's nose. "About so. What's that, about five-foot-something?

"Close enough," said Parker. She found the next blank page in her notebook and wrote "5'4"."

"What colour is her hair?" said Willows.

"Blond, streaked with red, and black roots. Her eyebrows were black. And I bet . . ." Pinky trailed off. He smiled goofily up at the lobby's ceiling.

"Eye colour?" said Willows.

"Brown, with gold specks."

"You happen to notice what she was wearing?"

"Yeah, but don't gimme no credit, 'cause she always wore the same outfit. At night, anyway. Fake leopardskin jacket over a pink or white T-shirt, jeans and boots."

Parker and Willows exchanged a quick look.

Willows said, "Was she five-something with or without the boots, Pinky?"

"With."

"She was hooking?" said Parker.

"I never asked her." Pinky saw the look in Willows' eye. "Except once," he amended. "She misunderstood my intentions, and told me she was already booked solid for the night." He spread his arms wide. "So tell me, do I look like the kind of guy has gotta pay for it?"

Both times, thought Willows.

Parker said, "Did you say anything to Chantal when she came down the stairs?"

"Asked her what happened, but she paid me no mind. Maybe didn't hear me. Then she took off, and I yelled at her to stop, but there was no way. What could I do? By the time I let myself out of the cage, she's gonna be blocks away. Could I catch up with her? Not unless I caught a taxi first. So, like I said, I grabbed the phone." Pinky smiled. His teeth were the same depressing shade of grey as very old concrete. "Before I know it, there's almost as many cops as cockroaches. Then you two show up. The detectives."

Mel Dutton's flash lit up the wall.

Pinky said, "D'you think he'd be interested in taking my picture?"

"Depends how much you're willing to pay for the privilege."

Pinky's optimistic grin slumped back into his face. "I was hoping he'd pay me."

"Is that what happened last time a cop took your picture, Pinky?"

"What're you saying?" Pinky sighed wearily. "Okay, I done a few crimes. Nothing heavy, and I been clean as a Boy Scout's ears for more'n two years. I turned in every last nickel, if that's what you're worried about. And I swear to God I almost stopped drinking during the daytime hours."

Willows glanced at Parker. She shook her head. Willows said, "That's it, for now."

"You done with me?"

Willows nodded. "Yeah, but we'll need your master key, Pinky. So we can get into the room without kicking the door in."

"That what you're gonna do now, go upstairs to look in their room, see if you can find any important clues?"

"You should've been a cop, Pinky."

"I ain't gonna argue with you, but I doubt it." Pinky dug deep into his pants pocket and came up with a brass key attached by a short length of rusty steel chain to a block of wood painted dark green. He handed the key to Parker. "Should I go up there with you? I mean, Uncle Morty told me that I should always be in the room if I let the cops or a lawyer or whatever go in without a warrant, to make sure nothing disappears, so we don't get sued."

Willows said, "If Uncle Morty arrives, send him upstairs. But don't call him, understand?"

Pinky frowned. "I hope so." His mother had been right; there were days when he wished he'd stayed in school. About three of them, so far. He said, "If you don't need me any more, is it okay if I get back in my cage?"

"Sure," said Willows. He smiled. "But only if you promise to behave yourself."

"You got it," said Pinky. Had he sniffed Willows' ironic tone? Yes, but he felt safe in the cage, and that was all that mattered.

14

The hospital's big stainless-steel-walled elevator was crammed with relatives and friends of the merely sick and deathly ill, assorted harried doctors, a scattering of insomniac patients in rumpled jammies, and half a dozen semi-gorgeous young nurses. The doctors and nurses eyed each other as the metal box plunged towards the depths. The air reeked of sex and death. Nurses probably did okay, payroll-wise, but Marty was willing to bet they had to work shifts, and that most of them burned out decades before the pension kicked in.

Doctors, on the other hand, were universally known to be overpaid. True, they bitched constantly about their incomes, but more often than not they paused in mid-sentence to take a long putt. Marty shook his head, irritated with himself. Why was he thinking about these things?

So he wouldn't have to think about Carlos and Hector.

The elevator slowed, then stopped. A bell pinged. The doors slid apart. Nobody moved. The corridor was empty. A patient chuckled nervously. The doors slid shut and the bell pinged again. They resumed their descent.

Marty fished out his Startac and speed-dialled Pedro, who picked up between the first and second ring.

"¿Qué pasa?"

"Fire it up." Marty disconnected as he heard the Hummer's starter motor whine. He speed-dialled his favourite number. Half a ring this time. Marty said, "Melanie, can I come over?" He smiled. "Yeah, I got a couple bottles of Crystal Brut, that okay?" Her reply made him laugh out loud. The nurses were watching him, every last one of them. Or maybe it was the suit, three pieces, five grand worth of dark-blue silk cut from one of Hermann Maglio's favourite bolts. But more likely it was Marty himself: the uncompromising way he carried himself, the way his two hundred and twenty pounds of hard bone and bulging muscle were artistically packed onto his six-foot-two-inch frame, his broad shoulders and narrow hips. Or it might have been his smooth skin and healthy complexion, his glossy hair and flawless teeth, ruthless, good-natured mouth, and the look in his dark eye that promised all comers anything, anytime, anywhere they wanted it. But especially right here, right this minute.

Marty hoped Melanie could help him figure out what to do about Carlos and Hector. He was his own man, and nobody else's, but when Jake put the finger on somebody, that was it, end of story.

Until now.

The elevator pinged again. Everybody got off except Marty and the pick of the nurses.

She gave him a nice smile. "What a night!"

Marty tugged at an earlobe.

She said, "That's a really nice suit. Is it silk? Are you a doctor?"

"Thank you," said Marty. "Yes, and no."

"Was that your wife I heard you talking to on the phone?"

"No, that was Pedro, my wheel-man." Marty saw he'd confused her. He said, "Guy who drives the car."

She shook her head, blond curls bouncing. "No, I mean the second call you made, to Melanie. Is Melanie your wife?"

"Just a friend," said Marty. It was the saddest truth he knew.

The nurse offered her small hand. "My name's Gwynneth, but my friends call me Gwen."

"Marty," said Marty. They shook. He half expected her to move in for a kiss, and then drive a knife into his guts. Not that she looked homicidal; it was just one of those situations, and the time was right, what with Jake gasping his last. Marty smiled. Was that why Jake wanted him to squib Carlos and Hector, so people would know he was in charge?

Gwynneth said, "Would you like to take me somewhere for a drink?"

"Yeah, sure, but I can't. I already got a commitment."

"Dump her."

"No, I couldn't do that."

Gwynneth gave him a teasing smile. She licked her lips, and he saw that she had a pearl stud in her tongue. How appealing. She said, "You've got no idea what . . ." She frowned, and then her brow cleared. She continued, ". . . you're missing . . ."

Marty smiled. He'd met women like Gwynneth many times before, and knew exactly what he was missing, and that he didn't miss it one little bit.

The elevator pinged one last time. Never ask for whom the elevator pings, because the elevator pings for you. The doors split apart. Marty stepped aside, and then followed Gwynneth out of the elevator. The matte-black Hummer was waiting for him, Pedro slouched over the wheel picking dried blood out of his fingernails with one of his switchblades. He glanced up from his copy of the *New Yorker*, and unlocked the door. Good ol' Pedro. A bilingual gem, except his English wasn't too wonderful and seemed, somehow, to keep getting worse. But despite this handicap he somehow always managed to make himself understood, and, when necessary, feared.

Gwynneth said, "Which way are you going, Marty?"

"Up, I hope."

Gwynneth chuckled throatily. "No, I mean what part of the city are you headed towards."

"False Creek."

"Me too. What a coincidence, huh? Is that Pedro? He's quite handsome, in a dark kind of way. Would you mind giving me a ride?"

"You don't have a car?"

"Of course I've got a car. Sort of." She pointed towards a late-model white Neon.

Marty thought about it, but not for long. He said, "We can give you a ride, but for reasons that probably wouldn't surprise you, Pedro's gotta pat you down first."

"Frisk me?"

"If that's how you want to put it."

"How would *you* like to put it?" said Gwynneth archly.

Marty got Pedro's attention. It wasn't hard. He introduced Gwynneth and asked Pedro if he'd mind patting her down. Pedro climbed down out of the enormous Humvee and sauntered over. The top of his shaved head was roughly level with Gwen's dilated pupils. It occurred to Marty, none too soon, that his new acquaintance had squandered a good part of her shift dipping her pearl-studded tongue into one of St. Paul's numerous medicine cabinets.

Gwynneth leaned against the Hummer. She pressed her splayed hands on the hood. Pedro eased up behind her and roved his hands over her body.

Gwynneth said, "Take your time, *señor*." Pedro rolled his eyes, being cute.

In the car, Gwynneth in the middle and Pedro behind the wheel, Marty said, "Drop me off at Melanie's."

"Big surprise."

Marty gave him a look.

Pedro said, "Ever' time you visit Mr. Jake, den you go see you sweetie."

Marty nodded thoughtfully. It was true that Melanie was his island in the storm. Since Jake had snuggled into his deathbed, Marty had required a lot of succouring. He said, "Take the long way around, Pedro."

"Hokay!"

Marty considered himself a decent fellow, given the nature of his profession. Even so, there were a lot of guys who'd prefer to think of him in the past tense, especially now that Jake was, from a vulture's point of view, pretty much ripe for the picking.

Predictability had been the death of more than one gangster. From now on he'd minimize the risk of a loud and bloody ambush by taking a variety of routes to Melanie's semi-luxurious apartment.

But the grim truth was that only a few roads led to her highrise on the water. Any thug with half a dozen lesser thugs on his payroll could easily cover all the routes. When you came right down to it, a lone thug could do the job, simply by waiting for him in the hallway outside Melanie's door. Or some murderous creep in a FedEx uniform could bull his way into her apartment.

Maybe, until Jake recovered his health, he should find her someplace else to live.

Or she could move into one of the many spare bedrooms in Jake's enormous house. No, that was a terrible idea. If she moved in, they'd start eating breakfast together, talking about stuff that was in the morning paper . . . Marty did not wish to become a domesticated animal, not even if Melanie was holding the reins.

The Hummer had stopped. Marty glanced up and saw that they'd arrived. He said, "I'll be a while. I got something I gotta talk over with Melanie, see what she thinks."

Pedro nodded. He said, "You wan' somebody snap-crackle-and-popped, just gimme the word, 'cause I always wanna be a cereal killer."

Gwynneth poked Pedro forcefully in the ribs. "That's so funny!"

Pedro blushed. He said, "I read it onna T-shirt. Lemme tell ya a joke I saw in a magazine. Dis bald guy inna business suit is standin' at a pearly gates, an' St. Peter's lookin' down at him. He asks da businessman in a great big voice, 'So what did you do that wasn't so terrible?'"

Gwynneth said, "Yeah . . . ?"

"Dat's it," said Pedro.

Marty got out of the car. He said, "Have fun, kids."

Pedro fetched him a sly wink.

Marty said, "Be good, Pedro."

"The best," said Pedro. He made a vile motion with his hand. Marty slammed the door.

He knew Melanie so well. By now she'd have changed the sheets, taken a shower, dabbed a little perfume here and there . . . Then she'd slip naked into the ankle-length ocelot coat he'd given her a few birthdays ago, step out on the balcony and smoke Gitane cigarettes until she saw the Humvee. He pictured her flicking her cigarette butt into the wind, going back inside the apartment to unlock the door for him. Pouring the wine, lighting the gas fire.

If he was lucky, he'd find her on the couch, in a pose far too provocative for his imagination to anticipate.

Funny how sex clarified the senses, but dulled the mind. He hoped Melanie could help him with his problem. If Jake hadn't told him to whiff Carlos and Hector, he'd be as close to contented as he ever could be.

15

Mel Dutton had graduated from the Vancouver Art School, now known by the more highfalutin name of the Emily Carr Institute of Art & Design. He'd shown a lot of early promise, and snagged a position with a renowned local photographer. His job was essentially that of an eighteenth-century apprentice, but without any of the usual perks. His salary was abysmally low. No, even lower. He was expected to be available to perform the most menial of tasks, at all hours of the day and night. Light my cigarette. Fetch my shoes. No matter how diligently he toiled, his employer never spoke an encouraging word to him. Dutton stuck it out for eighteen months, until he'd gained enough confidence in his abilities to strike out on his own as a freelancer. That part of his life had lasted deep into his twenties. He met a lovely woman, Emily, and they were married and had four children, all of them girls as sweet and brave as their mother. Dutton opened a small portrait studio. In his spare time – and there were times when he had an awful lot of spare time – he prowled the back alleys of the city's seamier side, and took thousands of starkly beautiful black-and-white photographs of dime-bagger drug addicts and desperate nickel-a-pop whores.

The photographs were in demand, but never for sale. Dutton's ethics prevented him from making a dollar out of the nearly dead.

Over the years his growing family's expenses mounted steadily, but Dutton's income remained constant. His talent was prodigious, but his twitchy temperament and unyielding insistence on absolute perfection of detail was not suited to his posed subjects, or his profession. Emily was endlessly supportive, but Dutton was a man, in the best sense of the word. He knew himself, and was acutely aware of the many involuntary sacrifices his wife and children made on his behalf, in the name of art. Gradually, he came to see that his situation was indefensible. The time had come for him to give up his tattered dream of artistic independence and step out in the real world, and earn a living.

What Dutton didn't tell Emily was that, on the advice of a pal who happened to be a VPD superintendent, he applied to join the Vancouver Police Department. The cops needed a recruit who could snap professional-quality photographs, and Dutton was fated to be their man. In less than a week he'd begun training at the police academy, which was located at that time in a big barn of a building on Point Grey Road. Dutton had traded in his suede sports jacket and shabby cords for a spiffy new uniform, blue steel .38-calibre Smith & Wesson revolver, and a Speed Graphic.

He had become official photographer to the horribly maimed, and recently dispatched. He'd turned his back forever on strained smiles and "watch the birdie," and would spend the rest of his working life knee-deep in bloody exit wounds, multiple stabbings, stippling and splash patterns. The first time he saw a body, he knew there was no turning back. Because he was an intelligent and perceptive person, he quickly realized that his primary role was as spokesman for the dead. He thrived in his work, its endless surprise and variety, and the certain knowledge that what he was doing was worthwhile, a benefit to his fellow man. But all that violence took a toll.

Two days earlier he'd photographed the aftermath of a domestic dispute. A bald man had died of a single powerful blow to the head from a cast-iron frying pan. The pan's bottom, twelve inches in diameter, had a pattern of heat-dispersing concentric circles. The homicide dicks had known the frying pan was the murder weapon because the pattern was deeply embedded in the man's skull. How unlucky for his murderous wife that he suffered from male-pattern baldness. That case had been interesting primarily because of the lighting problems, but the point was that they were all different, all had their unique little charms.

Several years into his new career, Dutton's wandering mind had stumbled on the idea of publishing a fat coffee-table book of a selection of his crime-scene photographs. The very best of the best. He put together a portfolio and contacted the major Canadian publishers. Everybody was fascinated but nobody would commit.

Dutton, who considered himself a fast learner, signed on with a powerful Toronto-based literary agency. Before the ink was dry on the contract, his high-powered agent switched personas to that of a reclusive, low-energy deaf-mute. His wife claimed he was in emotional hibernation. What did that mean? Dutton tried to get out of his contract, but the head of the agency threatened him with a massive lawsuit. All cops have a deeply ingrained fear of lawyers. Dutton was no exception.

A few years passed, and finally his contract with the agency expired. He rewrote his c.v. and managed after several more years and hundreds of dollars' worth of postage to attract a red-hot agent headquartered in New York City. The agent promptly got him a three-book deal and a huge cash advance. A few days later, Dutton got a polite phone call from a New York cop. His agent had been arrested for fraud and grand larceny, and his empty bank accounts had been frozen solid. A week later, his editor had a stroke, and took early retirement. The publishing dates were set back and back again, and then, following months of frantic long-distance phone calls, cancelled.

Dutton soldiered on. He was unable to recover the hundreds of glossy photographs he'd couriered to New York, but consoled himself with the knowledge that he had the negatives, which was undeniably a positive.

He was thinking about his next book, working title *Stiffs*, as he crouched over Nick Partridge's body, which lay face up on the tiles in the classic position, right arm extended above the head,

left arm close by the side, left leg straight, right leg slightly bent
at the knee. Dutton meant to shoot an extreme close-up of Nick's
glazed, rapidly dulling eye. He'd changed to a macro lens so
powerful it would allow him to damn near climb inside the guy's
cornea. He was so close that he was aware of a slow wash of heat
coming off the corpse. Or was the sensation merely a by-product
of his overworked imagination? He'd often idly wondered if the
global-warming phenomenon was due in large part to the earth's
burgeoning population. All those hundreds of billions of pounds of
meat walking around at 98.6 degrees Fahrenheit *had* to be a factor.

He grunted a terse reply when Claire Parker said hello to him
on her way to the broad staircase leading to the hotel's upper
floors. As usual, Willows was dead quiet. Mr. Personality. What
Parker saw in him was a mystery to Dutton. Maybe it was one of
those shallow, purely physical attractions. Dutton hoped so. He
took his shot, and then two more, bracketing the exposures.

The night clerk, Pinky, scruffy, moronic, with an alcoholic's
firecracker nose and the squinched-up eyes of a latent psychopath,
a character out of almost anybody's worst nightmare, was yelling
at Parker to watch out for the dog. Dutton couldn't *see* a dog, but
that didn't mean it wasn't solid advice. He dropped the Nikon,
letting it swing from its strap, and snatched up his Pentax, loaded
with fast 800 ASA film, and equipped with a 135-millimetre lens.
He got off three quick shots and they all felt good, the night clerk's
bloated face a jigsaw puzzle in black and white, his shouting mouth
a black hole spiked with broken stumps of teeth, strings of saliva
and irregular white blotches of something akin to fungi that were
obviously not symptomatic of a rigorously healthy lifestyle.

Dutton stepped away from the corpse. Crouching, his knee on
the black-and-white tiles, he took a shot of Willows and Parker
just as they reached the first turn in the stairs.

Parker glanced back when she heard the click and whir of the
camera. She blessed Dutton with a nice smile, and, just as he got
off his second shot, tossed her hair and gave him the finger.

Perfect!

16

Three uniformed cops loitered in the hallway, each of them somehow contriving to take up more space than was necessary, all of them managing the cop trick of simultaneously looking as if they had a God-given right to be there and absolutely no reason to be there.

The cops were there simply because they were there. No reason required, because they were in uniform and lethally armed. Nobody in his right mind would ever think to question their presence, or legitimacy. It was the very thing that Willows, who would never have described himself as a slumbering civil-rights activist, did not much like about his fellow officers. Not that it was their fault. Civilians got exactly the level of policing they deserved. If they didn't mind being shooed home at midnight on New Year's Eve or pepper-sprayed because the wind was favourable or having security cameras on every street corner, well, that's what they'd get. Promptly. He smiled. The idle cops reminded him of his father's talent for discovering unnecessary chores. He tossed the hotel-room key to the cop with the worst posture. "Unlock it."

The cop frowned down at the key as if he were unsure as to its purpose. After a moment he said, "There's no room number on the key. What room are we supposed to be watching?" He pointed with a blunt finger. "It's that one, isn't it?"

Willows glanced at the other cops. "Didn't Pinky tell you what room you were supposed to be watching?"

"Yeah, he told us. But the rooms don't have numbers. And like I already said, neither does this key."

"It's a master key," said Willows, too patiently. He spread his arms wide. "It opens the doors to all the rooms."

The cop flushed. "I know what a master key is!" He wasn't quite pouting, but it was a near thing. He inserted the key in the lock and turned it, withdrew the key, and punched the door open with his fist. He started to pocket the key, caught himself, and tossed it back to Willows. His mouth was clamped shut, but his face shouted his embarrassment and humiliation.

Willows had visited the hotel many times before. He was familiar with the layout of the rooms, and there was nothing in this one that surprised him, other than the large dog curled up on the bed.

Parker said, "Hey there, Tripper." The dog wagged it's stubby tail. "She looks friendly."

"So do I," countered Willows, not entirely accurately.

Parker cautiously approached the bed. Tripper lifted her head and tentatively licked Parker's hand. Parker scratched the dog behind an ear, and Tripper made a low growling sound that had nothing to do with aggression, but was more like a canine purring. She had a collar and a tag, a disc of plastic with a clear face. Beneath the plastic somebody had written a name and address in black ink. Parker wondered if the lab, or somebody with 20/20 vision, would be able to read the smudged writing. Squinting, she angled the tag to the light. It was no use, she was wasting her time. Tripper licked her hand again, and rolled over on her back. Parker gave her a tummy rub. The dog moaned with pleasure, and gave Willows a smug, self-satisfied look.

The room was furnished with a low coffee table, a battered chest of drawers, and the bed. Willows and Parker searched the place quickly but efficiently. It didn't take long. In a matchbox hidden in a rolled-up pair of dirty white sports socks, Willows found a few grams of what was almost certainly cocaine. Parker lifted a soiled pillow and found a switchblade. The knife was made in China and had a red plastic handle. The blade was pitted and rusty, but showed the marks of a recent sharpening. She said, "What kind of a person leaves a switchblade under his pillow, with the blade out?"

"Somebody who thinks he might find himself in a situation where every second counts."

Parker nodded. The dog jumped off the bed and followed her as she made her way into the bathroom. A bar of green soap squatted on the sink. She searched the medicine cabinet, bracing herself against the weight of the animal leaning on her leg. If proximity is the mother of fondness, her relationship with Tripper was a done deal. Parker had hoped for a vial of prescription medicine, with a neatly typed name and address, but all she found was a strangled-to-death tube of toothpaste, a tiny barrel of unwaxed dental floss, and a toothbrush with a fluorescent-pink handle. She glanced down. There was a fawning, take-pity-on-me-I'm-helpless-and-alone-and-may-starve-to-death-at-any-moment-if-you-don't-feed-me look in Tripper's chocolate eyes. Parker believed Tripper knew that something cataclysmic had happened, and that it would be wise to make as many new friends as possible.

She looked down at the dog and said, "Sorry, but we're full up. We already have two cats."

Tripper wagged her tail. Loved cats, obviously.

"Vicious cats," said Parker.

Tripper pressed even closer. Her soft brown eyes sought to assure Parker that she loved all animals of the feline persuasion from the very bottom of her heart, unconditionally.

As Parker continued to search the bathroom, the three-man crime-scene unit trotted up the stairs. The men were all about the same height and weight, and were dressed in identical flimsy white coveralls and elasticized white caps.

As they reached the landing they broke into an absolutely precise dance step, moonwalking across the linoleum, arms jerking, heads bobbing. The dance was over almost before it had begun. A cop by the door brought up his hands to applaud, then thought better of it. Just as well, because the CSU guys had their game faces on. They might have been in the mood for precision dancing, but they were in no mood for levity. They paused to wriggle white cotton slippers over their heavy protester-squashing cop boots, and entered the room in single file.

Willows spoke briefly to a CSU cop named Hugh Stevens, and then he and Parker and Tripper left the hotel room and trotted down the wide staircase towards the lobby.

Outside the hotel, the crowd had continued to grow despite the seasonally inclement weather. Parker's eye was drawn to a middle-aged couple wearing identical nylon jackets. The jackets were yellow with vertical red stripes on the sleeves. Parker suddenly realized that couples who sported identical jackets were never accompanied by children, nor looked as if they had children or ever intended to do so. Did the jackets signify an additional level of commitment that was a direct consequence of their decision not to have children, or an inability to have children? A tremor ran through her. Nick Partridge was somebody's beloved son. Chantal was someone's cherished daughter. How could Willows not realize that she was pregnant? What in hell was *wrong* with him?

A City of Vancouver street-cleaning truck roared by, brushes swirling, blasts of water chasing cigarette butts and used condoms and discarded hypos into the gutters. A few bystanders warily eyed the flood of water, but nobody gave ground. Word had spread that there was a body inside the hotel, that someone had died violently and bloodily. The corpse was coming out, sooner or later, and the unspoken consensus was that a close look at it was well worth a below-the-knee soaking.

Parker watched the miniature tsunami race along the gutter. Tourists and other newcomers considered the city immaculately clean, but she'd been around a long time. She'd noticed, over the past few years, that the streets were a lot dirtier than they used to be.

Parker moved slowly around the periphery of the crowd. A woman in a tattered nightgown tugged at her sleeve and demanded to know who'd been killed. Parker shrugged.

An elderly man wearing a ski jacket that was leaking puffs of pink insulation said, "That alky night clerk tossed a guy down the stairs and killed him."

"Where'd you hear that?" said Parker.

The man shrugged.

Parker said, "Does Pinky have a reputation for violence?"

The man eyed Tripper. He looked wildly around, and then ducked his head and lit a home-rolled cigarette. "Pinky who?"

Parker moved on. Every last person in the crowd looked guilty of some small transgression, but nobody looked like a murderer, and none of the women she could see remotely resembled Pinky's oddly detailed description of Nicholas Partridge's girlfriend, Chantal. Parker noticed Dutton discreetly snapping available-light photos of the crowd, in the faint hope that, if somebody had pushed Nicholas Partridge over the banister railing, he'd loitered to admire the effects of his handiwork.

"Butterbean!" The man in the breached ski jacket was pointing excitedly at Dutton.

Parker turned and stared at him.

"It's Butterbean!" shouted the man, rushing towards Dutton. "Butterbean, the heavyweight, the boxer! That's him right over there, that's Butterbean!" The man raised his fists and jabbed harmlessly at the woman in the nightgown. "I seen him on TV, he's a ball of suet, and a terror!" He swung again, meaninglessly. The woman stepped inside his looping punch and hit him in the ribs and belly with a flurry of hard shots. He fell to his knees and was dealt a chopping blow to the ear. Parker stuck out her foot, saving the man's face from the concrete. The female pugilist sized her up. She raised her fists. "You lookin' for a piece of me, sister?"

The crowd stirred. A worm of blood trickled down the defeated fighter's upper lip and trickled into his yawning mouth. Parker held tight to Tripper's collar as the dog growled, and showed her teeth. Laughing, the woman turned away and disappeared into the crowd.

Dutton nudged Parker with his elbow. "I got the whole damn thing, first punch to last. Interested?"

"I don't think so, Mel."

"I'll make a few extra prints, send 'em over and you can take a look."

Dutton glanced up as Pinky Koblansky shouted at him from the Lux's dimly lit doorway. Pinky's hair was in disarray and his eyes were wild. When he'd learned that Dutton was planning to publish a series of lavishly produced books based on his morbid crime-scene photos, Pinky had shamelessly begged Dutton to immortalize him for, as he put it, "all time." Dutton made his way back into the hotel, hustled Pinky over to the corpse, shot a half-roll of film, and sent the night clerk on his way.

Dutton turned towards the stairs. He was thirty pounds over-weight. Okay, forty. Worse, he'd started smoking again, effortlessly getting up to his previous speed of two packs of unfiltered Camels a day. He felt so bad about the smoking that he'd started drinking heavily, and, of course, when he smoked he drank. It was why God had given him two hands. Because there was a province-wide ban on smoking in bars and other enclosed public spaces, he did a lot of drinking at home. It was cheaper than going out, and he didn't have to worry about getting behind the wheel afterwards. So he drank even more. It was a closed loop and a Möbius strip, and it was hell.

Dutton lit a cigarette and started slowly up the stairs. By the third step, his heart was pounding like a sledgehammer, and he was wheezing like a trout in a frying pan.

Man, oh man, was he ever out of shape. Maybe he should think about switching to filtertips . . .

17

She'd sprinted to the end of the hall, unlocked the window and pushed it open and stepped outside, onto the rusty iron bars of the fire-escape landing. The window had opened easily and that had surprised her, so she lost her balance and almost fell.

She wondered if fear had given her the strength of ten women, and then she looked down, into the dimly lit alley, and her knees and heart turned to jelly. It had stopped raining, for now. The night air was cold and damp and smelled of the ocean.

She looked down again. Narrow iron steps zigzagged into the gloom. She turned and looked behind her. The hotel corridor was warm and familiar and inviting. She thought about the terrible sound Nick had made when he'd hit the floor. A meaty, irreparable thud, like nothing she'd ever heard before but instantly recognized, a terminal impact that shouted of broken bones and sudden death.

Poor Nick. Her eyes flooded with tears. The streetlights and distant lights of the office towers blurred and staggered. She wiped her eyes with the back of her hand. Nick was dead and she'd killed him. Hadn't she? That weasel Pinky had probably already called the cops. They'd find drugs in the room, maybe enough to convict her of possession with intent to traffic. Was that worth worrying about? She clutched the railings with both hands, and took that first crucial step towards freedom. The metal was shivery cold and

vibrated alarmingly with every painstakingly slow and tentative
step she took.

Heights had never bothered her, until now. A part of her knew
it was the vivid, jangling memory of Nick's swift and easy fall that
robbed her of her courage and strength, but it was one thing to
analyse the situation and quite another to have to deal with it. She
slammed her foot down, freshened her grip on the railings, and
took another step. The wail of an approaching siren drifted on
unseen currents, ebbed and flowed and suddenly gained enormous strength, climbing to a deafening, accusatory shriek.

Chantal leaned far out over the railing. Her stomach muscles
clenched involuntarily. Sparkling blue and red lights were reflected
off dozens of plate-glass windows, and it was as if every police car
in the world was after her in hot pursuit.

She scurried down the shuddering fire escape, moving faster than
she could think. Ten feet above the alley the ladder came to an
abrupt end. Chantal knew that this was to stop thieves from gaining
entrance to the hotel and that there had to be a mechanism to allow
a ladder to descend all the way to the alley, but the light was so poor
that she couldn't see the ladder, much less how to release it.

A patrol car turned in to the alley, headlights tossing a handful
of shadows, making them tumble like dice. The sirens were all
around her, deafening in their intensity. The patrol car's brakes
chirped. The vehicle stopped almost directly below her. The
backup lights flashed white and then the man behind the wheel
shifted into gear and the car surged forward, rocketed down the
alley and vanished around the corner at the end of the block.

Chantal sat down, her legs dangling. She grasped a rod of rust-
pitted steel, twisted her body and lowered herself cautiously, all
her weight in her arms. The ladder chose that moment to rattle
down, the crash of steel echoing off the brick walls of the buildings.
She lost her grip and tumbled sideways, instinctively protecting
her head with her arms as she hit the asphalt, and rolled.

A handful of distraught pigeons launched themselves heavily
into the night sky, wheeled uncertainly above her and returned to

their roosts. She stood up, shaky but unhurt. The rain was coming down again. More sirens and lights. She stared up at the dimly lit fifth-floor window, almost hoping a cop would stick his head out and yell at her not to move.

No such luck. She walked down the alley to the street and turned right, towards the railway tracks and the harbour. She had no plan beyond taking the next step. At the corner she waited as a patrol car howled past, tires slithering on wet pavement. The cop in the shotgun seat winked at her, and was gone. The light turned red. She waited patiently for it to turn green again. There was a crowd in front of the hotel, cops shouting at them to keep their distance. Good advice, and Chantal intended to take it. The light turned green. She hurried across the street, but not too quickly.

Nick's friends weren't her friends – not any longer. She had to stay away from them. She needed a hidey-hole, somewhere safe to pass the night. In an alley off Water Street she found what she was looking for, a warehouse doorway with a wide, overhanging roof that offered shelter from the elements. On the far side of the alley, acres of freight yards were protected by a high chain-link fence topped with razor wire. Powerful lights glittered high up on one of the monstrous cranes used to unload the ships that converged on the city from all over the world. Beyond the freight yard was the harbour, and then the mountains. It was a good place to spend the night: noisy, but out of the weather.

An overhead light protected by a wire cage illuminated a stack of wooden packing crates and a dumpster full of flattened cardboard boxes. Chantal glanced warily around. The loading dock was a prime location but it was unoccupied. In ten minutes of hard work, she made herself a snug little nest of crates and cardboard. She stepped back, and critically surveyed her work. She'd done a good job. Her tiny home couldn't be seen from the alley.

Secure in her hideaway, she emptied the pockets of her jeans and jacket and took inventory of her possessions. She searched frantically through her pockets, but somewhere between the hotel and the loading dock she'd lost the American money she'd held back from Nick. Was it in her leopardskin jacket? What difference did it make now? There was just enough light to count the money she found in Nick's leather jacket – eight dollars and ten cents. She still had the straight razor he'd made her carry when she was working. Curled up in the tight space she'd made, she was cold, but getting warmer. She listened to the sounds of the nearby trains shunting back and forth. The cops would roust her if they found her, but she was more likely to be caught by a private security guard. Some brainless chunk of testosterone riding a mountain bike. The guards were everywhere, in their black pants and yellow rain slickers. They were mean-hearted sons of bitches, some of them, armed with pepper spray and nightsticks.

Chantal opened the razor and put it down where she could get it fast, if she needed to. The security guards were bad enough, but all they'd do is slap her around a little, and force her to move on. What worried her was the possibility of being found by some wandering punk who thought he saw a chance to get laid. She wasn't about to risk a venereal disease, or AIDS. Some asshole tried to get into her pants, she'd slice him wide open, no hesitation.

Freight cars banged together, the immense, hollow, metallic sound of them thundering and rattling across the yards, startling her and suddenly making her afraid. She curled up in a tight ball, adjusted her clothing for maximum protection from the weather, and rested her head on her arm. She was physically and emotionally exhausted, but she knew she wouldn't be able to sleep because she couldn't stop thinking about Nick.

An hour slowly passed, and during that time the cold and damp penetrated her bed of cardboard and crept stealthily into her body. She lay there, shivering. She had no watch, and could only guess at the time. The police wouldn't stop looking for her until they found her. But they didn't really know who they were looking for, did they? All they had was a name.

Reassured by this thought, she'd almost drifted off when she heard a low muttering, accompanied by a shrill squeak. The sound

drew nearer and nearer, and then a bulky shape materialized out
of the darkness, pushing a grossly overloaded shopping cart down
the alley. Chantal twisted her body for a better view. She was cold,
and her joints were stiff. She flexed her muscles, and fumbled for
the razor. The squeaking slowed, then stopped.

A tremulous voice said, "Anybody in there?"

"Fuck off, I've got a knife!"

The squeaking started up again, and then the mumbling, louder
now, and with undertones of bitterness and aggression. The cart,
a mountainous junkyard on wheels, slowly disappeared from view.

Chantal waited until she couldn't hear the wheels any more,
and then she waited a little while longer, until her heartbeat had
steadied, and she was breathing normally. She wanted to climb
out of her tiny little room and look down the alley to make sure
the homeless person was gone. But at the same time, she didn't
want to risk exposing herself. Her hands trembled uncontrollably.
Was she frightened or was she cold? Both. Most of the vagrants
she'd met were harmless, interested only in their own cramped
lives. If they shouted or threatened someone it was because they
felt threatened themselves. Basically, they were more disoriented
than dangerous. If you left them alone, they'd leave you alone.
Chantal lay down, and closed her eyes.

When she opened her eyes, she found herself in her mother's
warm and cozy kitchen. They were preparing a meal together; her
mother mashed potatoes while Chantal prepared a salad. She heard
a burst of canned laughter from the television and knew her father
was in the living room, stretched out on the sofa in his red-and-
white striped terrycloth bathrobe, nursing a bottle of beer while he
watched the big Magnavox TV that they'd had forever.

Her mother told her to add a tomato to the salad, and she made
the mistake of saying she hated tomatoes. Why couldn't they for
just once in their lives have a salad without a stupid tomato in it?
Her father must have heard her, because he called out to her the
way he did, stretching out her name until he ran out of breath.

"Channnnnnnntaaaaal, is that you, honey?"

He thumped the sofa, the familiar sound of his big fist slamming into the padded material rising above another round of canned levity.

Chantal looked pleadingly at her mother, but all she did was mash the potatoes a little harder.

"Channnnnnnnntaaaaal, ba-by, I know you're in there, hiding behind your mommy's skirts. Come and say hello to your sweet papa, ba-by!"

Chantal got a knife from the rack and then hurried over to the fridge and crouched down and hunted through the crisper until she found the plastic bag containing the tomatoes. She chose the largest, slid the crisper shut and then closed the fridge door. When she turned around, he was standing right there in front of her, towering over her.

"You gonna tell me you didn't hear me calling you, ba-by?" His hot, beery breath enveloped her like a sour fog.

"I heard you."

"Heard me but ignored me, is that what you're sayin'?" His smile was no smile at all. They'd had this same discussion so many millions of times before that they both knew exactly where it was going, and that there was no way Chantal could wriggle or squirm her way out of it, no matter how ingenious she was or how hard she tried.

Her father said, "You sashay into my house, you can't bother to poke your head in the door and say hello?"

"I thought you might be resting."

He gripped her shoulders, and moved close up against her, so they were touching all along their bodies. He squeezed her flesh, roughly massaging her. "I'm always glad to see you, ba-by, you know that." He squeezed a little harder, and she flinched. "Don't you, ba-by?"

Chantal craned her head so she could see past him to her mother.

"Never mind her, she's busy mashin' potatoes. Now you c'mon into the living room with me, and watch a little TV."

"I can't. I have to make the salad."

"You mother'll do that. She'd be glad to do it, so I get a chance to talk to my sweetie."

He took the tomato from her and squeezed it until it burst. Juice and seeds and chunks of red pulp dripped from his fingers. He opened his fist and flung the ruined tomato at the floor. His eyes were dark. His mouth twisted into a mocking smile. Turning to Chantal's mother, he said, "Clean that up for me, will you, honey?"

The potato masher banged noisily against the pot.

"Honey?"

Chantal's mother nodded, but didn't look up.

Her father said, "How long until dinner?"

Her mother shrugged with her shoulders and then with her entire body.

"Half an hour sound about right?"

Her answer was a mute, terrible shudder.

"Good," said her father firmly. He reached out his dripping fingers and took Chantal by the hand. The living-room curtains were drawn, and the room was lit only by the TV's flickering light. The door to the kitchen swung shut behind them. He stretched out on the sofa and told Chantal to turn the TV up a notch, then come and sit down on the floor beside him.

The creak of the sofa's springs rolled into the squeak of an errant wheel on an overloaded shopping cart. Chantal snatched up her knife. The squeaking grew louder, and slower. She jumped to her feet. Light sparked off chromed metal. Something out there in the murky darkness shuffled sideways, shuffled back.

Chantal raised her arm, let whoever was out there see her razor. "Get away from me, go away, or I'll cut you!"

The wheel squeaked. The space between the loading dock and the grocery cart was filled with a tumult of muttered words. How many people were out there, one or a dozen? She shaded her eyes against the light. A bottle shattered on the concrete. She ran to the far end of the loading dock and jumped. She landed hard, the impact jolting her from her heels to the base of her skull. She ran, stiff-legged and clumsy, her head throbbing, towards a distant streetlight. A bottle burst at her feet, spraying chunks of glass and droplets of warm liquid.

Chantal ran until she was winded and hurting, and then slowed to a rapid, crippled walk. She had no idea where she was going, but she sure as hell wasn't going home, because *anywhere* was better than that, even jail. She walked for hours, parallel to the waterfront and then into the city. From time to time she rested in a doorway for a few moments, her head darting from side to side as she glanced anxiously around.

As dawn silently broke she found herself back on Granville Street. Sometime during the night the rain had stopped, but the street was still wet. Distorted neon gleamed and rippled on black pavement. Halfway down the block a storefront mannequin raised and lowered her arm in empty greeting. A few scraps of paper hurried down a side street. Overhead, a cold wind hummed in the orderly tangle of wires.

Chantal walked south on Granville to the largest of the three bridges that spanned False Creek. It took her twenty minutes to reach the apex of the bridge and in that time she saw almost no traffic. She hooked her arms over the grey-painted steel railing. It was a long way down to the water. Much farther than Nick had fallen. Chantal spat. Her spittle was carried away by the capricious wind, veering sideways and then swirling around as if in a whirlpool, falling, falling, falling.

Chantal imagined herself tumbling through the air, dropping towards the cold black water and then being magically lifted up, flung through the air like a leaf, spiralling dizzily around, rising up above the bridge and the city, through the clouds and into blue sky, and sunlight . . .

Off to the east, the morning sun was gaining in strength and the clouds along the horizon were beginning to break up. The sun warmed her face. In the space of just a few minutes, the ruffled water far below her turned from impenetrable black to a velvety blue.

She hooked a leg over the railing, braced her hand against a steel post, and hoisted herself up. She swung her other leg over the railing and looked out over the water at the orderly rows of boats moored in their slips. Her boots kicked against the vertical steel rails. If she leaned forward, she'd be gone.

She let go of the steel post, and spread her arms wide. A gust of wind hit her, pushing her off balance.

There was no time even to scream.

18

Steller's jays cavorting and yakking in the Japanese plum trees lining the boulevard made Carlos roll over on his belly, glare at his alarm clock, pull his stolen Motel 6 pillow over his head, stick his fingers in his sticky ears, curse foully and punch the wall a few times. None of this helped. Infuriated, he jumped out of bed and snatched his .22-calibre Ruger semiautomatic pistol from beneath the mattress. He worked the slide and made sure the silencer was screwed on good and tight. The bedroom window was nailed shut, so he made his way through the gloomy apartment to the living room.

The window was open and unlocked.

He wondered, not for the first time, how he'd been stupid enough to choose a fresh-air fiend for a partner. Their two-bedroom unit was on the third floor, facing the street. Didn't Hector realize his moronic actions made them both plump fodder for any passing burglar who was sufficiently alert to notice the open window and conveniently located fire escape?

Carlos pushed the window all the way open, for a wider field of fire. Five or six jays were goofing around in a tree about eighty feet away. They were in constant motion, hopping energetically from branch to branch to no obvious purpose, as if mimicking a workout class. Maybe they somehow sensed what he had in mind. Carlos was a piss-poor shot, but lucky. He glanced up and down the street. It was early, more or less dawn, and he saw no approach-ing cars or insomniac pedestrians or eighty-year-old erstwhile paperboys. A dark-blue Neon parked on the far side of the street was somewhat in the line of fire. He aimed as carefully as he knew how, and squeezed off a single shot. The bullet chopped through a small branch. One of the jays squawked in alarm, but was ignored by his companions. The bullet, carrying on, struck the road at an acute angle and hummed into the unknown distance as softly as a lounge singer. Carlos fired again. Realizing he'd segued from being murderously annoyed to having a little fun, he tossed the gun on the sofa and went into the kitchen for a beer and his smokes.

When he went back into the living room, the jays were still bois-terously goofing around, raucously insulting each other, pogo-sticking from branch to branch, generally acting as if they were a flock of kids hanging around the local burger joint. Carlos took a slug of beer. He swilled the beer around in his mouth, flossing his teeth the workingman's way, and then put the bottle down on the windowsill and seized the Ruger.

He aimed and fired without preamble.

The shot was a clean miss, but passed so close to several of the birds that they instinctively crouched low. The bullet's errant flight path carried it across the boulevard and down the street, where it ricocheted off a steel manhole cover and up into the tread of the Neon's left front tire. The car sagged like a mortally wounded buffalo. The alarm hooted, and the headlights flashed on and off. Carlos was tempted to fire a few more rounds into the damn thing, to put it out of its misery. But there was no predicting what kind of unwelcome attention a bullet-riddled vehicle might draw, assuming he managed to hit it. If the cops thought to work out the trajectories, they were sure to come a-pounding on his door . . .

The car alarm had frightened the jays, and they were gone. Carlos slammed the window and adjusted the drapes. After a few minutes the Neon's alarm system automatically deactivated, and an eerie silence descended. He reloaded the pistol and tossed it on the sofa. A spent shell casing lay on the carpet. He picked it up, toyed with it as he finished his beer, and then dropped the casing into the empty bottle.

It was ridiculously early, but the plinking had given him an adrenalin rush, and he knew he wouldn't be able to get back to sleep until he'd calmed down. Mid-afternoon, if the pattern held. He looked up a nearby White Spot in the Yellow Pages and ordered home delivery of a Nat's Breakfast: two eggs easy over, hash browns and bacon and sausages, delicious sourdough toast and blackberry jam, two large cups of coffee with cream and lots of those little packets of sugar. The chirpy woman who took his order and Hector's credit-card number told him his food would arrive within twenty minutes, guaranteed. Before she hung up she told Carlos to have a nice day, and he politely told her to have *three* nice days, minimum.

He hung up, went over to the door and peered through the circular glass peephole. The hallway was empty and silent. He unlocked the door and stepped outside. Three people on his floor had home newspaper delivery. Acting on the principle that it was unwise to soil one's own nest, Carlos usually did his stealing on some other floor.

Two levels down, the hallway was littered with rolled-up papers. He had his choice of the *National Post*, the *Vancouver Sun*, the *Globe and Mail*, and the *Province*, a tabloid that was locally infamous for its rabble-rousing headlines.

He hesitated, and then snatched up a pristine copy of the *Globe and Mail*, which he believed had the wittiest and most erudite sports columnists in Canada. But what the hell, in for a penny . . . He grabbed a copy of the *Province*, attracted by the lurid black forty-point headline. PREMIER A CROOK?

Holy jeepers, what was the world coming to?!

19

Chantal grabbed the metal lamp post with both hands and held on tight. Her stomach churned. A weakness ran through her, as if her muscles and bones were dissolving. In a moment she was better. She leaned her forehead against the cold metal of the pole. She'd almost been blown right off the bridge. It was okay to think about jumping, something else to be given a near-lethal push. She could just imagine the headline: MURDER SUSPECT SUICIDE!

The pole was wet and slippery. Gingerly, Chantal swung her legs back over the railing and stood up. Her knees buckled.

"You okay?"

She lifted her head. A uniformed cop stood a few feet away from her, ready to pounce. His marked car's headlights and red, white and blue lightbar were flashing bright as a circus. He was young, and good-looking, in a comically square-jawed kind of way.

Chantal straightened up, ran her fingers through her hair. The cop was watching her closely. She said, "I'm fine, just fine."

He didn't believe her, she could see it in his eyes. Moving cautiously towards her, he said, "You were up there on the railing . . ."

"Just for the hell of it." Chantal gave him her best smile, not holding anything back. "My big brother did it, years ago, on a dare. He said I'd never get up there, that I was chicken."

The cop started to relax.

She said, "Did you think I was going to jump? I don't blame you. Anybody might've thought that. And you guys are trained to notice stuff like that, aren't you?"

The cop nodded. He was so close now that all he had to do was reach out and take her in his arms. Chantal sized him up, trying to see past the uniform. He had pale-green eyes, a wide mouth and a snub nose. He wasn't wearing his hat, and his hair was black and curly. It was entirely possible that his last name was Murphy. She wondered if he liked to dance. She couldn't believe he hadn't arrested her. She *knew* Pinky had dialled 911. He must've given the detectives a pretty accurate description of her, given all the time he'd spent staring at her, his buggy little beady eyes sticking out of his ugly face.

She said, "My brother died . . ." His eyes widened. She smiled bravely. "No, not recently. Years ago. Today's his birthday. He would have been twenty-five. I wanted to celebrate his memory, and I know it sounds crazy, but taking his dare after all these years, climbing up on the railing, somehow seemed like a good idea."

The cop nodded solemnly. He was even younger than he looked. She smiled shyly. "I bet I must've given you a scare, huh?"

"A little bit. I mean, it's not like something you see every shift, a girl up on the railing . . ."

Something inside his cop brain clicked, darkened his pale-green eyes and made him emotionally withdraw, step back and see her differently. He unbuttoned the breast pocket of his uniform and pulled out a notebook and pen.

"I'll need your name, please."

"What for?" Chantal was alarmed. Why wouldn't she be? She let it show.

"I have to file a report. It's illegal to climb up on the railing."

"I wasn't doing anything!"

"What if somebody driving past had seen you, and had an accident? An older person might've had a heart attack."

In a split second, he'd gotten himself all worked up, shifted into pure cop mode, his dominant no-fun side.

The tip of his pen hovered over a blank page. Page one, she guessed. The smart thing would be to give him what he wanted and get the hell out of there.

She said, "My name's Linda Rider, okay? I live at apartment 10, 1814 Bute. Look, I'm late for work. Can I go now?"

"What was that address again?"

He'd written it down; she'd seen him do it. The suspicious little prick. She said, "Apartment 10, 1814 Bute. Do you want my phone number?"

"Yeah, you better give it to me."

Chantal gave him a seven-digit number. Her parent's number, if he'd had the area code. He wrote that down too, and asked her to repeat it. He tapped the pen against his teeth. "Got any ID, Linda?"

"No, I don't. I don't carry a wallet or purse because there's no place safe to put it where I work."

He nodded. "If I phoned this number now, and asked for Linda, what kind of response would I get?"

"*Meow!*" She smiled. "I live alone, except for my cat, Festus."

"Nice name."

"My boyfriend thought so, before he split."

The cop's smooth forehead wrinkled as he registered the fact that this dishevelled but undeniably pretty girl standing in front of him had just told him she lived alone.

Chantal cocked a hip.

The cop said, "Where did you say you worked?"

"Right over there."

Chantal jerked her thumb down and to the left. The cop took a cautious step closer to the railing. At the entrance to the Granville Island Market, several foreshortened figures were busy unloading cardboard boxes from a truck.

The cop turned back to Chantal. "You work at the market?"

"Yeah, that's right."

"Doing what?"

"Selling vegetables. Maybe you've seen me down there, doing my thing." She smiled. "I'm a juggler. I juggle fruit all day, to bring in customers."

"You kidding me?"

"No, I'm not. I can juggle any kind of fruit or vegetable you can think of. Bunches of carrots, apples, a grape . . ." She held out her hand, palm up. "Lend me your gun and handcuffs and car keys and I'll show you."

The cop laughed. He had a nice laugh, hearty and strong and genuine. Not at all like Nick's low, dangerous chuckle. The cop had nice teeth, too. Were cops unionized? He was probably on a dental plan. Chantal ran her tongue along the inside of her lower jaw. She hadn't seen a dentist since she'd run away from home, almost two years ago.

The cop said, "Tell you what, you're going to be late for work and it's my fault. Why don't I give you a ride?"

"No, it's okay, really. I can make it."

Too late, because the cop had taken her arm and was leading her to the patrol car. He opened the door and leaned past her to shift aside a bunch of cop stuff lying on the passenger seat. She fought down a rising panic. He hadn't busted her. He was just taking her for a drive, that's all. Like in a cab. But what was she supposed to do when she got to the market?

The door slammed shut, and a part of Chantal that was deep inside her crumpled and fell away. The cop touched her shoulder. "Buckle up!"

He was right, she *had* been thinking about jumping. Because Nick's death had been all her fault, just like every other bad thing that had happened to her during her short, completely fucked-up life.

Tires squealed as the cop gunned it. He said, "We'll get there faster if I leave the lights on." He grinned. "Better not use the siren, though. Don't want to overdo it. What're you going to tell your boss?"

"That I slept in. It's what he's used to, so it's what he'll believe."

The cop glanced at her, alert to habitual deception, and all it implied.

They were on an off-ramp when she finally noticed her name at the top of the on-board computer's screen.

There was a fairly accurate description, except it said she was wearing her leopardskin jacket, not Nick's red leather.

They were cruising along at a rock-steady forty kilometres per hour. She was late for work, but the cop was taking his time getting her there. Why was that? Random possibilities skittered like waterbugs across the rumpled surface of her consciousness. A blast of warm air from the heater washed across her knees. She was as tired as she'd ever been in all her life. If she shut her eyes, she'd fall asleep in an instant.

The cop tapped the brakes, slowing to make a left. They cruised past a high-rise apartment complex in the late stages of construction. They made another left, and then another, and then a right. Now they were passing under the bridge. The cop seemed to know where he was going. They drove past apartments and then a span of open ground. Geese gnawed at the grass. The car bumped across a set of railway tracks. The bridge's concrete pillars were enormous, and Chantal was running out of time. She glanced around, trying to make sense of her surroundings, work out an escape route. What if he asked those people moving boxes if she was who she claimed to be? Linda Rider. But why would he bother?

He made another turn, and the market came into view. There were several large trucks parked in front of the building. Half a dozen men and women, all of them Asian, were busy unloading heavy waxed cardboard boxes full of fresh vegetables.

He stopped the patrol car a few inches from the rear bumper of the nearest truck. He gave her a nice smile.

"Close enough?"

"Thanks for the ride. I really appreciate it."

"No problem." He let her see in his eyes what was on his mind. She said, "Yeah, I'd like that."

"Like what?"

"I'd like it if you gave me a call. What's your name?"

"John."

Perfect. Chantal said, "Give me a call, John. Any time after seven."

He smiled uncertainly. "Seven at night?"

She nodded. Dimwit. She unfastened her seatbelt and got out of the car. Amazingly, nobody was paying any attention to her. She shut the door, waved goodbye, and swung her hips hard as she walked towards the market. Now an elderly woman was watching her, looking vaguely unhappy. The woman started after her, and then the market's glass doors swung open and an Asian man about Chantal's age started towards her, dragging a dolly behind him. She smiled, and he smiled back. She said, "Can I ask you to do me a teensy little favour?"

He eyed the patrol car.

She said, "That cop over there thinks he just drove me to my new job. He's wants to go out with me, but he's way too old, and I'm trying to lose him. Is there something I can do, just for a few minutes, so it looks like I work here?"

"Uh, I don't think so . . ."

"Please help me. I'm not asking a lot."

The kid glanced nervously over her shoulder again, at the idling police car.

Chantal played the only card she had. "Tell me the truth, would you help me if I was Asian?"

Exasperation turned to guilt, defeat, and raw defiance. He shouted something in Cantonese at the elderly woman, who looked sharply up.

The cop rolled down his window.

20

The Public Safety Building, the depressingly solemn granite-sheathed building that houses the heart and soul and self-serve kitchen of the Vancouver Police Department, is located at 312 Main, a Sammy Sosa blast from the scabrous corner of Main and Hastings, open-air home to hundreds of the city's drug addicts and dealers, and one of only two functioning public toilets in the entire city. Why the cops can't shut down the drug trade on that one corner, given its close proximity to police headquarters, is a mystery to many of the city's citizens. Theories abound. Some people think the cops are on the take. Others blame soft-hearted judges and grossly inadequate sentences.

The city's homicide-squad offices are on the building's third floor. There's a nice view across the alley of the remand centre's red brick wall, a fistful of gracefully looping electrical wires and the area's resident pigeon population. In the summer, in mid-morning on a clear day, wide beams of sunlight pour in through the tinted windows, highlighting motes of dust and gold badges.

Willows and Parker's beige, enamelled-steel desks butted up against each other. When Parker was sitting at her desk and Willows wasn't in the way, she had a nice view out the window. When Willows was sitting at his desk, he had an excellent view of the open-plan office's far wall. If Parker was sitting at her desk, he had a wonderful view of her.

The dog, Tripper, lay on the carpet beside Parker's desk. A brand-new leash kept her from wandering. She was gnawing on a wide leather belt generously donated by Detective Dan Oikawa.

Willows watched as Parker searched Nick Partridge's wallet for the third time that morning.

The wallet contained a single five-dollar bill, a couple of squashed-flat marijuana cigarettes, and the laminated picture ID that Partridge needed to collect welfare. Nick wasn't in CPIC, the database most frequently used by the VPD to locate unidentified moral stragglers. Neither did either of the two missing-persons cops know anything about him.

Parker had come to think of Partridge as the Bird Who Could Not Fly. She hated herself for it, but the phrase had taken up permanent residence in a dark corner of her mind, like a noxious jingle for a deodorant, or a particularly irritating hook from a popular song.

Willows flipped through Mel Dutton's scene-of-crime photos. No matter how many times he looked at them, he could find no clue in any of the shots that indicated one way or another whether Nick Partridge had died as a consequence of an accident or an act of malice. Willows was working on only a few hours' sleep. He was bone-weary, and growing increasingly frustrated.

"Claire?"

She glanced up.

"Want a coffee?"

"Sure, but not badly enough to get you a cup."

Willows yawned. He covered his mouth with his hand. "I'll get it."

The coffee pot was down at the far end of the squad room, on a low bench set against the wall. On weekday mornings, for a minute or two, there was a selection of fresh doughnuts. Civilian support staff were responsible for providing the doughnuts and brewing the coffee, but the detectives were expected to pay for whatever they consumed – fifty cents a doughnut, maximum of three per detective, and a quarter for each cup *or partial cup* of

coffee. The three-doughnuts-a-day rule was regularly abused by
Detective Eddy Orwell, whose gorgeous wife, Judith, had recently
left him for the fifth time. Orwell, grief-stricken and ravenous,
had fallen off the health-food wagon and landed hard, on his knife
and fork. There was nothing worse than a born-again glutton. In
six months, he'd gained more than thirty pounds, all of it lard.
Every morning, Orwell paid for his own doughnuts, and chipped
in another dollar-fifty for Parker's, and gobbled them down one
after another, lickety-split.

Willows poured two cups of coffee, added milk and a packet of
sugar to his own cup and walked back to his desk.

"Thank you," said Parker.

"You're welcome."

Willows sipped his coffee. Old and bold, but not too cold. He
looked at the pictures again, first the colour shots and then the
black-and-whites. In Willows' opinion, Dutton could be wilfully
pretentious, inconsistently hostile, and bone-lazy. But there was
no denying that he was a genius with a camera, capable of photo-
graphing a view of the world that no one else could even see.
Dutton's crime-scene photos had yielded countless vital clues, or
somehow contrived to hint at an unlikely but fruitful turn in the
investigation. But this time, as far as Willows could see, Dutton
had come up empty.

Willows glanced up as the squad-room door buzzed. One of
the two civilian staff hit an under-the-counter button, releasing
the lock. The door swung open, admitting homicide detectives
Dan Oikawa and Bobby Dundas. Oikawa nodded to Willows.
Bobby tried in vain to catch Parker's eye. He shucked his pure-wool
overcoat and silk suit jacket. His chunky gold cufflinks glittered
almost as brightly as his gelled fifty-dollar haircut. His crisp white
shirt had a blue-striped collar and matching cuffs. Bobby dressed
so extravagantly that, when he had transferred to homicide from
vice, his fellow cops had assumed he was on the take. As it turned
out, Bobby's father was a successful tailor who owned a small but
wildly profitable chain of clothing stores. Careful of the creases in

his pants, Bobby sat down at his desk. He said, "You and Claire *still* working the Gastown no-bouncer, Jack?"

Willows nodded.

Smirking, Bobby said, "Me 'n' Dan got the Kerrisdale shooting. Guy goes into his garage and his BMW's full of dead illegals, eight of 'em."

"I heard about it."

"Two in the front and three in the back, three more in the trunk," said Bobby. "Multiple wounds, and we know that at least five weapons were used, all of them nines."

Nine-millimetre semiauto handguns, the weapon of choice for gangsters all across the continent. Police forces, too, although the VPD were armed with ten-millimetre Glock pistols. Bobby leaned away from his chair, towards Parker. "Claire, I could probably swing it if you'd like to work with us on this one."

"Thanks anyway."

"You sure? Eight bullet-riddled bodies." Bobby ignored Willows' baleful glare. "We could have an awful lot of fun."

Parker said, "I don't think so."

"Maybe you should stop thinking."

Parker looked directly at him for the first time. "Knock it off, Bobby. Stop pestering me."

Bobby tried to laugh off the remark, but the dark rush of blood to his face gave him away. He swivelled his chair around so his back was to Parker, and got busy shuffling paper. Oikawa sighed heavily. Bobby was notoriously slow to recover from an insult, real or imagined. He was a miserable prick at the best of times, but when you partnered Bobby, there were no best of times. Oikawa knew that the rest of the day would be pure misery.

Parker's phone rang. She picked up, listened a moment, and then said, "No, keep him there, I'll come down and get him." She cradled the phone. "Pinky Koblansky's downstairs."

Willows checked his watch. Pinky was right on time. He said, "Want me to get him?"

"No, I'll do it."

Willows understood that Parker wanted to get away from
Bobby. He said, "I'll meet you in the interrogation room."

Parker stood up, moved away from her desk. Bobby kept his
head down as she walked by. Willows shuffled the crime-scene
photos together, put them in a folder and locked the folder and a
few related documents away in his desk. Bobby was watching
him. Willows spun his chair around so he was directly facing him.
"Something on your mind?"

"Not at the moment."

Bobby had been nibbling on a pencil. A fleck of yellow paint
hung from his lower lip. What else was Bobby chewing on?
Willows didn't care nearly enough to ask.

The interview room was equipped with a playschool-sized
wooden desk and matching wooden chair, and a stacked pair of
Sony VCRs. Two wide-angle cameras recorded everything that
went on in the room.

Pinky wore a pair of dirty Adidas sneakers, badly worn dark-
brown wide-wale corduroy pants, a black T-shirt and a gold-
coloured corduroy jacket with an ink-stained breast pocket. He
had the bearing of a man who'd dressed in his best clothes for a
job he really didn't want. He sat awkwardly in the wooden chair,
staring up at a camera, but jumped to his feet as Willows entered
the room. He was nervous as a mouse in a cathouse. He'd chain-
smoked for a good twenty minutes before walking into the Public
Safety Building. His nicotine levels were borderline lethal, but it
wouldn't last, and he'd soon need another hit.

Pinky hoped the cops would get straight to the chase, and not
toy with him too much. He wriggled his hips. Where'd they steal
this chair, from some kid's dollhouse, a midget convention, or
Ikea? He wasn't going to ask if he could stand up, because they'd
say no, so what was the point? He knew how cops' minds worked.
They wanted to dominate him, show him that they were in total
control of his fate. Like he had one.

He said, "Can I take off my jacket?"

Willows nodded.

Pinky took off his jacket, folded it neatly, lifted his butt off the chair and slipped the jacket underneath. He sat back down, and sighed contentedly.

Parker said. "C'mon, Pinky. How are Jack and I going to make you sweat when you're nice and comfortable?"

"Don't worry about it, you'll find a way."

Parker laughed. She said, "We appreciate your coming in. Did you think of anything, since last night?"

"Not really." Pinky frowned mightily. Acting, because he was being taped. He said, "If I *was* to think of something, like a clue that could lead to Nick's girlfriend, would I get a reward?"

"You bet," said Willows. He leaned forward and patted Pinky lightly on the back. "There you go."

"'Scuse me?"

"You wanted a pat on the back, you got it. Now, what can you tell us?"

"Nothin'!" Pinky's forehead wrinkled up as if disturbed by a brisk wind. "It was a ... what d'ya call it ... *hypocritical* question."

"Gotcha."

"So, what did you want to talk to me about?"

Willows glanced at Parker. She said, "Tell us about the money, Pinky."

"What money?" Pinky smelled richly of tobacco smoke, cheap wine, sweat, fear, and hard living, all of it overlaid with a liberal sprinkling of compost. He blinked rapidly, and used the tips of his fingers to brush away the thin film of oil that gave his forehead a glossy yellow sheen. "You mean the coins, right?"

Parker nodded, congratulating him.

Pinky's face was squinched up as if his head were being pulled through a too-small hole. He struggled with the problem for the better part of a long minute, and finally said, "I guess you're gonna tell me I shouldn't of taken any of 'em, right?"

Parker said, "What else did you take?"

"Who, me? Nothin', absolutely zilch!"

"How many coins did you pick up off the floor?"

"Not many. A few quarters, a couple dimes . . ."

"What'd it add up to?"

"Hardly anything, A few bucks . . . You tell me, 'cause I gave you every last penny. Say, are you accusin' me of theft?"

The sound of Parker's beeper drowned her sigh of discontent. She glanced down at the tiny screen. Missing persons. She said, "Come on, Pinky, quit wasting our time. What else did you take from the crime scene?"

"Like I told you, nothin'!"

Parker said, "Tell us again what happened last night."

"Okay, fine. I heard Chantal yelling, and Nick laughing, and all them coins came rattling down, and the next thing I know, boom, there he is, so still and quiet that he coulda been there forever."

Willows said, "And you didn't take anything, except the coins you gave us?"

"I swear on a stack of Bibles."

Or pancakes, thought Willows.

"Look at me and tell me you didn't take anything except a fistful of coins," said Parker. "Lie, and I'll know you're lying."

Pinky stared blankly into her eyes. He said, "On my dear mother's grave, all I took was a couple of bucks' worth of coins."

Willows and Parker had told Pinky to come in because they'd both thought he was lying when they'd talked to him at the Lux. Parker still thought he was lying, or at least holding something back. She could see that Willows thought so, too. He jerked a thumb at Pinky. "Let's go. I'll get somebody to walk you out of the building."

"Fine, but then what? Could you lend me cab fare back to the hotel?"

"What else did you take, Pinky?"

"Nothin'! You keep at me, I'm gonna need a lawyer."

As Willows led Pinky out of the squad room, Parker went to her desk and dialled 525, the missing-persons extension.

"Broadhead."

"Geoff, this is Claire Parker. You rang?"

"Yeah. That girl you were asking about, Chantal? A rookie traffic cop spotted her about seven this morning, on the Granville Street bridge. He thought she was a jumper, and he could've been right. Anyway, she told him she was on her way to work, and the poor sap gave her a lift."

"Christ," said Parker. Tripper nuzzled her. She pushed her away. "Where'd he drop her off?"

"At the market. I already checked: a guy works there said she hung around until the cop left, and then beat it."

"The cop," said Parker. "Who was it?"

Broadhead hesitated, and Parker suddenly remembered that his youngest son had just graduated from the Academy. She said, "Get a description, and send it up right away, will you?"

"Consider it done," said Broadhead. The relief in his voice was palpable.

Parker disconnected as Willows sat down at his desk. Her phone rang, and she picked up.

Inspector Homer Bradley wanted Willows and Parker in his office *now*, right this minute.

21

The interior of the rectangular stainless-steel box was so black that Nick wouldn't have been able to see a slow-moving fist coming at him even *after* it smacked him on his nose.

Voices rose as several people drew near. The box moved a fraction of an inch, sliding easily along on nylon runners. The far wall, just beyond his feet, was rimmed in a soft, golden fire, like a gorgeous sunrise on the horizon of a squared-off world.

A woman's voice rose above the others. The box moved briskly back to its original position. Metal clicked on metal, and the light was extinguished.

It was cold in there, in that cramped space. So cold it thickened Nick's blood, fogged his eyes, and congealed the fatty marrow in his bones. It was so cold that, if there'd been any light, and – important point – Nick had been alive and breathing, he could've seen the warm, wet, roiling vapour of his breath.

The babble of voices rose again. This time the metal box was pulled violently into the light and the pale-blue rubberized sheet covering Nick's body was rudely flipped aside.

The morgue attendant turned over the stiff brown cardboard tag attached to the big toe of Nick's right foot by a loop of coarse butcher's twine.

The toe was vigorously wiggled. The attendant triumphantly said, "See, wrong guy. What'd I tell you!"

The stainless-steel box slammed shut. Nick's body trembled, and was still.

22

The Chinese kid's name was Jerry. Jerry was bored with his job, and probably his entire life. Chantal had seen that he was hot for her, and encouraged him to believe she could hardly keep her hands off him, too. Love at first sight. How fucking romantic. She laid bundles of asparagus for about thirty seconds, and then glanced up. The cop car was gone. She lined up a few more bundles and asked Jerry if there was a washroom she could use. He pointed at a nearby door. Chantal went inside and held the washroom door open a crack. She waited until Jerry grabbed his dolly and went outside for another load of vegetables, and then made her move. The cash register was unlocked. She punched buttons until the drawer slid open, grabbed a handful of bills and shut the drawer and stuffed the money in her pocket. Outside, Jerry was involved in a heated discussion with the old woman. He saw Chantal and stared at her as she walked diagonally away from him. The old woman turned and glared at her. Chantal blew Jerry a kiss. The old woman started shrieking at him, waving her arms. Wait until she discovered the plundered cash register. *Plunder*. That was the word Nick used when he wanted to make love to her, and it had made her laugh, but she wasn't laughing now.

She passed between two huge metal-clad buildings. As soon as she was out of view of the market, she started running as fast as she could, knowing the kid would come after her, and not just for the money. No athlete, Chantal was winded in minutes. Holding her aching side, walking as quickly as her burning lungs allowed, she turned a corner and hurried past a microbrewery. The ponderous bulk of the bridge was directly overhead, the sound of the traffic a steady, monotonous drone.

Chantal glanced wildly around. They'd have discovered that the money was missing by now. She shouldn't have been so greedy; if she'd left a few bills in the cash register it might have given her a lot more time to get away. She kept walking towards the mouth of the single road that fed into the market. Her breathing was still out of control and the pain was like a knife between her ribs, hot and sharp. She hurried past a restaurant, and several other businesses, but saw no sign of life. To her right the harbour opened up, but she could hardly see any water, because of all the boats in the crowded marinas. There was a wide, paved pathway that followed the contour of the waterfront, miles of drab condominiums with ridiculously small windows, considering the views. She was tempted to follow the seawall, to avoid the cops, but decided in favour of the warren of streets that lay just ahead.

She continued on, up a slight incline, past a motorcycle dealership, and then followed the road as it curved to the right. A taxi sped past, and she shouted and tried to wave it down. The driver smiled at her but didn't stop. She swore at him and gave him the finger. The car's brake lights flashed and the tires shrieked as the driver slammed on the brakes. He reached across and pushed open the passenger-side door. Chantal had gotten lucky; maybe he hadn't seen her upthrust middle finger. She hurried up the street, climbed into the cab and slammed the door. The car surged forward.

She said, "Aren't you going to ask me where I want to go?"

"Doesn't matter." The driver was a huge, bearded Sikh wearing a black suit, white shirt and black tie, pale-blue turban. He turned to look at her, his eyes bright and full of mischief.

"What d'you mean? Stop the car, I want to get out!"

"I am stopping the car right *now*." He pulled into a parking lot in front of a stucco building painted dark blue with bright yellow trim. They were surrounded by taxis; the place was like a taxi graveyard.

The driver said, "I have been working twelve hours, and now I am going off duty, home to my dear wife and blessed children. But when you shouted at me and then signalled your distress and anger, it occurred to me that you must need a ride very badly. So I am giving you only a short one, but it is with my compliments, no charge whatsoever. Now you may leave, or rest comfortably while I gas up this vehicle and turn it over to my dear wife's wonderful brother, who is almost as good a driver as me. His name is Paul and he will gladly take you wherever you desire, but the meter will be running. Now tell me, do you wish to stay in the taxi?"

"Please," said Chantal demurely.

"Very good. And did you wish to apologize for your sharp tongue and pointed finger?"

"Sure, okay. I mean . . . I'm sorry."

"Most excellent." He smiled. His teeth were very white. "In future you may wish to consider the possibility that God sees these angry fingers and mistakenly believes they are pointed at him. Should he be a vessel for our rage? I do not think so!"

Chantal stared out the windshield, willing him and his bright eyes and warm, spicy breath out of the car. She watched him in the mirror, but lost sight of him when he went into the blue-painted building. She slouched low, and shut her eyes. A few minutes later the car rocked on its springs. She'd dozed off. She opened her eyes, disoriented. Sitting behind the wheel was a smaller and younger version of her driver, complete with turban. He smiled and cheerfully thumped the steering wheel.

"No sleeping! You snooze, you lose!" He started the engine. "Where to, valued customer?"

"Broadway and Main."

"Very good, a wonderful destination. Tell me now, and make me wiser, do you think the word *destination* comes from the same root as *destiny*?"

"I never thought about it."

"Well, what better time?" He backed the car onto the street, braked to avoid a passing patrol car. He chuckled. "Have you observed that the police are like taxi drivers? Never around when you want one, always there when you don't." He pulled in tight behind the pretty white-with-scenic-blue-and-green-trim patrol car. Nick had told Chantal that Vancouver cops used to wear pale-blue shirts and drive black cars. Now they drove white cars and wore black shirts, like the infamously brutal LAPD thugs. What, Nick asked, did the local cops' wardrobe tell you about their mindset? Nothing you really wanted to know. Chantal relaxed a little as the police car turned left and the taxi made a sweeping right.

In a few minutes they were on Broadway, heading east into a pale, silvery glow in the clouds, and thickening traffic.

Chantal pulled crumpled bills out of her pocket. Three twenties, two tens, and four fives. One hundred dollars, exactly.

The cab stopped for the red at Granville. A woman was led across the road by a large poodle so ornately clipped it more closely resembled a carefully tended plant than a living animal. The poodle tossed its head, giving the leash a yank, hurrying the woman along. So little time, so many fire hydrants. Tears welled up in Chantal's eyes. Poor Tripper! But she was on her own now, and so was Tripper, because Nick was dead and he was going to stay that way forever. So there was no turning back, and anyway, Tripper was a handsome and reasonably obedient dog, so she'd probably land on her feet. It wasn't as if she'd been living in doggie heaven. Chantal was pretty sure Nick made a habit of slipping a little coke into Tripper's dinner dish. Not everybody had a dope addict for a pet. In certain circles, it was probably considered hip.

They were cruising along Broadway now, driving past the big Toys "Я" Us sign. Broadway was a main artery, but it was weird how it physically dwindled, the stores and shops shrinking and somehow becoming less and less interesting as you drove east, until finally you reached the city's boundary, home to the last McDonald's in town.

Had they buried Nick yet? Probably not. He'd be in the morgue. The phrase "cooling his heels" slipped unbidden into her mind. She shuddered.

Chantal concentrated on cataloguing what she knew about the disposition of bodies, the few facts at her disposal. The police would locate his parents, and make them identify the body. Then what?

They'd stopped. The driver turned towards her. He smiled good-naturedly. "Broadway and Main, correct?"

Chantal nodded. She passed him a twenty, told him to add a couple of dollars for a tip. It took him a long time to make change. What was he up to? She pushed the door open and climbed out of the car. He glanced up, startled. She slammed the door behind her and walked hurriedly away.

"Lady, your change!"

She waved dismissively, without looking back. She had no idea why she'd asked to be let off at Broadway and Main, and then, as she walked around a corner, it hit her. This was where she'd first met Nick.

Right there, at that bus stop.

She'd been sitting on the wooden bench when he walked up to her and asked her for a light. He sat down at the far end of the bench and smoked quietly for a couple of minutes, then introduced himself, and asked her name. He had a nice smile, cocky but warm. They talked for a while and she told him she was new in town, had been staying with a friend, but it hadn't worked out, and now she was basically homeless, on her way downtown to try to find a job . . .

Nick told her, fuck that, she was too pretty to sling burgers. He asked her how old she was. She lied and told him nineteen, just a couple of days ago.

A bus came along and they both got on, not saying anything, Nick slinging her backpack over his shoulder. As they rode downtown he told her he made a living on the street, hitting people up for spare change, sometimes moving a little dope. Not smack, he assured her, as if she cared one way or the other. They got off the bus at the south end of the bridge and walked down the street, past the bars, porno joints and clubs. He'd been in the city almost a month, and as they walked down the strip, it seemed to Chantal that he knew just about every street person in the city. Twice he left her to duck into a doorway to make a furtive exchange of cash and drugs.

They walked for a few more blocks and then he said he was hungry. She followed him into a restaurant, they sat down at a booth and he ordered two big breakfasts, bacon and eggs and hash browns, coffee, without looking at the menu or asking her what she wanted.

Later, as the waitress was refilling their coffee cups, Nick told her he had a room in a nearby hotel. He asked her if she'd like to move in with him, since she didn't have a place to stay. He somehow made it clear that she wouldn't owe him anything for the favour. He told her to take her time thinking about it, but reminded her that the streets could be dangerous.

But really, what was there to think about?

Chantal waited for the light to change, and then crossed the street, hurried past the bus stop and turned into a mini-mall in the middle of the block. There was a chain convenience store, a drug store, liquor store and low-end clothing store, and a small restaurant named Jack's. Inside the mall, the liquor store was closed but the restaurant was open. She sat down at a booth with a view of the street. The waitress yawned as she slapped a menu down on the red Formica table. Chantal ordered coffee and toast.

"What kinda bread you want? We got . . ."

"White."

"Cream with your coffee?"

Chantal nodded. The waitress went away and came back with the pot. Chantal poured a container of cream into her coffee, stirred it with her knife, just like Nick.

She stared out at the street, concentrating on the people walking by, seeing as many details as she could, trying to think of names, occupations, anything that would stop her from thinking about him.

Her toast arrived, and a plastic container of jam the colour of dried blood. She called the waitress back, and asked for peanut butter.

Outside, a woman wearing a dark-green coat walked past. She wore a pink scarf laced with silver threads, and her hair was in curlers. Pink curlers. Her chin was tucked into the scarf and her eyes were on the sidewalk. She was about fifty years old, maybe sixty. Old was old. Chantal thought she'd probably worked as a secretary but was now on welfare. Her coat was several sizes too large, which meant she'd lost a lot of weight recently. Was that because of grief or poverty or sickness? Maybe a social worker had given her the coat. Take it or leave it, look scrawny or be cold. Chantal thought that sometimes a long life was no great blessing.

The waitress dropped a couple of packets of peanut butter on the table. Squirrel, Chantal's favourite brand. She opened one of the packets and picked up her knife.

She'd ordered white toast but this was whole-wheat. She looked up and caught the waitress staring at her, smirking as if at some great triumph.

Chantal's sudden anger twisted into her like a corkscrew and faded away in an instant, leaving her feeling empty and tired. She stared blankly down at her plate. Maybe she should turn herself in. There was a pay phone by the door to the washrooms. All she had to do was walk over there and dial 911.

A burst of laughter made her look up. A quartet of girls in their early twenties sat down a couple of tables away. She sipped her coffee and secretly studied their plump, well-fed faces. They looked, if not exactly happy, then self-contained. How did you get to be a normal, everyday person? What did you have to do to get there?

Probably you didn't run away from home at age sixteen, sneak into the barn and kiss your 4-H calf goodbye, and not even give a thought to your parents because you hated your father and didn't care about your mother any more than she cared about you.

The girls ordered coffee and toast, a cinnamon bun. One of them ordered pie, and her friends gave her a hard time about it, poking and giggling. The waitress knew them. Her broad back was to Chantal as she effortlessly joined in the conversation, made a joke that was well received, and laughed loudly at her own wit.

Two of the girls wore dark-blue sweaters with the mall grocery store's name embroidered on it in white letters. So they were checkout girls, trapped in dead-end jobs, their youth and brains withering away day by day. Just look at them. What were they so fucking happy about, a special on dairy products?

Chantal nibbled her toast, sipped at her lukewarm cup of coffee. She wished desperately that there was someone she could talk to, someone she could trust. She missed Tripper more than anything. She missed her dog even more than she missed Nick.

Tears welled up in her eyes. She wiped her face with a fistful of napkins yanked viciously from the chrome dispenser, blew her nose and tossed the napkins on the floor. The stupid waitress and stupid checkout girls were staring at her as if she had a major infectious disease. Fuck them all.

23

Marty sat on Melanie Martel's enclosed balcony, looking down at the harbour. If his mind were viewed as a pie chart, a large slice of it would have been occupied by warm sexual thoughts of his gorgeous blonde sweetheart. A much smaller wedge of the chart busily counted the sailboats neatly arranged in the slips almost directly below him.

But the largest slice of all was scurrying around in a cage, chasing Carlos and Hector. It was a futile exercise, because there was no point running them down until he'd decided what to do with them. Marty gulped the last of his champagne and fresh-squeezed orange juice and put the glass gently on the patio table.

He had lived on the West Coast, hilariously referred to by newcomers as the *Wet* Coast, his entire adult life. He still wondered how the sky could hold such a vast weight of rain.

Marty had seen enough rain in Vancouver in one winter to flood the Amazon basin. No wonder the city had been built on the ocean. There had to be *someplace* for all that water to go. He'd been told stories of first-generation Vancouverites who had moss growing on them.

Half the buildings in town leaked so badly they'd been covered in mammoth blue tarps. The eternal dampness had turned thousands of apartments into mushroom farms. What did the unlucky people who lived under those tarps think about, as they drifted through their deep-blue worlds?

Never mind all that. Carlos and Hector – what should he do with them?

Melanie pushed open the sliding glass door and sat down opposite him. She wore a tight black skirt, a silvery sleeveless T-shirt kind of thing with spaghetti straps, and stilettos in shiny translucent blue plastic, generously sprinkled with red and blue and silver and gold sequins. She helped herself to one of his Camels and lit up. Her hair was still damp from her shower, and hung in loose curls. Her lipstick and impossibly long nails were Spontaneous Combustion Pink and she wore just a tad too much eyeliner.

Marty loved her for it.

She exhaled and said, "What d'you think?"

"About what?"

"Me." She held out her arms, stretching the silvery fabric. No bra, but then, as far as he knew, she didn't own one.

He studied her for a moment. "What're you trying for?"

"You tell me."

"Sexy, and cheap. But pricey."

Melanie leaned across the table, flash of cleavage, and kissed his mouth. "Thank you so much." She saw he was preoccupied, and frowned prettily. "Still worrying about Carlos and his dimwit pal?"

Marty nodded. There were about three dozen sailboats moored down there. Most of them were in the thirty-foot range, but a few of them were big fifty- or sixty-footers. What was a sailboat worth, about two grand a foot? He started to do the math and then let it go, seeing that it would take more time than it was worth. Lots of money down there, for sure.

He said, "Is there any more coffee?"

"I just put on a fresh pot. Here, let me get it."

Melanie started to get up, but Marty put a gentle hand on her shoulder. "Stay put, I'll get it." What smooth, creamy skin she had.

Inside, the off-white berber carpet was soft and warm to his bare feet. He got the sterling-silver creamer from the fridge, found the matching sugar bowl, poured cream into a cup and tonged in half a dozen sugar cubes. In his youth he'd eaten anything he saw and liked the look of, and never gained an ounce. Now that he was in his late thirties, he had to let his belt out a notch every time he glanced at a dessert tray. He poured the coffee. Time was a train that never missed a passenger. The main thing, as you got older, was to maintain a relentless fuck-you attitude.

As he stepped onto the balcony Melanie said, "I meant to ask you, and then we got caught up in all that other stuff, but how's Jake coming along?"

"Not too bad." Marty stretched out his arms and heard and felt his joints creak. Gotta join one of those fitness clubs, get sweaty. The treadmill was originally a means of punishment in Victorian-era prisons, but so what, because he didn't remember seeing pictures of chubby Victorian-era prisoners. Things sure had changed in the past hundred years. Nowadays, prison was where hardened criminals went to relax, play a little golf and get focussed on the next big scam.

He said, "Jake's okay, for a guy who'd draw a big crowd at the 'Antiques Road Show.'" Melanie giggled, and Marty managed a wan smile. He said, "They got him on morphine, and that pisses him off something awful." Like most high-level dealers, Jake was deathly afraid of drugs, contemptuous of addicts.

"You talk to him about Carlos and Hector?"

"Yeah, on the phone, about an hour ago. Told him straight out I didn't understand why he wanted them squibbed."

"What'd he say?"

"Nothing much. Thought about it for about an hour, while I read the paper, and then told me to forget it, but keep a close eye on them."

"How you gonna do that?"

"I wish I knew."

"Whatever you decide, please don't invite them over here."

"You're a real mind reader, aren't you?"

Melanie laughed, a nice, throaty chuckle. She reached out and patted Marty on the knee, and Marty lifted her hand to his mouth and kissed her fingers each in turn. He'd just phoned Carlos on his Pay As You Go cellphone, tried to make an impression without saying anything incriminating. He'd arranged a meeting with him and his five-watt partner for later that afternoon. He hoped it would go well.

A few months ago he'd recruited some fresh muscle, a couple of North Korean thugs recommended to him by a chartered accountant he more or less trusted. The C.A. had described the Koreans as tough, brutal, and completely lacking in imagination. Marty liked the N.K.s, because he knew that imaginative muscle was muscle that couldn't be trusted. A person cursed with a lively imagination was a person who knew fear, and the first-born child of fear was foul betrayal.

He sipped his coffee and studied the landscape, how all the disparate and clashing parts of it merged effortlessly together to form a pleasing panorama. Funny how the long view was pretty much black and white and shades of grey. Where did all the colour go? He wondered if he'd enjoy sailing; decided he probably wouldn't, but that it might be fun to own a sailboat. He imagined making love to Melanie on the frolicking sea, and then realized there was no imagining involved, because she *was* a frolicking sea, restless and full of motion. What had that Irish guy with the skinny face and glasses written about the ocean? *The great grey mother of the sea.*

Marty butted his cigarette and resumed kissing Melanie's soft hand. He licked wetly at the little flap of skin between her fingers, and then snuck an under-the-eyebrows look at her to see how he was doing. Her eyes told him he was doing great. He stood up, helped her to her feet, scooped her up in his powerful arms.

"Bedroom?"

She leaned into him, and whispered into his ear that she didn't think she could make it past the couch.

24

Homer Bradley had started losing his hair in his mid-forties. Baldness attacked him from all sides. He dreaded stepping in front of the shaving mirror in the morning. His hairline receded so fast he was surprised he didn't get a ticket. The widening expanse of worm-white, glistening skin never ceased to shock him, even though he came to expect it. He learned to comb his remaining hair as delicately as if it were made of spun glass. He stopped using the hair dryer because the blast of hot air seemed to have the effect of clear-cutting his scalp. Soon his time in the barber's chair was reduced from half an hour to less than ten minutes. No drop in price, however. He took to wearing a fedora, soon discarded it in favour of a beret. He secretly wasted a great deal of money on restoratives and other arcane, laughably unlikely treatments. Finally he bought a cheap wig, which he tried on in the safety and comfort of his bathroom. Oops. He burned it in the fireplace, and had to open all the windows to air out the house. After sulking for a week or so, he went out and bought a hairpiece so expensive that he had to finance it with his Visa card, over ten equal monthly payments.

He wore the wig for the better part of a month, until he happened to overhear a halfwit Crown prosecutor compare his head to a clear cut.

That same afternoon, he drove miles out of the city, nailed the wig to a tree and spent the better part of an hour and three twenty-round boxes of nine-millimetre hardball ammunition blasting the damn thing to pieces no larger than a vole.

That was it for Bradley. No more pills or ointments, pricey fad diets, hats, toupées, or comb-overs. He suffered from male-pattern baldness because he was a *man*!

His hairline continued to recede until he had an ear-high fringe of hair around the sides and back, like a villain in a Charles Dickens novel. As the years slipped by, his hair turned from a murky brown to a pristine, snowy, high-altitude white. For two decades he looked old before his time, but then his age caught up with him, and he was transformed almost overnight into distinguished and wise. A flurry of articles relating premature balding to astronomically high testosterone levels made him feel even better about his new self.

But now, suddenly, without warning, he was losing what little hair he had left. His GP nervously referred him to a specialist, who told him a transplant was his only hope. Bradley paled, and for good reason, because the only decent-sized patches of hair he had left were under his armpits and smack dab in his pubic region.

Bradley leaned back in his chair. Oak creaked under the weight of his body. He folded his arms across his chest, and contemplated his future. Eddy Orwell and the rest of his crew were already referring to him as Inspector Picard behind his back. Soon they'd start wearing sunglasses to shield their eyes from the glare of his naked scalp, casually ask him technical questions about the likelihood of an eclipse, and so on, endlessly.

Speaking of Orwell, where was he? Bradley shot the cuff of his crisp white uniform shirt and squinted at his analog-style Timex.

Now that he was older, it took his eyes time to adjust to changes in distance. As the numbers on his watch swam slowly into focus, a scarred and callused fist rattled his door. He sat up straight.

"Come in!"

Orwell stepped into the room with Bobby Dundas close behind

him. Bradley noticed that Orwell was dressing better now that he and Dundas were partners. No more black-shirt-and-orange-tie combos, thank God. The black leather porkpie hat Judith had given him the previous Christmas seemed to have permanently disappeared, together with his collection of Popsicle-coloured double-breasted suits, and patent leather shoes. Bradley preferred the old Orwell, though he wasn't sure why.

Bradley leaned down and scratched his ankle. He made a mental note never to wear a new pair of wool socks without washing them first. He pushed a large white envelope across his desk. Morgue photos of Nicholas Partridge. "Canvass the east side of Granville from The Bay to the bridge, and back again. On foot."

Orwell picked up the envelope. He tried to put it in his jacket pocket, but it wouldn't fit.

Bobby pinched a speck of lint off the sleeve of his coat, scrutinized it for a long moment and let it drop. "Both of us?" he said.

"Yeah, both of you, on both your feet." Orwell and Bobby had solved the BMW-full-of-bodies case – mainly because one of the killers' mothers had turned him in. Bobby acted as if he expected to be rewarded with a paid holiday. Fat chance. The chair creaked. "Talk to the street kids. Show 'em the pics of Nick, try to get a lead on the girl, Chantal." He pointed a finger at each of them in turn. "Be polite. No strong-arm stuff."

"We'll give it our best shot," said Bobby. He was the only cop Bradley knew who could speak clearly while sneering.

Bradley said, "Has Chantal got any brothers or sisters or other relatives in the city? Close friends, another boyfriend? Where does she like to hang out . . . ?" He flicked his hand in a gesture of terse dismissal.

Bobby lurched towards Bradley's pebbled-glass door. He was red-faced and angry. He believed that the canvass was a complete waste of time, because most of the street punks were dealers and the rest of them were junkies and dope fiends. He and Orwell would get zero co-operation, and that was being

optimistic. He knew it and Bradley knew it – everybody but
Orwell was in on the joke.

Twenty minutes later, Orwell parked their beige unmarked Ford
in an alley behind a multi-tiered parking lot. They worked their
way down Granville as far as Robson Street, home of the city's first
covert police-surveillance camera.

Orwell broke stride. A few kids loitered nearby, but he ignored
them in favour of a Wendy's fast-food restaurant. "Hey, Bobby,
want a bite to eat?"

"What've you got in mind?"

Eddy jerked a muscular thumb towards the restaurant. "How's a
couple cheeseburgers, side of fries and a Diet Coke sound to you?"

"Like terminal indigestion." Bobby patted his perfect slab of a
stomach. "Go ahead, enjoy. I'm not hungry."

Orwell swung wide the restaurant's glass door. "You sure?"

Bobby wrinkled his nose as a blast of air heated by a deep fryer
smacked him in the face.

"Don't want a coffee, or . . . ?"

"Beat it, Eddy."

Bobby crossed the sidewalk, stopping just short of the curb. He
turned his greedy eye on the women walking by, trying to guess
which among them were wearing thong panties, and so on. His
fetid brain was in turmoil but his face was a perfect blank, giving
away none of his vile carnal thoughts, because he'd been in kinder-
garten when he'd first learned the value of keeping his sluggish
cesspool of a mind to himself.

He lit a cigarette, his third of the day. If you told him that
smoking was a disgusting, self-destructive habit, he'd agree with
everything you said and mean every word of it. But a few months
ago a girl he'd thought he could trust had given him herpes and
he was still feeling a lot of anger and tension. Okay, not anger,
rage. So far, comforted by the fact that time wounds all heels, he'd
managed to resist a nearly irresistible urge to empty his Glock into
her gorgeous but treacherous body.

He'd promised himself that, as soon as he calmed down, he was going to give up the evil weed. In the meantime, whenever he saw someone smoking, he couldn't help wondering if they suffered from the same disease.

He glanced behind him, into the restaurant. Orwell was waiting patiently in line, studying the illuminated menu board. Large fries or small? It would probably be the most important decision of his day. Bobby hoped he'd eat his meal inside, because he was sick to his soul of watching Eddy wipe gobs of special sauce or whatever off his bloated face. And if he walked out of there playing kissy-face with another one of those goddam plastic toys, Bobby was going to pop him one, or suffer a creeping tremble-fit.

Bobby tired of looking at women he would never in a million devolving reincarnations get his hands on. He turned his attention to the street kids and their lame circus of stale delights. Like most cops, he was familiar with all the stats relating to broken homes, abusive parents, the toxic stew of violence and despair that drove ordinary kids to risk the streets, but he had no sympathy for any of them because of how they wasted the days that conspired to make up their lives. Hell, how could anybody in his right mind hope to earn a living out of a foam cup? Worse, the damn kids had no respect for the authority of the law. Losers, every last one of them. Bobby stared hard at a kid perched on a metal garbage can. You'd think he owned the damn thing.

Orwell's broad back pressed against the glass door, which then swung open, and he pivoted onto the street, a massive hamburger in one hand, a large milkshake in the other. Bobby smiled. What fun it would be to wait until Orwell had a mouthful of milkshake and then give him a swift kick in the nuts. The hilarity meter would go right off the scale.

Orwell said, "Want a bite?"

Bobby sighed heavily. Orwell's breath smelled faintly of fresh-turned soil.

"Is that a no?" Orwell patted his jacket pocket. "I got fries, and extra ketchup."

"When was the last time you saw a mirror, Eddy? You look like the Michelin Man with a water-retention problem."

"'Scuse me?"

"When did Judith leave you?"

"I dunno . . ."

"A couple of hundred pounds ago," said Bobby. He brought up his fists, jabbed Orwell twice in the belly.

"Cut it out!"

"Why, did it hurt?"

"Not that I noticed."

"Course not, not with all that padding. You got the body of a haystack. If I tossed you off the roof of a ten-storey building, you'd hit the pavement and all you'd do is *bounce*."

Orwell shoved a fistful of french fries into his mouth, licked a gob of ketchup from his fingers.

Bobby started walking down the street. Orwell trailed along, a few cautious steps behind. Bobby was an in-your-face-type guy. When he was mad, he had a voice like the feature soloist in a frog choir. Bobby picked up the pace. Orwell took turns huffing and puffing. It wasn't easy to walk fast while you were chowing down, especially if you wore a size-48 belt.

They approached the refurbished Orpheum Theatre. The sidewalk in front of it had been a favourite location for street musicians, until the city buried them in bylaws and fines. Now you needed an expensive, next-to-unobtainable permit from City Hall before you dared to publicly amuse people. The only form of artistic expression that was countenanced was begging. Parker had said it was like the Middle Ages, but with less compassion.

Orwell homed in on a trio of kids sitting on rolled-up sleeping bags. Crouching, he showed them Nicholas Partridge's morgue photo. "Anybody recognize him?"

A kid whose skinny, dirt-smeared face was adorned with a dozen silver rings of various sizes glanced at the picture and then said, "What flavour is your milkshake?"

"Chocolate."

"Can I have it, please?"

"Well, it's about, uh, a third gone."

"That's okay."

Orwell handed over the milkshake. The kid threw away the plastic top and straw. His throat moved as he gulped down the shake.

Orwell showed the picture around again. "C'mon, help me out. Anybody recognize him?"

A girl with mauve hair said, "What's his name?"

"Nick," said Orwell.

"Is he dead? He looks dead. He's dead, isn't he? What happened to him?"

Bobby loomed over her. "We shot him to death for refusing to answer questions. Did you know him?"

"Not really. I mean, he was around. We might've smoked a jay or two together, but I never fucked him or anything."

Bobby smiled. "You'd remember, would you?"

"Depends. Can I have a cigarette?"

"No, but you can stand downwind when I exhale."

Half the piss-poor beggars on Granville were the genuine article, but the other half wore expensive leather jackets and Doc Martens, and had driven downtown in Mommy's Volvo, looking for drug money, cheap thrills, a kick in the face, anything that was marginally more exciting than watching TV. Bobby had no respect for them: they were leeches, poseurs.

Orwell said, "We're looking for Nick's girlfriend, Chantal."

"You want the rest of that burger?"

Orwell tossed his double cheese with bacon to the third kid, who reached down inside his sleeping bag and pulled out a small, sleepy black dog. The dog sniffed the burger and woke up fast.

The girl said, "How come Nick had to die before anybody cared about him?"

"Nobody cares about him now," said Bobby. "If somebody told you otherwise, they lied."

The kids stared insolently at him. He resisted the urge to kick in some teeth. He hadn't been surprised when the dog came crawling out of the sleeping bag. A lot of these kids had dogs. The fucking bleeding-heart liberals thought it was real cute that these homeless kids were willing to take on the responsibility of a pet. But were the dogs properly licensed? Had they had their rabies shots, or any of that? No way. Bobby knew damn well that the only reason any of these kids owned a pet was as a last-resort source of cheap protein.

The two detectives continued south along Granville towards the bridge.

Bobby said, "Got a dog, Eddy?"

"I had one, but it ran away."

"Just like Judith, huh? Tell me something, which one of them was first out the gate?"

Eddy wondered why Homer had partnered him with Bobby Dundas. Was he being punished for some heinous crime he was unaware of?

Bobby said, "I had a dog when I was a kid."

"Yeah?"

"A little white one. I got it for my birthday. It's name was Jackie, after Jackie Gleason. I had him for about six weeks, and then one day I came home from school and he was gone."

"What happened to him?"

Bobby shrugged. "How should I know?"

"You never asked?"

"What would be the point? My dad would've just lied to me, like always."

Orwell waited until a bus roared by, then said, "You never got another dog?"

"Too much trouble. You come home, looking to grab a beer and fall down in front of the TV, the goddam dog's in your face. Who needs it? I had a girlfriend who had a dog, but . . ."

Orwell glanced diagonally back across the street, towards the McDonald's. Lots of people preferred Wendy's, but McDonald's had always been his favourite. Don't ask him why. He looked for Dan Oikawa and Farley Spears, but couldn't see either of them.

Maybe they were inside, grabbing a quick bite to eat. He was short half a burger and most of a milkshake, and he was so hungry it hurt. He said, "I'm going into McDonald's for a sec, I gotta use the can."

"Bullshit, you're gonna get something to eat."

Orwell was too famished to argue.

25

The McDonald's at Granville and Robson has a seating capacity of less than a hundred. Because of the nature of the location, the washrooms are sometimes locked. Orwell pushed the restaurant's glass door open and strode directly to the counter, snapped his pudgy fingers and demanded the key to the washroom.

The counter girl, who was about half as tall as Orwell, and a fifth as wide, told him the key was for customers only.

Orwell said, "I'm a regular customer."

A scruffy-looking pensioner standing in the lineup said, "If you're regular, how come you're in such a big rush to use the john?"

The girl smiled, and turned her attention to another customer. "Can I help you, sir?"

"I'm not a regular at this outlet," said Orwell.

"Cheeseburger and a small coffee," said the man.

"Cream in your coffee?"

Orwell said, "Look, I'm kind of in a hurry . . ." Waterfalls of pop streamed gurgling into waxed cups. Orwell had always been the suggestive type. He pressed his thighs together. Losing patience, he said, "Okay, gimme a cheeseburger."

"You'll have to wait your turn, sir."

Orwell shifted his weight from foot to foot. Fuck it, all they could do was fire him. He badged her. "I'm a police officer. Gimme the damn key!"

She was back in a moment, beaming. "I'm sorry, somebody's already using the washroom."

"Which is where?"

She pointed towards the rear of the restaurant. Orwell spun on his heel and hurried towards a narrow, open corridor. The door was locked. He pounded on it with his heavy fist, then both fists.

From the other side of the door, a heavy voice yelled, "Fuck off, asshole!"

Orwell was suddenly sundered by a lightning-bolt of déjà vu. He'd played out this exact scene hundreds of times before, in his own home, pleading with Judith to unlock the door and let him in, oh *please please please*.

He stepped back, and gave the door a swift kick. "Police officer, open up, or you're busted!" Behind him, the door to the women's washroom swung open. Orwell was still trying to decide whether he should take advantage when the door swung shut. Bobby was right, he did have the reflexes of a sloth. He reared back to give the men's-room door another kick. It opened before he could deliver the blow. He found himself standing face to face with Dan Oikawa. Though he was a good six inches shorter than Orwell, Oikawa managed to look down at him. He stepped aside. "Come on in, before you wet yourself."

Orwell was mystified. Oikawa had always been so scrupulously polite. His Japanese background, presumably. Orwell sidled around him and stepped up to the urinal. He unzipped. Like they said, point and shoot. It was so easy, unless you made the mistake of thinking about it. He zipped up and went over to the sink. Behind him, the door to the washroom's lone stall swung open and Farley Spears stepped out.

Spears looked like a six-foot-tall, one-hundred-and-eighty-pound definition of a trapped rat. Orwell was startled and taken aback by the look of shame and humiliation and anger on his lined face. Then he saw the smear of white powder on Spears's upper lip, and the feverish look in his watery eyes.

"Jeez, you're a fuckin' dope addict!"

Oikawa stepped between Orwell and Spears. "Eddy, what's the matter with . . . ?"

Orwell pushed him away. Harder than he meant to. Oikawa's feet skidded on the wet tile floor. His arms windmilled like a demented air-traffic controller's, and he lost his balance and fell. Orwell snatched at him, but he was too fat and too slow. Oikawa's close-shaven head bounced off a sink, and then the tiled floor. He bounced once, and was still. Oikawa must have bitten his tongue, because his teeth were glazed with red.

"Danny!" shouted Spears. He turned on Orwell. "You killed him, you prick!"

"It was an accident!" Orwell knelt and placed his ear to Oikawa's mouth. Nothing stirred. He lifted an eyelid. The orb that stared blindly up at him was nothing but white. He knew he should get down there and apply mouth-to-mouth, but Oikawa was bleeding, and . . . He loosened Oikawa's tie and rested his hands on Oikawa's muscular chest. Danny had told him a long time ago that he was related to David Suzuki, the internationally famous environmentalist and do-gooder. What if it was true? Orwell pushed down on Oikawa's chest. Behind him, Spears capered and moaned. Orwell pushed harder. He shouted, "Farley, get a goddam ambulance!"

No response. Orwell glanced up. Spears sat cross-legged on the floor, the muzzle of his Glock buried in his mouth. Not a pretty sight. Orwell lurched sideways. He snatched at the gun with his left hand, while simultaneously delivering a vicious roundhouse right to Spears' temple. The pistol clattered on the floor. Spears sagged backwards, victim of a knockout punch. The sound of his skull smacking against the tiles reminded Orwell of the time a Domino's pizza slipped out of the box and landed gooey-side down on the kitchen floor. Man, Judith had just about ripped his head off. He stood up. In the space of less than ten seconds, he'd eliminated one-quarter of the city's homicide squad, and given the rest of the unit plenty to keep them occupied. Somebody was pounding on the door. He opened it a crack.

"What?"

"I'm the manager. What's going on in there?" The guy was in his early twenties, with all the charisma and force of personality of a cardboard cutout.

"Police business." Orwell tried to shut the door, but the weasel had stuck out his foot. Orwell glared at him. "What's your name?"

"Brian Kenwood." The manager's fingernails chattered against his plastic nameplate.

Orwell said, "Brian, you're obstructing a police officer in the course of an investigation. Step back, right now, or I'll arrest your scrawny ass!"

"You can't talk to me like that!"

But as he spoke he withdrew his foot. Orwell slammed the door shut. The sound of running water made him spin around.

Oikawa leaned against the sink. He splashed water onto his face with his cupped hand. His eyes, reflected in the burnished metal mirror over the sink, caught Orwell's.

"Nice work, Eddy." He spat. A gob of blood slithered down the porcelain wall of the sink.

Orwell turned his solemn eyes on Farley Spears' corpse. The corpse sat up, looking befuddled. It glared at Orwell. "What'd you hit me for?"

"You were going to smoke yourself!"

With that?" Spears kicked the pistol across the floor and Orwell bent and scooped it up. The thing was light as a feather. He pulled the trigger and a blue flame shot out the barrel.

Orwell said, "It's a lighter."

"Really? That probably explains why I was using it to light my cigarette."

Oikawa spat another mouthful of blood.

Spears said, "Why in hell would I want to kill myself?"

"Because you're a fucking junkie!" shouted Orwell.

Spears' mouth fell open. "I'm a . . . what?"

"Cocaine addict," muttered Orwell, uncertainly.

"What're you talking about?"

"That smear of powder under your nose!"

Spears wiped his upper lip with the tips of his fingers. He peered down at what he'd found. "That's sauce from my Big Mac."

Spears wiped his fingers clean on Orwell's lapel. It was Big Mac sauce, all right; Orwell should have recognized it anywhere. His face twisted. He was emotionally conflicted, and didn't know why.

Bobby Dundas shouted at them through the locked door.

Orwell said, "How're you guys doing on the sunny side of the street? You getting anywhere, or what?"

Oikawa and Spears exchanged weary, disgusted glances. Oikawa spat more blood into the sink. Spears said, "Scram, Eddy."

Orwell nodded. "I can do that."

As the washroom door shut behind him, Orwell heard Oikawa say, "When Judith sees what he did to me, she's gonna go crazy."

Judith? What Judith? His *wife* Judith? *That* Judith? Orwell couldn't believe it, because Judith had told him she was leaving him for another woman. Yet he knew it was true.

He consoled himself with a strawberry milkshake, and a piece of piping-hot apple pie.

His monthly nut included payments on two cars, rent on two apartments, massive bills for booze and junk food, and killingly expensive child-support payments. He could live to be a thousand, and never save a dime. How was he going to pay for Oikawa's tooth?

On the other hand, if Oikawa was dating Judith . . .

A block down the street, as Bobby rousted another pack of street kids, Orwell realized that he'd somehow acquired the key to the men's washroom. The philosophers were right – every cloud did have a silver lining.

26

A preternaturally buoyant disc jockey chattering about the weather had wakened Hector at seven sharp. Why did he think it was such a big deal to tell you what it was like outside when any fool who looked out his window could see it was raining so heavily it warranted a quick trip to the lumberyard for sufficient material to build a one-man ark?

Hector head-butted the wall until his neighbour turned the radio off. Thank you. He lay back and shut his eyes and tendered his return ticket to dreamland.

No way, because the couple next door, who happened to be newlyweds, had apparently been sexually aroused by the DJ's peanut-butter-smooth voice. Bitter experience had taught Hector that, once the lovebirds started smooching, they could go at it for hours. And, man oh man, were they ever *loud*.

Hector pulled his sleeping bag up over his shoulders and pressed his ear against the wall. Grunts and groans, sighs and moans. It was like trying to follow a heated conversation in a foreign language. How strange it must be, to have sex with a woman who wasn't being paid for her services. Though the cynic in him supposed, people being what they were, that there was always commerce of one kind or another, even if no actual cash changed hands.

Something else bothering him was the fact that the woman was gorgeous, a real knockout, while her husband was short and flabby, with mouse-brown hair and a potato nose. What did a dame like that see in such a loser? And how did somebody so weak and puny manage to keep it up for hours at a time? Hector had complained about the noise to the building's manager. The guy had laughed in his face, possibly because he, too, was short and flabby. Hector consoled himself with the certain knowledge that nobody else liked him, so why should the super be any different. Even so, it was vexing. He got out his indelible-ink pen and wrote the super's name on the miles-long revenge ledger in his brain.

What was it like to "make love," as opposed to "get laid." Was there really any difference? His mother had told him that sex was a base physical act, brutal and painful, but necessary for procreation. Hector was twelve years old at the time. He wondered aloud, if this were true, why he didn't have more brothers and sisters, since Mom and her boyfriends went at it so much. The question cost him a fat lip and his first broken nose.

The noise on the far side of the wall subsided. They must be catching their breath, or taking a smoke break, or wringing the sweat out of the sheets. Roger wasn't around much because he worked, but Hector had bumped into his wife lots of times, in the hallway or elevator, or downstairs in the lobby checking her mail. She liked to wear tight jeans or skirts, tank tops, and lots of silver jewellery. He'd asked her once if she'd bought the silver in Mexico, and she gave him a look cold enough to freeze a hot tamale. Hector had given her a look right back, his special I-can-see-through-your-clothes look. She'd brushed him off like a speck of lint. Stung, he loitered in the lobby out of a strong sense of immobility. If she felt vulnerable and threatened, was that his fault? He followed her into the elevator, leaned in close beside her to press the button for their shared floor.

She looked straight at him and said, "I used to work at a downtown bar, the high-tech crowd. IPO creeps."

Hector had no idea what she was talking about. He said, "Yeah?" Sounding tough, nonchalant. He hoped.

"Sick assholes like you, who get a kick out of intimidating women."

She sure had him pegged.

She said, "You ever look at me like that again, I'll kick the living crap out of you."

Hector's face hurt. His armpits were damp and his face was feverishly hot. His eyes stung. He said, "Just like that, huh?"

She spat on his boots and, when he looked down to verify the impossibility of what she'd done, hit him in the belly. He doubled over, winded. She pulled back his head and hooked a finger into his eye socket. The pain was dizzying.

"Next time you give me a reason to hit you, you'll wake up in a fucking emergency ward. Or not at all."

When he regained consciousness, he was lying face down on the elevator floor, in a tepid pool of vomit.

Somehow the super found out who'd messed the elevator, and came ranting after him. Hector had to give him fifty to avoid an eviction notice. He never told Carlos about the woman, because he knew that, if Carlos went after her, she'd slaughter them both. So he kept his mouth shut, sat around steamin' and schemin' for a few days, and then got lucky and stumbled across a drunk in a Gastown alley and pummelled the living bejesus out of him. There now, didn't he feel better? You bet your ass he did. The drunk turned out to be the degenerate boozer son of a city alderman. Icing on the cake.

Those jungle drums started beating again. They sure did go at it.

Hector lay there in his lonely bed, all floppy ears and imagination, trying to figure out what perversions they were up to now. On and on it went, the volume of their marathon lovemaking ebbing and flowing as did the tides, but a lot more frequently.

Finally he couldn't take it any more, and rolled out of bed. In the kitchen, he boiled water for instant coffee, and fussily cut the spongy green mould off a sesame-seed bagel, then sliced it in half and dropped it in the toaster.

He was licking the crumbs from his plate when his neighbours uttered a series of overlapping whoops and shrieks followed by a kind of yodelling that went on for a long, long time.

This was what he really hated about his rabbity neighbours: their obnoxious habit of bursting into song when they'd finished doing it. Were they in the music biz? He'd asked the super, who told him to mind his own business, if he had any. Were they going to go at it again? Hector tongued the last few crumbs off his plate. He suspected that they sometimes went off to some other part of the apartment to do their pleasuring. Man, he sure wished he had one of those spy-type devices that let you peek through walls, so he could videotape them, make a fortune selling copies to the porn market, and retire to Mexico.

He spent a few minutes imagining himself lolling around some small town on the ocean, sipping cold beer and messing with the local beauties, then went back into his bedroom. Standing in front of the cheap mirror hanging from the bedroom door, he sucked in his belly and puffed up his chest and flexed his biceps. Lookin' good, Hector. He turned sideways to the mirror and clenched his butt muscles and struck another pose. If he weren't so damn tough, he'd scare himself silly.

Somebody pounded on the door, and he jumped a foot. His heart ricocheting all over his chest, he yelled, "Who is it?"

Carlos. He'd managed to lock himself out of the apartment, but what was he doing up so early? Hector unlocked the door and let him in. Carlos was wet, from the rain. He was carrying a plastic Home Hardware bag.

Hector said, "What'd you get?"

"Steel wool," said Carlos.

Hector shut the door and shot the bolt. He stared at Carlos for a long time. Finally he asked the million-dollar question.

"Who'd you shoot?"

Carlos told him all about it, holding nothing back.

27

It was Parker's idea to get Tripper a guest shot on a local TV station's noon news. The station regularly hosted an SPCA spokesperson, accompanied by two or three photogenic cats or dogs in need of a loving home. The program director, caught up in a ratings war with a rival network, jumped at the chance to entertain an orphaned pooch whose teenage pimp owner had come to a gruesome and untimely end.

Parker had no television experience and was a bit nervous, but Tripper seemed to enjoy herself immensely. Dogs, like people, get a kick out of being the centre of attention.

Parker also had a composite drawing of Chantal. The police phone lines started ringing the moment the segment ended. One call came from a veterinarian who lived in Abbotsford, a small town in the Fraser Valley about an hour's drive east of Vancouver. The man claimed to have treated Tripper several times. Suspecting the dog was maltreated, he'd reported his suspicions to the SPCA and the police.

The vet gave the dispatcher the name and address of the dog's owner. The dispatcher passed the information on to Willows, who immediately notified Homer Bradley.

Bradley contacted the Abbotsford detachment of the RCMP. His tale of an orphaned mutt and unlucky drug addict did not get the duty sergeant's pulse racing. Bradley politely declined the sergeant's unenthusiastic offer of backup. He phoned Willows at the TV station, and gave him the green light to make the long but intermittently scenic drive into the valley.

It took Willows half an hour of hard driving to get onto Highway 1, the Trans-Canada. Traffic was fairly thick, but he was able to take advantage of the HOV lane, and so they made fairly good time all the way to New Westminster, where he was slowed by heavy commercial traffic, and the two-lane Port Mann Bridge, which spanned the Fraser River.

Rain and a mist over the half-mile-wide river obscured the tugboats, log booms and other water-borne traffic. Parker flinched, her thoughts disrupted, as Tripper shoved her wet black nose up against her neck.

"Tripper, sit!"

Tripper tried to crawl over the bench seat into the front of the car. Parker pushed her back. Tripper whined piteously, and lifted a helpless paw. Where had she learned such manipulative behaviour? From watching "Lassie" reruns? Parker pushed her back again. There was no room up front, and Tripper was shedding like a bale of hay in a hurricane.

"Tripper, lie down!"

The dog turned her back on her and stared forlornly out the side window. Parker tried not to feel guilty. She made a mental note to stop somewhere and pick up a box of dog biscuits, or at least a prefab hamburger.

Willows said, "Did you see Annie this morning?"

"No, why?"

Willows waited until he'd passed a semi. When the roar of the truck had dwindled to a level that permitted normal conversation, he said, "I thought I heard her come home about three, but when I looked in her room this morning, she wasn't there, and her bed hadn't been slept in."

"No, she was home," said Parker. She wondered if Annie had

made her bed because she'd found it necessary to change the sheets.

"Good." Willows hadn't said anything to Claire, but he hadn't been sleeping well lately. He often woke at three or three-thirty in the morning, and couldn't get back to sleep for hours. He was worried about Annie, but it was his ex-wife, Sheila, that he spent most of his time thinking about. When Sheila left him, he'd been a workaholic, completely immersed in his job, with no time for her or the kids. He'd blissfully ignored her repeated warnings that the marriage was falling apart, and flat-out refused to go to a family counsellor with her. When she finally packed her bags and walked out, he'd been taken completely by surprise.

Sheila stood tall against his rage and grief. She coolly told him that the children were all his. She'd raised them from infancy without any help from him. Now it was his turn to be a single parent. When he learned that she was romantically involved with another man, it hit him like a sucker punch to the heart.

He'd pleaded with her to give him a second chance, but at the same time he was honest enough to admit that he was motivated more by vanity than love. As a consequence of years of neglect, he and Sheila had drifted irrevocably apart. Plus, joker in the pack, he had already begun to fall in love with Parker.

Sheila had run through the two hundred thousand Willows had sent her in less than a year, and wired him for more. Over the following years, he'd sent her a few hundred dollars here, a thousand there. Whatever he and Claire could afford, and sometimes a little bit more.

Willows hadn't heard from her in almost a year. He had a premonition that something terrible had happened to her.

"Jack?" Parker's hand was on his shoulder. He started, as if waking from a dream. "You okay?"

"Yeah, fine."

Parker pointed up the highway. "It's the next turnoff, about a kilometre away."

"Got it."

"If you see a grocery store, pull over, I want to get some biscuits."

Willows gave her a look. Mock consternation. Parker never dieted, but she was always watching her weight, which as far as he could tell never varied by more than an ounce or two.

Smiling, she said, "For Tripper."

Willows told himself to be strong. They already had two cats, and all they did was eat, shed, and demand to be let in or out of the house. If Parker asked him if they could keep Tripper, the answer was going to be a resounding no.

But what if she didn't bother to ask?

Nicholas Partridge had run away from a rundown cottage on ten acres of farmland that had gone fallow. The cottage might have qualified as quaint thirty-odd years ago. Willows doubted it had seen a fresh coat of paint or new roof since it was built. Now it looked like a prime candidate for a bulldozer. The chimney was smoking, but that was the only sign of life. Three cars squatted in the mud and weeds by the side of the house. Two more cars and the gutted remains of a Chevy pickup graced the front yard. A sixties-era Ford Falcon parked at an angle in the muddy driveway had two flat tires, but current plates. All the other vehicles had been reduced to lawn ornaments. Tripper's growl was like the low rumble of nearby thunder. Her ears lay flat on her head. White teeth gleamed.

Parker said, "She recognizes the place."

Willows nodded. He parked his unmarked Crown Vic behind the Falcon. The home's scabrous front door opened slightly as he and Parker gingerly climbed the rotting front-porch steps.

"Beat it, you're trespassin'!"

The door slammed shut.

Willows crossed the porch, and gave his knuckles a workout. He held his badge up to the door's peephole.

The door was again opened a crack, against a thick safety chain. "If you're lookin' for Nick, he ain't here."

Parker slammed the palm of her hand against the frame. "Open the door!"

"Christ almighty!" The door was slammed shut, the chain rattled, and then the door swung wide. Parker tried not to look surprised. She thought they'd been talking to Nicholas Partridge's father, but it was Mrs. Partridge, her voice aged and deepened by cigarettes and alcohol, who'd greeted them. She wore dark-blue men's coveralls, a baggy black sweater and ratty bedroom slippers with fur trim. She was in her mid-sixties, and had not aged well.

She peered suspiciously up at Parker. "Nick in trouble again? What'd he do this time?"

Parker introduced herself and Willows. She said, "Can we come inside, Mrs. Partridge?"

"Nick's my son by my first marriage. The name's Steadman, now. What'd he do?"

She reluctantly stepped aside as Willows and Parker eased into the house. Willows shut the door behind him. The house smelled of mould. The wallpaper was peeling and the cracks between the bare wooden floorboards were black with accumulated grime.

Parker said, "Is your husband home?"

"Bob? Where else would he be?" She led them through a doorway and into the living room. She introduced them to Bob Steadman, who lay comfortably on the sofa, and clearly wasn't about to get up. He had an alcoholic's bloodshot eyes, emaciated body, bulging, hell-red nose. He eyed Parker and acknowledged Willows with a terse nod, but didn't offer his hand. The wood stove's metal chimney had been jury-rigged to the fireplace chimney. The room was uncomfortably hot. Willows thought about taking off his jacket; decided against it.

Parker glanced at him. He took the morgue photo out of his pocket, unfolded it and showed it to the Steadmans. "Is this your son?"

Bob said, "Yeah, that's Nick."

"Mrs. Steadman, you might want to sit down, because I'm afraid I have some very bad news."

"Is Nick hurt?"

Willows nodded. He said, "Nick's had an accident. At least, we think it was an accident. You didn't know about this?"

"About what?"

"I'm sorry, but Nick fell down a stairwell. He was killed instantly."

Bob Steadman said, "My God!" He didn't put much into it. His wife glanced sharply towards him, and looked away.

Willows said, "If it helps, I can tell you with certainty that he didn't suffer."

Mrs. Steadman was pale. She fished in her pocket and came up with a bedraggled Kleenex. She dabbed at her eyes, grasped a steel poker, swung open the stove's metal door and jabbed furiously at the fire, raising a storm of sparks. She banged the door shut but didn't relinquish her grip on the poker.

Bob Steadman's fingers rolled a cigarette. He said, "Weeks would go by and he'd never say a goddam word. Not one word. You knew he was gonna blow his stack sooner or later, it was just a question of when." His tongue trolled down the length of the paper tube. He pinched away the excess tobacco and stuck the cigarette in his mouth, sucked smoke into his lungs. "You got any idea what it's like to live with somebody like that? I'm here to tell you it's no fun at all."

"When did you last see him?" said Parker.

The Steadmans frowned. Bob studied the ceiling while his wife peered out the dust-clouded window. Finally Mrs. Steadman said, "It's been a while now, must be getting on to about a year."

"Not that long," countered her husband.

It seemed to Parker that Mrs. Steadman was about to say something but decided against it.

Parker said, "Did you ever meet any of his Vancouver friends?"

Bob Steadman shook his head. "He never had any, as far as we ever knew. If he did, he sure as hell wouldn't have told Agnes or me about it." He flicked his cigarette in the general direction of a dark-green glass ashtray. "Hell, it wasn't like he phoned every week to tell us how he was doing. I mean, he left home to get shut of us, and we were glad to see the back of him."

"Why is that?" said Parker.

"Drugs and more drugs. He was smokin' dope in his bedroom, moved on to cocaine. We figured heroin was just around the corner. It'd be fair to say he left just as I was gettin' set to kick his ass out the door."

"He left because you disapproved of his drug use?"

"That's right, and we never saw him or spoke to him again. Not once. It was like he went to Mars."

Agnes Steadman couldn't take it any longer. She turned on her husband, her face tight and angry. "You hit him! Chased him away and told him to never come back! My only child, and you treated him worse than a rabid dog!"

"To hell with you, Agnes!" Steadman started to push himself up off the sofa, changed his mind and sank back. "You treated him like a goddam halfwit child, doin' every damn thing for him that you could think of. No wonder he never grew up."

Parker stepped between them. "Mrs. Steadman, we're here because we need you to identify your son's body."

"Where is he? Please don't tell me you brought him with you!"

"No, that's not how it works. Nick's in the city morgue."

"Well, we ain't going way the hell out to the city and back," said Bob Steadman.

Parker was shocked by the Steadmans' response to the news that Nick was dead. His experiments with drugs were no reason to abandon him. She knew serial killers in maximum security whose parents had moved thousands of miles to be near them. She suspected there was more than drugs involved. Had Steadman sexually abused his stepson? She'd never know, because Bob wasn't about to confess anything, and neither was his wife. Despite her brief outburst, Agnes Steadman clearly wasn't about to defy her husband's wishes.

Parker took a shot at it anyway.

"Mrs. Steadman – Agnes – will you let us drive you into the city to identify your son?"

"Are you sure Nick's dead?"

Parker nodded.

"Then what's the point of me identifying him?"

"You want to be sure it's him, don't you?"

"No, I don't." Mrs. Steadman had surprised herself with her candour. "I'd rather believe he might be alive, even if I never saw him or heard from him for the rest of my life."

Willows stepped in, at last. "It is Nick, Mrs. Steadman, and this is your last chance to see him."

Bob Steadman said, "Well, she ain't gonna take it."

"What about the disposal of the body," said Willows. "How do you want that handled?"

"We ain't wasting our hard-earned cash on a funeral," said Steadman, "and that's a brass-plated fact."

Willows kept his face blank. He glanced at Mrs. Steadman, and saw he could waste the rest of the afternoon on her and never gain an inch. He said, "Thanks for your time, folks."

"You're welcome," said Steadman.

Mrs. Steadman surprised Parker by stepping out on the porch and shutting the door behind her. She said, "I'm sorry I can't help you, but you have no idea what Nick put us through, all the trouble he caused." She looked across the yard towards the Crown Vic. "Is that a police dog? I thought they were trained not to bark."

"That's Tripper, your son's dog."

"Nick had a dog?"

Tripper's paws scrabbled at the Crown Vic's side window. She snapped furiously at the glass.

Parker said, "Tripper seems to know you, Mrs. Steadman."

"No, that isn't possible."

"Your son never came out here with the dog?"

"No. I already told you we haven't seen him since he ran off to the city."

"When was the last time you or your husband were in Vancouver?"

"Years and years ago, long before Nick left."

"Why *did* Nick leave, Mrs. Steadman?"

"He never told me, and I never got the chance to ask. I woke up one morning and he was gone. I looked in his bedroom and all he'd taken was the clothes on his back." Mrs. Steadman's cheeks began to quiver. Tears welled up in her eyes.

Parker gave her one of her cards. "Call me if you decide you want to see your son. But don't put it off for more than a day or two, or it'll be too late."

She and Willows walked down the sagging steps and got into the car. Parker had her hands full with Tripper. She held tight to the dog's collar as Willows backed the car down the muddy driveway and onto the road. He hit the gas hard enough to make the tires chirp. Tripper didn't stop barking until the house had disappeared from view.

Willows said, "Nice family. There was a TV. D'you think they already knew Nick had died?"

"I have no idea." Parker reached back and gave Tripper a reassuring pat. She said, "It was like a damn 'X-Files' episode – that awful house, and the way Tripper went crazy."

Willows nodded agreeably, though he had only a vague idea what she was talking about. He'd never watched Scully and Mulder at work, and he didn't intend to until the show was cancelled. Then he'd watch the reruns, if he found he liked the show. Reruns were the only way to go. He'd first used this strategy on "Seinfeld." When Jerry quit, millions of loyal viewers were disappointed. Not Willows, though. Now, two years later, he still stumbled across the odd episode he'd never seen.

Parker said, "Over there!"

Her tone was sharp. Willows hunted for a purse-snatching or fist fight, or at least a jaywalker, but Parker was pointing at a corner grocery store. Willows turned into the parking lot. He pulled up beside a black Camaro in the handicapped zone.

Parker opened her door. "I'll be right back."

Willows watched her as she strode past banked rows of flowers. She vanished into the store and he found himself thinking about the Steadmans' ruination of a marriage, and then he was thinking about Sheila, and all the terrible things that might have happened to her, in the gaudy wilderness of Mexico.

28

A scum had formed on the surface of Chantal's coffee. The quartet of checkout girls soon went back to work. The waitress, left alone with her conscience, had a change of heart and took pity on her. She brought Chantal a fresh cup of coffee without being asked, and then left her alone. Chantal sat quietly, but her mind was in turmoil. Nick hadn't exactly been Mr. Perfect, but he hadn't deserved to die such a terrible death.

She shut her eyes against a sudden memory of the mean, teasing look in his eyes as he leaned away from her, tumbled backwards over the banister railing, the smug look on his face turning to raw terror. The memory of his scream flailed her.

She knew she'd never forget the terrible thud of his body's impact on the hotel's marble floor.

She squeezed her eyes shut, trying to block out the scene, and her deceitful imagination treated her to a flickering montage of happy moments with Nick.

Nick at the park, laughing crazily as he and Tripper chased a dog that had stolen their Frisbee. Nick frolicking on the beach at Spanish Banks, wading fully clothed into the water.

She remembered lying on the bed in his arms, the steady thump of his heartbeat against her breast, listening to the discordant soothing music of the city, watching the light fade in the window.

Once, on the street, Nick had horrified and thrilled her by jumping a big-boned kid twice his size who'd made the mistake of talking dirty to her.

She put the fight out of her mind. Nick at the beach had been Nick at his best. He'd happily made himself look like an idiot, just to make her smile.

The waitress tapped her on the shoulder. "Look, I'm sorry, but we're getting pretty busy."

Chantal glanced around. The restaurant was almost full.

"You don't have to leave, but you should order something . . ."

"I'm not hungry."

The waitress patted her shoulder. "I know, but . . . you'll feel better if you have something to eat." She smiled. "Scrambled eggs and toast, how does that sound?"

Chantal hesitated.

"If you don't have any money . . ."

"No, I do, it's okay."

"Because if you're broke, it's my treat."

Chantal looked up at her, looked directly at her, seeing her as a person, a fellow human being. She said, "That's really nice of you, but money isn't a problem."

"Okay, fine." The waitress picked up her untouched coffee. "You just relax, and take it easy. I'll be right back with a fresh cup."

Chantal was still waiting for her breakfast when a man walked up to her and shyly asked her if he could share her table. She glanced around again. All the other chairs were occupied. She ducked her head, accepting the situation but not happy about it. The man was in his early twenties, not all that old, really. He sat down opposite her, unfolded a newspaper and began reading. The waitress arrived, and he ordered a BLT and a pot of tea. Chantal covertly sized him up as he read his newspaper. He was thin, and only a few inches taller than her own height of five-foot-four. He had long blond hair and an open, unremarkable but pleasant face. His blue eyes were his best feature. He wore a brown corduroy jacket over a dark-blue T-shirt. Chantal leaned sideways. Jeans and a pair of well-worn Adidas sneakers. A red backpack was slung over the back of his chair.

She sipped at her coffee. "Excuse me."

He was so engrossed in his paper that he didn't hear her. She leaned across the table. "Excuse me."

He glanced up, startled, uncomfortable at being singled out.

She said, "Would you mind passing the cream, please?"

The metal jug of cream was midway between them. Head down, he pushed it towards her.

She poured a little cream in her coffee and pushed the jug back towards him.

"Thank you very much."

He nodded but didn't look up. His cheeks were pink. Chantal gained confidence.

"What are you reading?"

He risked a quick look at her. "A newspaper."

She forced a laugh. "I can see that. I mean, what are you reading about?"

"Nothing, really." He studied her with his lively blue eyes and then turned back to his paper, as if to confirm what he'd just said.

"Nothing?"

"Well, nothing important." He put down the paper. That was a start. He said, "I was just reading about Tiger Woods." He saw the name meant nothing to her. "He's a golfer. The best golfer in the world."

Chantal nodded. She said, "Do you play golf?"

"No, I'm no good at sports. I don't even like reading about sports, to tell you the truth. Tiger Woods is kind of amazing, but the only reason I read the sports section is so I can keep up with the other guys."

"What do you do for a living? Have you got a job?"

"I'm a student."

Chantal smiled. "What are you studying?"

"Law. I'm in my final year. In a few months I'll be finished, and then I'll move back to Toronto to article."

"I don't know what that means."

"Basically, it's like an apprenticeship. I'll be working for a law firm, but for the first year I won't get paid much more than I'd make flipping burgers at McDonald's."

"That doesn't sound fair." She leaned forward and offered him her hand. "I'm Janie." And she was, too, because Jane was her middle name.

"Tim Shepherd." He shook her hand but didn't put much into it. He said, "Articling isn't really that bad. Everybody has to do it, and in some ways it makes it easier to find a job, get the ball rolling."

"And I guess the money's pretty good, after that first year."

"It can be." He smiled, and it transformed his whole face; he had the warmest and most sincere and kindly smile Chantal had seen in her whole life. "In fact, the money better be good, because I owe a small fortune in student loans."

Their food – her late breakfast and his early lunch – arrived together. As they ate, Chantal worked hard to keep him talking.

"D'you live around here, Tim?"

He nodded, chewed and swallowed, wiped his mouth with a paper napkin. "My apartment's just a few blocks from here, on Eleventh."

"You have your own apartment?"

"Well, sort of. It's a basement suite, and it's pretty small." He smiled again. "The ceiling's so low that, if I was any taller, I'd feel like a basketball player."

Chantal laughed. "There you go, talking sports again. Do you live alone or do you share it with your girlfriend?"

"I live alone." He took a big bite of his sandwich and chewed furiously.

"But you do have a girlfriend, don't you?"

"Not at the moment, no."

"Did you just break up with somebody?"

"Not really." Tim drank some coffee. He wiped his mouth with the napkin again. "How about you? Do you live around here?"

"Are you kidding? This is my first day in Vancouver. I just got here a couple of hours ago."

"You did? Where are you from?'

"Winnipeg. I ran away from home. My dad beat me, and I couldn't take it any more."

"Your dad *beat* you?" He was astonished. "What about your mom? Didn't she protect you?"

"She died in a car accident when I was ten. That's why Dad started drinking." Chantal picked at her eggs. Tim stared fixedly at her. He'd forgotten all about his shyness. She said, "I came to Vancouver because I've got a friend here who said she'd put me up for a few days until I found a job. But when I phoned her, the operator said the number had been disconnected."

"That's too bad."

"It gets worse. I had to change buses in Calgary, and when I was in the washroom some creep stole my suitcase, with all my clothes and most of my money, three hundred dollars it took me almost a year to save. All I've got is the clothes on my back and enough money to pay for breakfast."

"I'm so sorry . . ."

"Hey, it's not your fault. I'm nineteen, and that's the legal definition of an adult, so I must be able to take care of myself, right?"

"You're nineteen?"

"Don't look my age, do I? Want to see my driver's licence?"

"No, that's okay." He toyed with his coffee cup. "I moved to Vancouver when I was eighteen, straight out of high school. It seemed like the far side of the world."

"Why did you move?"

He shrugged. "My dad's a lawyer, and he went to UBC. I guess he wanted me to carry on the family tradition."

"It must be nice to have a father who cares about you, and has your best interests at heart."

"Yeah, I guess so."

He'd almost finished his sandwich. Chantal wolfed her breakfast, keeping up. When she cleared her plate, she said, "Tim?"

"Yeah, what?"

"I'm a good worker. I know I can get a job, waiting tables or whatever. But it's probably going to take me a few days, and I don't have anywhere to stay, or any money."

"I'm sorry, I really am. But I'm living on a shoestring." He looked out the window and then directly at her. "It's my birthday. This is the first time I've eaten at a restaurant in more than a month."

"Happy birthday. I'm not asking you for money, I'm asking if I can stay in your apartment for a few days."

"No, I . . . I don't think I could do that."

"Why not? I just need a place to sleep, that's all."

"No, I don't think that would be a good idea . . ."

"Yes, it is!" Chantal suddenly reached across the table and squeezed Tim's hand. "It's just a complete fluke that we ran into each other. I can be your birthday present!" She tightened her grip on his hand. "I'm not letting go until you say yes."

He jerked his hand away. "*I said no!*" Her fingernails had left white indentations in his flesh. He refused to look at her. Now he was pulling out his wallet.

"Tell you what, I'll treat you to breakfast."

"No thanks!" Chantal pulled a five-dollar bill out of her pocket and threw it on the table.

29

Carlos finished telling Hector the story he called "The Jays and the Neon." He peeked out the living-room window and saw that the dark-blue car was still parked in the same spot. But now both front tires were flat and there were several bullet holes in the windshield. There was something else he'd have to clean up, too: the dead bird caught in the branches of one of the plum trees lining the boulevard. He got a beer from the fridge and sat down on the sofa, tore apart the pads of steel wool he'd bought at the twenty-four-hour market, and repacked his pistol's homemade silencer. It was still early, relatively speaking. Way too early to be up and at 'em. But if there was one single thing in the world that got his adrenalin pumping, it was gunfire and live targets. Going back to bed would be a waste of time, because he knew from slim past experience that he'd just lie there, tossing and turning, uncomfortable and unhappy. He'd take a nap in the afternoon, if he ran out of juice. Scratching his belly, he headed for the bathroom to take a leak, and a shower.

The bathroom door was closed, and locked. He could hear water beating against the shower curtain. What in hell was going on? Hector *never* took a shower in the morning, unless he had to meet with his parole officer – but that had been last week. Carlos pounded on the door with his fist, but to no avail. He pressed his ear to the door. Hector was mauling a vaguely familiar tune.

"Send in the Clowns." Carlos pounded on the door again, but how could Hector hear him over the penetrating wail of his wretched voice? Hector was a goddam shower fiend. He wouldn't come out of there until his skin started to pucker up like an albino prune.

Carlos went into the kitchen and urinated copiously into the sink. He gave himself a discreet shake, tucked himself back in.

Shuffling sideways along the counter, he grabbed the coffee pot and dumped the cold, black, bean-greasy contents into the sink. The filter and grounds went into the overflowing garbage. He filled the pot with cold water and fitted a clean filter into the machine. So far, so good. He pawed through the refrigerator and cupboards, top to bottom and back and forth.

Fucking Hector! They were out of coffee, bread, milk, eggs, and grapefruit juice. Every last necessity he could think of. How was he supposed to get himself cranked when they were out of grape-fruit juice?

He filled the sink with hot water, got the last clean towel out of the hall closet, went back into the kitchen and washed his hair and body with Sunlight dish soap. The soap generated a lot more suds than he'd anticipated. He rinsed himself clean with potsful of water. It took a long time, because of the spillage. He finger-combed his hair and studied his reflection in the glass door of a kitchen cabinet. He liked the way he looked with a two- or three-day growth of beard. Tough, like a hockey player. That manly Mark Messier look.

He ambushed Hector as he came out of the bathroom, snuck up behind him and flipped his soapy-wet towel over Hector's head, at the same time driving his knee into his partner's spine, knocking him off balance and down. He wrapped the towel around Hector's empty head and dragged him kicking and gagging into the kitchen.

"Leggo!" Hector tried to stand up, but the floor was wet and slippery, and he was helpless as a turtle on a frozen pond.

Carlos said, "How do I like to start my morning, Hector?"

"Get your foot off my head!"

"Answer the question! How do I like to start my morning?"

"Late?"

"And then . . . ?"

"Fucked if I know." Hector twisted sideways, got out from under Carlos' foot, scrabbled across the floor and leaned against the refrigerator. "My neck hurts."

"Grapefruit juice, Hector. That's how I like to start my day, with a glass of cold grapefruit juice."

Hector's eyes brightened as the light went on inside his brain. He said, "If we're outta groceries, whose fault is that?"

"Okay, so I got a flamboyant personality. That's why I put up with you, because you're a responsible, clear-thinking type of guy. Situations like that, you're expected to save me from myself."

But still, Hector had a point. Carlos helped him to his feet. "Tell you what, why don't we go out for breakfast? My treat."

Hector thought it over, his brain working hard, chugging away as if on a steep grade. Where was the downside? Carlos was half Gila monster and half snake, all twitches and jumps and weird bends and curves . . .

Mom's was busy, for Mom's. Half a dozen seedy, down-and-out, doomed-to-be-a-loner-for-life types lurked in the gutted booths and at the grease-slick counter. Every last one of them looked as if he'd skipped out on a day pass as a consequence of a grievous bureaucratic error.

Carlos and Hector sat at the prestigious booth next to the fire exit. Hector brushed a thousand flakes of Budweiser label off the table. Carlos lit a cigarette and flicked away the burning match. The black cook slammed a plate of bacon and eggs and hash browns down under the heat lamps, and punched the bell with his fist. A toilet flushed noisily. Mom snapped her suspenders hard when she spotted Carlos and Hector, but otherwise ignored them, in favour of forcibly evicting a wannabe vampire she noticed sucking ketchup straight from the bottle.

She picked up the order of bacon and eggs and delivered them to a customer in a fly-specked window booth, veered towards Carlos and Hector's table wielding a pair of ragged menus and an ice-cold smile.

Carlos said, "How's it goin', Mom?"

"As if you'd know what to do if I told you. Coffee?"

"If that's what you call it. Mona quit?"

"No, she's in the can, preening."

Hector shifted in his seat, moving tight up against the dingy wall so he had a clear view of the door to the women's washroom. Mona came out with a tube of lipstick in one hand and a rat-tail comb in the other. Her mouth was the colour of a five-alarm fire and her shoulder-length platinum hair was a silvery, angelic halo that hung effortlessly above her, like a summertime cloud. Her hips strained the fabric of her tight black dress as she zigzagged up to the booth. She beamed at Carlos. Flakes of eyeshadow and pancake makeup rained down on the table. Her slim fingers disappeared into her hair and reappeared clutching a stubby pencil.

"Ready to order, gents?"

Carlos nodded. He said, "I couldn't help notice you're wearing an engagement ring."

"My other sweetheart gave it to me." Her eyelashes were batting a thousand. She thrust out her hand. "Tell me that ain't the biggest zirconium you ever did see."

Carlos looked away.

Mona said, "Okay, so it ain't a diamond. It's the thought that counts."

"Think so, Mona? Try counting your thoughts. What d'you get? Zero, because a thought is nothing. A thought is only there for as long as you keep thinking about it. The second you stop thinking about it, it's gone."

"I don't follow you."

"Like they say, a kiss is just a kiss, but a zirconium is forever." Carlos slid the menus across the table. "Me 'n' Hector both want the same thing – a double stack with blueberry compote, and I'll have a large grapefruit juice, easy on the ice."

Carlos had dated Mona and had a mild crush on her, though he'd never have admitted it to anybody, especially himself. He'd been born in the Age of Commitment, and he'd been born too soon.

The food arrived just inside the half-hour time span stipulated on the menu. Carlos and Hector ate quickly, in a moody silence. When Mona put the bill down on the table, Carlos pushed it towards Hector. He said, "He doesn't get much – but he'll get the bill."

Hector cocked a hip and slid out his wallet. He extracted a perfectly matched pair of crisp new American twenties, tossed the money on the table, and then leaned sharply back as Carlos let fly a roundhouse right that missed by inches.

"*You goddam moron!*"

"What'd I do?" But Hector knew, he knew.

Carlos snatched up the twenties and shoved them deep into his pocket. He tossed some real money at Mona, told her to beat it, reached across the table and grabbed a handful of jacket and pulled Hector towards him, overturning glasses of cloudy water and syrup-smeared plates and overflowing ashtrays, a vase of dusty plastic flowers.

"You got into one of Jake's boxes, didn't you?" Carlos' close-set eyes were dark as thunderclouds, spiked with lightning. He gave Hector a spine-rattling shake. "How could you be so fuckin' dumb?"

"I only took a few bucks." Hector was whining. He hated himself, but couldn't stop. "I taped the box back up just like it was."

"Jake finds out what you done, he'll cut us into pieces so small he could run us through a garden hose!"

"Jake's in intensive care. He's got about as much juice left in him as a June bug celebrating the Fourth of July."

Carlos frowned. What the fuck did *that* mean? There was no point asking Hector, because he wouldn't know. His head ached something fierce, and the sad truth was that he'd been so much happier scratching out a living breaking into parked cars. Ambition was a terrible thing. The higher you climbed the ladder, the farther you could fall.

He said, "Got any more of Jake's twenties on ya?"

"A few."

Carlos sighed. "Hector, we work pretty good together, but when you screw up like this, it makes me wonder. Jake or Marty find out what you done, they're gonna blame me, too. 'Cause we're partners. That's why you're gonna put every last one of them twenties back where it belongs. Understand?"

Hector nodded agreeably. It felt like a hurricane was playing with his heart. He'd heard that rumour about a guy being fed to Jake's Rottweiler, Butch, but he'd never believed it was true. He imagined himself in bite-size chunks, being poured into Butch's doggie dish. Those big teeth ripping into him, chewing him to a pulp.

Should he mention he'd paid that hooker, Chantal, with Jake's cash? No need. Hector decided that, if Jake somehow found out that Chantal had been paid with his bogus U.S. currency, he'd tell Jake it was Carlos' fault. Jake would believe him, because Carlos was always running around telling anybody who'd listen that he was the brains of the outfit.

Hector imagined dullard Carlos hanging from a sharp hook in Jake's basement.

30

Willows had skipped breakfast. His stomach had been complaining all morning long. Abbotsford was blessed with all the usual chain-restaurant suspects, but when he spotted a drive-in hamburger joint a block off the main road, he knew he'd found the right place to park his appetite. The place was called Fat Bob's. An animated sign towering over the parking lot featured Bob opening his jaws wide to accommodate a monstrous cheeseburger that kept slipping away from him.

Parker braced herself as the car hit a particularly deep pothole. The Fat Bob sign was in good working order, but the rest of the place looked pretty grim. A face briefly appeared in Fat Bob's dusty window, then vanished. She said, "Are you sure you want to eat here, Jack?"

"Takes me back."

"To what? The birthplace of ptomaine poisoning?"

"No, my frivolous, wasted youth. Did I ever tell you about Marilyn?"

"No, you were smart enough not to."

Willows parked under a covered walkway with enough angled slots to accommodate a dozen cars. He said, "Marilyn Weaver was the first girl I ever met who wore matching nail polish and lipstick. She had a beehive hairdo at least as big as Marge Simpson's, and thoughtless blue eyes I thought were mysteriously unfathomable."

Fat Bob's menu was painted on a sheet of plywood. The once-gaudy hamburgers and milkshakes had faded so badly they'd lost almost all their colour, but the prices, printed in black paint, were bright and sharp. Willows studied the menu for a few moments, decided on a cheeseburger and fries. And a chocolate shake, but he'd only drink half, because he was on an informal diet.

"Anyway, Marilyn had a part-time job, Friday nights and weekends, carhop at the local A&W."

"Is that how you met her?"

Willows nodded, remembering. "I'd worked all summer, spent every cent I earned on a second-hand '56 Dodge. A straight six, blue and white, with whitewall tires."

"Thought you were pretty hot stuff, did you?"

"At the time. You eating?"

"No thanks. I'll have a Diet Coke. In the can, unopened."

Willows turned on the headlights. Marilyn was a good-looking girl, but it was her snazzy A&W uniform that had really turned his crank. He'd gone out with her for two full years, and never understood one word in ten that she yelled at him. Not that she ever had any trouble making herself clear when that word was "no." The relationship had ended the day of their high-school graduation ceremony. Willows went straight into first-year Arts; Marilyn trained to be a hairstylist. Within a year, she'd married a telephone repairman, and started producing babies. Or so Willows had been told.

He was startled by a sharp tapping on his side window. He turned and damn near had a heart attack. The carhop was Marilyn Weaver, thirty-odd years older and fifty pounds heavier. Her cornflower-blue eyes had not been sullied by time – they were as vacant as they'd ever been. Her blond hair had some silver in it now, and roots black as Marilyn's windowless basement rumpus room with the lights turned off.

Her Fat Bob's uniform had a name tag stitched on the breast pocket. The material was folded and rumpled by her posture, but he could make out an "M" and an "r." He rolled down the car window, and forced a smile.

She said, "Hi, what can I get you?" Her voice had been deepened by a lifetime of booze and cigarettes, but was hauntingly
familiar. She dipped her head so she could see Parker.

Parker smiled. "A Diet Coke, please. In the can, unopened, if
you don't mind."

"Diet Coke to go," said the woman. She turned her attention to
Willows, gazed quizzically down at him as she waited for his order.

"I'll have a cheeseburger, hold the pickle. Side of fries, a chocolate shake, and a coffee."

"That's it?"

"Side of onion rings," said Willows. He could already feel his
cholesterol level shooting up. But how often did a man get a
chance to step backwards in time?

"Bob's making a fresh pot of coffee. Should be ready in a minute."
She gave her head a little sideways flick. "Cream and sugar?"

"Just cream, please."

She waved her hand at his headlights as she walked away. He
turned them off and rolled up his window against the damp.

Parker said, "Think that's her?"

"Who?"

"Marilyn. You should see the look on your face. Did you notice
that her name's stitched on her jacket?"

"Not really," said Willows unconvincingly.

" 'Ma . . .' something. I couldn't see the rest of it." Parker's laugh
was low and musical. "Wouldn't it be something if that's her? Are
you sure you didn't recognize her?"

"It was a long time ago, Claire. But no, I didn't recognize her."
Not that he was at all sure he would.

"Wouldn't it be a coincidence, though?"

"Yes, it would, but I don't have much faith in coincidences."

Parker was feeling mischievous, but let it go. She decided not to
say another word, even if the woman's name turned out to be
Marilyn. But if it was, could she resist asking if her last name was
Weaver? The answer to Parker's question was written across Willows'
face. Marilyn had been his first true love, and that was something

that she suspected nobody, man or woman, ever got completely over. If the carhop was Marilyn, it likely meant her marriage hadn't worked out and her children couldn't help her financially. Or wouldn't. How sad.

The glass door swung open and the woman came out carrying a brown plastic tray high over her shoulder. As she drew near she lowered the tray with a flourish, obscuring her name tag. Willows rolled down his window about halfway. The woman hooked the tray onto the glass, and told him his burger and fries would be ready in a few minutes. She said, "Did you want your milkshake extra thick or regular?"

"Extra thick's with more ice cream?"

"You got it."

"Extra thick," said Willows. He wanted to check out her breast pocket but was afraid she'd think he was ogling her, and so he maintained eye contact.

She smiled and turned away, but not before he caught a quick glimpse of an "r." How many names started with "Mar"? Only one that he could think of. He emptied a creamer into the coffee, stirred it with a plastic stick. She was about the right age, and the shape of her mouth was exactly as he remembered it. The odds were swiftly narrowing.

Parker said, "Thirty years is a long time, isn't it, Jack?"

He nodded, and sipped his coffee. It was hot, but weak. Unlike Marilyn, who had been cold and strong.

"Think that's her?"

"I doubt it."

"You mean, you hope not."

Willows didn't like to think of himself as the sort of person who wasted time dwelling on the past, and what might have been. He knew that his love for Marilyn had been an adolescent infatuation, rather than a true stirring of the heart. Even so, she'd meant a lot to him at the time, and he'd always wished her nothing but the best.

Parker checked her watch. "We're due at the school in half an hour."

"No problem."

"You sound pretty sure of yourself."

Willows tapped his head. "It's all in there, Claire. Burger in the left hand, milkshake in the right. Bite 'n' chew, gulp 'n' sip. Watch, and be amazed."

The door swung open again, and the carhop moved towards them, carrying her tray. She unhooked the first tray from the window and replaced it with the tray containing Willows' meal.

"Enjoy."

"Thank you," said Willows. The woman loitered. He still couldn't see her embroidered name.

She said, "You aren't by any chance Jack Willows, are you?"

Willows felt the blood drain from his face. He managed to say, "Marilyn, is that you?"

"No, my name's Martina." She turned so he could see the tag. "You were on the news a few months ago, at that shooting in the Korean restaurant, am I right?"

Willows nodded.

"Enjoy your meal. Flash your lights if you want more coffee."

Martina sashayed away. Willows balanced his milkshake on the dashboard, put the little waxed-paper bag of onion rings down on the seat beside him, and reached for his burger.

Parker watched him chew and swallow. "How is it?"

"Best burger I've had in thirty years."

"No, but really."

"I'm serious." Willows took a long pull on the milkshake. His tastebuds were on red alert. His stomach rumbled contentedly.

Nicholas Partridge's alma mater was three storeys high, made of brick that had been painted a pale sand colour. The building had a vaguely castle-ish look about it. Turrets high up on the roof were perfectly situated to provide a wide field of fire for a disenchanted student armed with a longbow and a quiver full of broadheads.

Willows parked in the guest lot. As he and Parker entered the building, all the paranoia and insecurity of his high-school years welled up inside him. He remembered the panic of that first week, when he couldn't find classrooms, remember his teachers' names or even the number of his locker.

Parker asked a passing student for directions to the office. The girl mutely pointed at a narrow flight of concrete stairs. Going ahead of them, she walked her manicured fingers up the stairs and then made a sharp left and finger-walked down a hall, made another left, and stopped. Glitter polish sparkled as her fingers waved goodbye.

The school principal, James Timmins, was a large man in his late fifties. His complexion was florid, the skin under his watery, dark-brown eyes loose and pouchy. He had the tobacco-stained teeth of a lifetime smoker, and the bulbous nose of a serious drinker. He stood to greet them, but sank back into his chair the instant he'd finished shaking hands. Waving vaguely at the pair of hard oak chairs in front of his desk, he smiled and said, "Grab a pew."

Parker tried to find a comfortable position, but it was impossible. The chair's design was subtly but horribly wrong. They'd have to get a couple of these for the interrogation rooms at 312 Main. Ten minutes perched on one of these slabs of pain would wring a voluntary confession out of the most hardened of criminals.

Timmins said, "I was terribly shocked to hear that Nicholas had died. But, paradoxically, I have to confess I wasn't terribly surprised he came to a violent end."

"Why is that?" said Willows.

Timmins pressed the tips of his fingers against his temple. The meditative look, but he didn't wear it well. He said, "Nicholas often came to school with various bumps and bruises, abrasions. Naturally we questioned him. He said he raced a dirt bike – a small motorcycle – on the weekends and after school. I checked with his parents, to verify his story. Not until some time after he'd dropped out of school did I discover that his story was a complete fabrication."

"How did you find that out?"

"Nicholas had a girlfriend, another of my students, a lovely young girl named Julie Myers. She told me that dirt-bike riders

wear full-face helmets. How could Nicholas break his nose and
blacken his eyes on such a regular basis when his helmet should
completely protect his face from injury? Nicholas had lied to me.
I'd talked to his stepfather on the telephone, and he'd lied, too.
But by the time I knew that, Nicholas had quit school and left
home, and was no longer in danger." He added, "I have to admit
that part of the reason I hesitated to get involved was because I
was afraid. Nicholas' father is a violent and unpredictable man.
He said that, if I stuck my nose in his business, he'd beat me to a
pulp. Those were his exact words. They made quite an impression, let me tell you."

Timmins waved away Parker's unspoken question.

"Of course I contacted the police. They said they'd send a car
around and have a talk with him, but there was nothing they could
do until he actually assaulted me." Timmins' smile was strained.
"Naturally I dropped the matter."

"Is Julie still in school?" said Parker.

"Yes, she's in her graduate year."

"We'd like to talk to her."

Timmins shrugged. "I have no objection, but if she doesn't want
to talk to you . . ."

"Is that likely?"

"Who can say?" Timmins' chair creaked as he leaned forward.
He pressed a button on his speakerphone, and told his secretary
to send a runner to bring Julie Myers to the office.

While they waited, Parker tried to imagine what could possibly
motivate a slug like Bob Steadman to make the long drive into the
city to murder his stepson.

31

Tim Shepherd kept the key to his basement suite on a length of string looped around his neck. He said, "I know this probably seems pretty dumb, but I've lost so many keys . . ." He crouched awkwardly so he could insert the key into the lock, and then stood up and pushed the door open. "Welcome to my humble abode."

Chantal followed him into the suite. He turned on a light. Humble was the right word, for sure. The kitchen and eating area were open to the living room. There was just enough space for a small couch and a TV.

Tim said, "The bathroom's just around the corner, and the bedroom's right over there." He pointed at a flimsy wooden door. "Not exactly the Taj Mahal, is it?"

Chantal smiled. "It's nice. Cozy. It must be great to have your own place."

Tim smiled. "Yeah, you're right. But the people who live upstairs have three kids, and sometimes it sounds like a stampede of elephants right over your head. And they *never* sleep in."

Chantal laughed. "You're a student. You have to get up early anyway, don't you?"

"Not if I can help it."

The windows were aluminum sliders, about eighteen inches high and two feet long. They were covered with brown curtains made of a rough-textured cloth and didn't let in much light. A red metal lamp stood on the kitchen table, next to a portable computer, the only sign of luxury in the whole apartment. Tim obviously both ate and studied at the table. Chantal noticed that there was only one chair, so maybe he'd been telling the truth when he said he didn't have a girlfriend. Another lamp, modern and cheap-looking, stood on a wooden crate at one end of the couch. The TV stood on the top shelf of a bookcase made of unpainted boards and large concrete blocks. A print of a musician Chantal didn't recognize had been push-pinned to the wall behind the TV.

"Who's that?"

"Mick Jagger." Tim made as if to open the bedroom door and then veered awkwardly away. "The TV's pretty old, but it works okay. There's no remote, so you have to . . ." He noticed that she was giving him an odd look. "What's wrong?"

"Nothing, but you're acting like a bellhop. I can figure out the TV, and how to flush the toilet, so don't worry about it. Just relax, okay?"

"Fine. Want a cup of tea?"

"No, but if I do I can make it myself."

Tim went over to the table and unplugged the laptop and picked it up. He jerked his thumb towards the bedroom. "I'm going to pack my stuff, and then I'm going over to my prof's house. I'll put some clean sheets on the bed."

"I told you, don't worry about it."

"I'm not, but the people upstairs let me use their washer and dryer, so you might as well sleep on clean sheets. Okay?"

"Fine. Thank you very much, you're too kind."

He gave her an exasperated look, and went into the bedroom and shut the door behind him. Chantal turned on the TV and sat down on the couch.

At the restaurant, Tim had finally caved in and said she could stay with him for a day or two. He'd told her he was going to Vancouver Island for a day or two, to visit relatives in Victoria. She was welcome to stay at his apartment while he was gone.

Maybe he hoped she'd put out for him when he got back. In the meantime, she could hardly believe her luck.

She was watching a soap when the bedroom door opened and he came out wearing his coat and carrying his backpack and a rolled-up sleeping bag.

Chantal said, "All set?"

"Yeah, I hope so."

"Got your toothbrush?"

"Not yet!" He hurried into the bathroom and came out carrying a clear plastic bag full of toiletries. He stuffed the bag into his backpack. "Okay, gotta go." He unslung the loop of butcher's twine from his neck and handed Chantal the key. "Promise me you won't lose it, because it's the landlord's. I was supposed to make a copy, but I forgot."

"I won't lose it."

"If Morris calls, tell him I'm in Victoria and I'll call when I get back."

"Morris. Got it."

Tim struggled into the backpack and scooped up the sleeping bag. "If you call somebody and they need to phone you here, the number's on the bill, on top of the bureau."

"Thanks, but I'm not going to want to call anybody."

He frowned. "I thought you were going to get a job."

Chantal said, "I am. But if you're looking for a job waiting tables, it's mostly a question of being in the right place at the right time. I'm hoping to walk in the door just as somebody else walks out."

"Right, right." Tim glanced at his watch. He opened the door. "I've got to get going, or I'm going to be late."

"Have fun."

"Keep the sound down on the TV, okay? Especially late, after eleven."

"No problem."

"Thanks, and good luck with the job-hunting."

He waved goodbye and left the apartment, shutting the door behind him. At last. Chantal gave him a few minutes and then got up and shot the deadbolt. She'd had a TV in her room when she was living at home. Since she'd run away she'd hardly watched any television at all, and hadn't missed it one little bit, until now. She went into the bedroom and searched the bureau. Tim was as poor as he seemed. There was no cash or drugs in the room, not even a handful of spare change. She doubted she'd find anything of value in the rest of the apartment. Not that she wouldn't look anyway, on the off chance she was wrong. She snatched the pillow and a wool blanket off the bed and went into the living room and made herself comfortable on the couch.

The apartment was chilly, and so quiet that she knew the rest of the house must be empty. Maybe both parents worked, and the kids were in school, or at daycare. She snuggled a little deeper under the blankets. She was safe, for now, but she was in a kind of trap. If she went out, there was a chance the police would pick her up, but she'd soon go crazy hanging around the apartment.

Maybe if she dyed her hair and changed her name, she could find somebody to take care of her. Somebody like Nick, but nicer. She got up and went over to the TV and muted the sound. Outside, she heard a truck pull up, doors slam and then the sound of angry voices. A shadow passed by the kitchen window, and then there was silence again. She went back to the sofa and curled up under the blanket. She'd never felt so tired in all her life. She shut her eyes and was soon sleeping soundly, oblivious to the low mutter of the TV, the intermittent drone of passing traffic, heavy foot-steps on the sidewalk, and the dark shadows that drifted slowly across the curtained window.

32

"Turn that damn thing off! I want to talk to you!" Agnes Steadman's lumpy face was twisted in a snarl of rage. Bob had seen that same look many times before, and he'd learned to fear it. Her hands were behind her back. Was she armed with a knife, rolling pin, or some weapon he couldn't even imagine? Years ago, she'd smacked him flush in the face with a blackberry pie fresh from the oven. His skin had blistered something awful. He thought he'd be scarred for life. It was almost a month before he'd healed up enough so she'd let him out of the house.

He pointed the remote at the TV and killed the sound. His eyes downcast, he said, "What's your problem? Weren't you listening? I never said a damn thing to them detectives, kept my mouth shut just like you told me to."

"And you better keep right on keeping it shut if they decide to come visit us again."

"They won't be back."

"You hope," said Agnes disdainfully. She brought her hands from behind her back and Bob saw that she had two shot glasses and a bottle of Queen Anne Scotch. His mood perked up, then plummeted. Agnes was at her most congenial when she'd had a couple of drinks, but she turned into a venomous bitch-monster if she downed one too many. And she *always* had one too many.

Agnes waddled towards him, her slippers dragging on the worn carpet. She lifted a foot and, for a moment, he thought she was going to give him a kick, but all she did was clear a section of the battered coffee table by shoving a pile of old magazines and newspapers to the floor. She slammed down the bottle and the glasses and poured them each a solid shot. Bob reached for his glass. Agnes banged her own glass against his forehead, hard enough to slop whisky into his hair.

"Here's looking at you, kid."

Bob emptied his glass. "D'you think there's such a place as hell, Agnes?"

"No, I don't."

Bob lifted his legs as Agnes made to sit down on the far end of the sofa. She knocked back her whisky and poured herself another. He reached for the bottle but she slapped his hand away. Quick, she was.

She said, "If there is a hell, I'll see you there, for sure."

"I never hit anybody. You're the one who . . ."

She shut him up with a cutting motion of her hand. "You pleading not guilty, Bob? If I punished Nicholas, it was because he had it coming. He was a bad seed. A bad seed, Bob, and he *needed* to be punished."

Bob reached for the bottle again, and this time she didn't stop him. He poured himself a fat measure, and lay back on the sofa.

Agnes wasn't finished. "He needed to be punished, and we both knew it. That's why you sat there on your fat ass while I did the dirty work, because you knew it had to be done." She eyed him in a way that made him nervous. "You kind of liked it when I hit him, didn't you?"

"No, never."

"You goddam liar! You *loved* to see the tears roll down his cheeks. If you had any guts you'd have hit him yourself, accepted the responsibility of being a parent, taken part of the load off my shoulders."

"I never . . ."

"Shut up!" Agnes poured an inch of Scotch into her glass, drank it down, and filled her glass again. The alcohol warmed her but it did not soften her. She stared at him, her eyes dark with loathing. "I don't know why I bother with you, really I don't."

Bob stared at the TV, the actors with their shiny hair and white teeth and perfect clothes. Sometimes the whole show was nothing but headshots of them yakking away at each other, and then the camera would pull back and he would see that they had bodies, and he'd be kind of surprised. It was hard enough to make sense of the plot when he could hear what they were saying. With the sound off, the never-ending drama was damn well incomprehensible.

Just like his own sweet life.

33

Carlos said, "Shut the door. Buckle your seatbelt. Keep your empty head down and your fool mouth shut!"

Hector didn't much appreciate Carlos' tone of voice, but he did as he was told, except for that part about keeping his head down. If Carlos expected him to sit there in full view of the public, staring at his crotch like some kind of pervert, he was nuts. Beside, one of his favourite things was sitting in the truck, looking out at the people passing by, and all the various stuff that was going down. The world was beautiful and it was ugly, but it was almost always interesting . . .

Hector's deep thoughts were interrupted by a blow to the back of his skull. His head snapped forward, and his filthy blond hair rose up off his scalp like a pheasant startled from a sun-bleached field.

Carlos had hit him with the shrink-wrapped bundle of bogus American cash that Hector had sliced open to pay Chantal for her services. He smacked Hector again, hard enough to drive Hector's face into the dashboard and bloody his nose.

"Cut it out, quit hitting me!"

Carlos reached past him and popped open the glove compartment. Out tumbled a can of pepper spray, a snub-nosed .38 revolver, a box of wadcutters, the brass knuckles he'd bought at that pawnshop on Hastings, a copy of one of his perverted sex magazines . . . There it was, the little packet of Kleenex he knew was in there. He tossed it at Hector, who flinched.

There wasn't much blood. Hector was a quick congealer. It was one of the very few things he'd always admired about himself.

Carlos said, "Gimme your knife."

"For what?"

"You worried I'll cut you? No way, 'cause there's nothin' stickier than blood, and you know how I hate to mess up my van. Hector. Now gimme the damn knife!"

Hector fished his switchblade out of his back pocket, hit the button and felt the sweet jolt in his hand as the blade locked in place. He passed the knife to Carlos, who used it to cut the rest of the way through the shrink-wrapped bundle of money. He tossed the knife down beside him on the van's carpeted floor.

Carlos started counting the loose bills.

"What're you doin'?"

"What's it look like?" There were supposed to be one hundred bills to a packet, but Hector counted only forty-four. Add the two bills he'd scooped off the restaurant table, the six that Hector had in his wallet. That made . . . fifty-two. Which meant, lemme see now . . . that forty-eight of Jake's bogus American twenties were missing.

Sweating, he counted the money again, twice, and then counted it a third time.

"Hector, there's forty-eight bills missing. Nine hundred and sixty bucks. Where is it?"

"Fucked if I know." Hector frowned. "You sure you counted it right?"

"Yeah, I'm sure." Fear had bullied away Carlos' rage. Not long after he and Hector had started working as couriers for Jake, Carlos had pumped Marty about the wild tales he'd heard, that Jake fed people who'd annoyed or disappointed him to his Dobermans. Marty had been embarrassed by the question. He'd hemmed and hawed, and Carlos had thought it wise to back off, tell Marty to forget it, he was just curious, that's all. Marty said it was okay, that it was probably a good idea for him to understand the situation. He told Carlos the rumours were absolutely true. If a guy pissed Jake off bad enough, Jake'd drag him down into the basement of his Point Grey house, duct-tape the guy's mouth shut and handcuff him to a cement post.

Marty said Jake used a meat cleaver to hack bite-sized chunks off the offending thug. That he fed him, piece by piece, to the dogs.

Carlos asked Marty if it was true that Jake kept cutting and feeding until there was nothing left but bones. Nah, said Marty, that was bullshit. As soon as the guy went under, Jake shot him, had him wrapped in a tarp and disposed of.

Carlos, hanging on Marty's every word, had been simultaneously terrified and thrilled. What a horrible way to go, how scary, and clever!

But now his perspective was somewhat altered, because he was the poor sap who was at risk of watching himself being chewed to death, vanishing chunk after bloody chunk into the hungry jaws of Jake's brutal pets.

Carlos ran the ball of his thumb lightly along the switchblade's finely honed edge. A thin-as-a-hair line of blood welled up. Say what you will about Hector's slovenly lifestyle, he took real good care of his tools. He touched the point of the blade to his thumb and was rewarded with a dot of blood. Now he had an exclamation mark on his thumb, drawn in blood. When he was a schoolyard bully he'd drawn unhappy faces on his thumb with a Bic pen. Those days were dead and buried. He wrapped his left arm around Hector's throat and pressed the knife's needle-sharp point against his chest. Hector squirmed and wriggled, but to no avail.

Carlos said, "I stick this into your stupid heart, you'll be dead inside a minute, hardly bleed at all." He gave him a little poke. "We work pretty good together, but I'm gonna feed you to Jake if you don't tell me what's up with them missing twenties."

"Listen, why don't we find a bank, buy some nice crisp U.S. twenties, shrink-wrap a new bundle and forget about it?"

Hector was smart, but not smart enough. Carlos said, "The Russians don't trust nobody. They'll check every bill. Sooner or later word'll get back to Jake that some of the money was real, and he'll come after us with blood in his eye."

Hector sighed. He said, "Chantal's got it."

"Who're you talking about?"

"The hooker. You told me to pay her, and then you went off to make that phone call. I was broke. What was I supposed to do, write her a cheque?"

"Those bills have one thing in common, Hector, and that's the serial number. Nobody trusts a hooker. She tries to pass any of that money, it's gonna get looked at real close. And she will try to pass the money, 'cause otherwise why would she work so hard to earn it?" Carlos snapped the blade shut and slipped Hector's knife into his pocket. "Nine outta ten hookers are junkies. Where do junkies get their dope, Hector?"

"From dealers."

"And who do most of the dealers in this city work for?"

"Uh . . ."

"Right, Jake. Word gets back to him there's funny money in the loop, it won't take him long to find out how it got there." He snapped his fingers. "What'd you say her name was?"

"Chantal."

"The cops nail her, who d'you think she's gonna give up?"

"Me 'n' you?"

Carlos frisked himself, found his cigarettes and lit up.

Hector was no fool. He'd worked all this out long before Carlos had even realized the money was missing.

Carlos said, "Okay, you're broke. That don't explain why you didn't throw her out on her ass. I mean, what's she gonna do, call the cops?"

Hector pecked at the crusted blood that rimmed his nostril. "You want the truth? Okay, here it is. I gave her the money because I *liked* her."

"Gimme a break."

"She was real nice, Carlos. Not hard, like all the other hookers I met. After you left, I asked her how long she'd been a working girl, and she told me she just got started, was ashamed of what she did. She said she wanted to be a vet, learn how to save wounded or sick animals. But her boyfriend was outta work, they had no money to live on."

"You moron!" Carlos' narrow, embittered face turned the colour of an industrial-zoned sunset. "We gotta find her, get the money back."

"Okay," said Hector passively. But it wasn't like her number would be in the book, even if they knew her last name. Or first. Most hookers he'd met had been born with names like Mary or Judy or whatever, but, being romantic types at heart, had unofficially changed their names to Tiffany or Venus or, say, Chantal. Funny how hookers and daytime soap-opera actors favoured the same names. Hector said, "So what're we gonna do now?"

"Where'd we pick her up?"

"On Richards, by that club . . ."

Carlos nodded, remembering. Richards was the best street in the city for picking up a certain class of whore. It was kind of depressing though, down at the south end where the boys hung out. Looking so sad and fucked-up and totally lacking in self-respect. Lazy perverts. Why didn't they get into armed robbery, or some other area of relatively honest work? Jeez, even purse-snatching would be a step in the right direction.

Carlos said, "We picked her up on Richards, that's where we'll find her."

"Good thinking," said Hector.

Carlos slid him a sidelong glance. As he put the van in gear and pulled away from the curb, he imagined Hector cuffed to a blood-splattered concrete post in Jake's soundproofed basement. He and Marty and a few other guys, a mix of Russians and Cubans, standing around smoking expensive cigars while they watched

Jake wield his machete magic. The dogs barking, jowls dripping pink drool. Bone chips flying as Jake cut too deep.

The look in Hector's eyes.

Carlos could hardly wait.

34

Principal Timmins let Willows and Parker use his office to interview Julie Myers, Nicholas' ex-girlfriend. Julie confirmed that Nick often came to school with unexplained bruises or contusions, but that he always insisted he'd been injured riding his motorcycle, or in fights with other kids. Julie had never been to Nick's home or met his parents, and he had made it clear he didn't want to talk about them. She hadn't heard from Nick since he'd quit school, and had never heard him mention Chantal's name.

During the drive home, Parker and Willows discussed the case at length, and then, inevitably, the conversation settled on Tripper.

Parker said, "What are we going to do with her?"

"I don't know. Turn her in to the SPCA, I guess."

"We must know somebody who'd take her." Parker gave Tripper a pat. The dog leaned forward, and rested her bony head on Parker's shoulder.

"How about Bradley?" said Willows.

"We can ask him, but it's only been a few months since his own dog died, so I doubt if he'd say yes."

Willows nodded. Ten years ago, Bradley had adopted a dog-squad dropout. The animal had never been sick, then suddenly lost its appetite. Bradley's vet examined the dog and diagnosed inoperable stomach cancer. Bradley had been devastated. He didn't come to work on the day he had to put the dog down.

186

It was the first time he'd booked off sick in living memory. Parker was right. Bradley wouldn't be ready to take on another animal.

Willows said, "What about Dan Oikawa?"

"Good choice. Why didn't I think of him? He owns a house in North Vancouver, doesn't he?"

"Condo," said Willows, "but I remember him saying that pets are allowed, and that his wife wanted to get a dog."

"Then maybe they already have one."

"Maybe." Willows made a head check, moved into the passing lane, and accelerated past a dump truck trailing a cloud of white dust. He said, "No, wait a minute. Dan's got an allergy. His wife did get a dog. She brought home a Weimaraner and it almost killed him. Watery eyes, sneezing, headaches . . ."

"A small price to pay," said Parker.

"Bobby Dundas?" suggested Willows.

"That creep? I wouldn't trust him with an ant farm."

"What about Orwell?"

Parker mulled it over. "I don't know. Maybe. Eddy's a decent guy, but he's so messed up over his marriage that he can barely take care of himself."

"A dog might be good for him."

"Maybe, but Tripper deserves a better fate than Orwell can provide."

"Ted Moffett?"

"In vice? No thanks, Jack."

A synapse in Willows' brain reached up and tugged a dusty cord. A light bulb snapped on, providing light enough for him to see his collar and leash, and the winding road down which Parker was inevitably leading him.

He said, "Forget it!"

"Excuse me?"

"Tripper wouldn't even get through the door. They'd tear her apart and spit out the pieces."

"Who?"

"The cats."

Parker smiled sweetly. "They'd get along just fine. The truth is, you don't want a dog."

"That's right," said Willows. "I don't want a dog. Not even a wonderful dog like Tripper."

Willows mentioned a few more names. Parker vetoed everyone he could think of. They were either too young, or too old, or too busy, or too lethargic, or already had one too many pets.

Parker said, "Tell you what, *I'll* take full responsibility for Tripper. I'll pay for her shots, and I'll feed and water her, and take her for a walk almost every single day, rain or shine. If we go on a trip and can't take her with us, I'll find a good kennel, and pay for her keep."

"And comb her, and pinch her fleas?"

"Tripper isn't the kind of dog who gets fleas, Jack. But if she picks up a flea, I'll deal with it."

"What about the cats?"

"They'll adjust."

"But what if they don't?"

"Then we'll find another home for her. But we've got to give her a chance. We can't just abandon her."

Willows sighed heavily. Parker had deployed every argument he'd himself used on his parents when he was in the fifth grade and a mutt had followed him home from school. His impassioned pleas had fallen on deaf ears. That night, the unfed and mostly unloved mutt was tied to the front-porch railing, to be picked up by the pound in the morning. Willows, shivering in his pyjamas, had sneaked it a peanut butter sandwich and bowl of warm milk. At dawn, the grateful animal had savagely attacked the milkman. An angry-faced man from the pound came with a long pole with a metal hoop on the end. He smelled of tobacco and sweat, and he had the snarling dog locked away in the back of his truck in less time than it took Willows to burst into tears and run to his room and hide in the closet. A few days later his mother told him the dog had found a home on a distant farm, where it would be allowed to run free and have a wonderful time. Until then, it had never even occurred to him that his parents were capable of deception, much less outright lying. The incident with the dog stripped them both of all their heroic qualities, and in the end all of them were the better for it. But it was another twenty years before Willows was mature enough to realize that.

He glanced across the seat at Parker. Her jaw was set, and she refused to look at him. Tripper was in the back seat but she had come between them, solid as a wall. He decided to concentrate on his driving. They were only a few miles outside the city, and the flow of traffic had taken on a dangerous urgency.

Bradley had left three pink message slips on Parker's desk. He wanted to see her and Willows immediately. There had been a time when Bradley would have left the messages with Willows, but he'd learned that Parker would respond to them promptly, whereas Willows claimed the pink slips magically disappeared before he ever saw them.

Parker looped Tripper's leash around a leg of her desk. She dug into her purse and came up with a rawhide chew toy. She tossed the toy to Tripper and told her to be a good dog. Tripper's mouth was full, but she managed a low growl. Willows wondered if the janitorial crew would complain about the drool stains in the carpet. Not his problem. He followed Parker down the length of the squad room, and reached past her to open Bradley's door as she knocked on the pebbled glass.

Bradley looked up from his desk, motioned them in and told Willows to shut the door.

"You drove out to the valley?"

"Just got back," said Parker. "We talked to Nick's parents, and his high-school principal, James Timmins, and also Nick's ex-girlfriend."

Bradley read the expression on Parker's face. "But you got nowhere."

"That's true, but we eliminated a few dead ends."

Willows said, "The kid's parents are boozers. His stepfather used him for a punching bag. But I don't think he's got the energy to kill him."

Bradley looked to Willows for confirmation. "What about the missing hooker, Chantal?"

"Still missing. We're working on it. The Granville Street canvass come up with anything?"

"We picked up a few leads. Nothing definitive. Spears and Dan Oikawa are working the other strolls, chatting to the girls and boys. Maybe they'll get lucky."

Bradley shifted in his chair, trying to make himself slightly less uncomfortable. Tonight, he was going to try very hard not to fall asleep on the couch in the middle of the "Late Show." "What about the night clerk, think it's worth spending more time on him?"

"Pinky? I doubt it." Parker glanced at Willows. He wasn't pounding his fist into the wall, so he probably agreed.

Bradley said, "Any other leads?"

"Not really."

"Whose idea was it to turn the dog into a TV star?"

Willows jerked his thumb at Parker.

"Nice work," said Bradley. "I saw the tape, and so did about a zillion other people. Unfortunately, about 10 per cent of them called in with leads. We've got three apparently rational couples claiming Chantal is their missing daughter. She's been gone five years, three years, and ten years. One kidnapping, two runaways."

Parker said, "Well, it seemed like a good idea at the time."

"It was, or I wouldn't have approved it." Bradley's chair creaked as he leaned forward and moved his carved cedar humidor half an inch to the left. The humidor had been a parting gift from his wife, who had left him without warning and divorced him without mercy. She'd told him she needed to discover her meaningful inner self, and had flown to California to join a cult. The life must have suited her, because she'd never come back. Now his goddam dog had died, and he was alone except for his son, whose last postcard had come from a tiny village in Mozambique that Bradley had been unable to find on any map.

Parker said, "Uh, about the dog . . ."

"What dog?"

"The girl's dog, Nicholas Partridge's dog."

Bradley waited.

Parker said, "She's a terrific animal, and we don't want to take her to the pound. But we don't know what else to do with her, and we were wondering . . ."

"The pound doesn't put animals down any more," said Bradley. He smiled. "So you don't have to worry about that."

"I know, but we were wondering . . ."

Bradley's door rattled. Pink blurs materialized into fists that pounded on the pebbled glass and then vanished and came back again.

Bradley said, "Get the door, Jack."

Willows opened the door. Eddy Orwell thrust his sports jacket in Willows' face. The jacket was a single-breasted model in such a rancid shade of mustard that it wouldn't have looked out of place on a real-estate agent or a golf course. Sharp teeth had cut the jacket to shreds. Orwell said, "Look what your dog did to my jacket!"

Willows looked Orwell over, head to toe. Smiling, he turned to Parker and said, "Tripper ought to be a surgeon. She ripped Eddy's jacket to ribbons and never laid a tooth on him."

"I wasn't wearing it at the time!" hissed Orwell. "It was hanging over the back of my chair, and your dog ruined it!"

Bradley pointed at the door. "Everybody out – and that means you."

In the squad room, Orwell violently threw the remains of his jacket to the floor. "Somebody's paying for this!"

Parker nodded. "That's fine with me, Eddy."

"I mean you! She's your dog, isn't she!"

Parker smiled. "Not yet she isn't."

Not yet, thought Willows, but soon.

35

Chantal slept for hours. When she woke she felt hungry and tired. The apartment was cold and dark. She couldn't find a thermostat, which meant the people living upstairs controlled the heat. She went over to the avocado-coloured stove and opened the oven door and turned the heat up to four hundred degrees, then turned on all four electric burners. In the bathroom, she splashed warm water on her face and dried herself with Tim's threadbare towel. A round shaving mirror hung from the shower nozzle. She took the mirror down and studied her reflection. There were bags under her eyes and her skin was pale. She thought, This is what I'll look like when I'm older.

She hunted through the cheap white-painted metal medicine cabinet, searching for whatever she could find. Rusty nail clippers, Irish Spring soap, several empty Aspirin bottles, an empty floss container . . .

She went back into the kitchen. The oven apparently didn't work, and neither did two of the four burners. She was starving, but there was nothing in the cupboards but a dented tin of tomato soup and an unopened box of Mini Ritz Bits, sandwiches made of Ritz crackers and peanut butter. The fridge was empty except for a litre of mineral water and a block of unsalted butter. The freezer contained a tray of shrunken ice cubes and a bag of Jolly Green Giant peas buried inside a huge lump of ice and frost.

She'd paid for Tim's lunch but still had almost a hundred dollars in her pocket. She went over to a window, pushed aside the curtain and looked out. The night sky was dark and close, and it was raining hard, beating down on the narrow sidewalk that ran between the houses, making the dark-green leaves of the bushes in the neighbour's yard shudder spasmodically. What time was it? The glowing red numbers of an alarm clock on the floor by the narrow bed tinted the white sheets pink. She knelt down and picked the clock up and turned it in her hand. It was just past midnight and the mall would be closed by now. She was too tired to wander around in the rain, looking for a convenience store, so she went back into the kitchen to heat up the soup.

After she ate, she watched an old black-and-white movie on TV for half an hour or so, then dragged herself off the sofa and undressed and crawled into Tim Shepherd's bed. The sheets were cold and felt slightly damp. She lay there, shivering, as the bed slowly warmed up. The floor above her creaked as someone walked past. A short burst of laughter was followed by a long silence. Shadows crawled swiftly across the ceiling as a car made a U-turn in front of the house. She shut her eyes, and there was Nick.

He'd told her his parents lived in a farming community a couple of hours' drive east of the city. Had they been contacted by the police? Not that it mattered, because Nick said they hated him, and didn't care if he lived or died. She imagined a pauper's funeral, cremation, an unmarked grave. She hadn't been to church since she was a small child. She hardly ever thought about God, and wasn't at all sure she believed in him. But there was no harm in a little insurance. She clasped her hands together and shut her eyes and prayed for Nick's soul. At times he'd been meaner than a snake, but there were other times when he'd been as kind and loving as an angel. Mostly, he'd been thoughtless and carefree. Was that such a terrible crime? She hoped not, for her own sake as much as for his.

Her prayer for Nick dissolved into tears. When she finally stopped crying, she flopped the pillow over, and curled up like a baby. Her face softened. Lines of tension faded. Her fleeting youth was recaptured. Her breathing steadied, and she eased into a deep and dreamless sleep.

36

Bradley's arthritic foot woke him at a few minutes past five. He lay there in the dark for a quarter of an hour, willing himself back to sleep. Not this time. The pain, sharp and persistent, ran in piercing, thread-thin lines through the joints of his toes and into the swollen ball of his foot. Defeated, he rolled out of bed and limped into the bathroom and turned on the shower, adjusting the water until it was as hot as he could stand it. Heat always offered a degree of comfort, but from day to day it was impossible to say how helpful it would be. Sometimes a few minutes' work with the hair dryer could blast the pain entirely away, but the next day the treatment would be useless. Bradley suspected it all depended on his state of mind. He knew from past experience that today was going to be about as bad as it got, no matter how many Tylenols he sprinkled on his breakfast-table Bran Flakes.

As it happened, Bradley's day started with such a flurry of activity that he forget all about his pain. The *Province* had somehow obtained a morgue photo of Nicholas Partridge, and a colour shot of his missing girlfriend, Chantal. Wedged into the bottom right corner of Chantal's picture was an inch-square black-and-white picture of Pinky Koblansky. Bradley's body temperature and pulse rate skyrocketed as he saw that Koblansky was credited with

Chantal's photo. He scanned the accompanying article, but it was just a rehash of known facts and contained no revelations.

Bradley flipped through the stack of pink message slips on his desk. The *Province* piece had resulted in a flurry of calls and sightings. So far, none of them had panned out, but that could change at any minute.

He picked up the paper again and turned to page five. A rookie crime reporter had interviewed Pinky Koblansky at length, but it was a puff piece, a waste of time unless you were looking for a little light humour as you rode the bus to work. Or was he wrong about that? He turned back to the page-one photo. The picture of Chantal had been taken from an odd angle, as if the photographer had been standing high up on a stepladder. Chantal's shoulders and upper arms were bare. The longer Bradley looked at the photo, the more it bothered him. It had been tightly cropped, and the background was a field of impenetrable black. Somebody had manipulated the print to eliminate the background. As well, the softness and intimacy of expression on Chantal's face made Bradley certain she wasn't aware that her picture was being taken. He tilted the page to the watery grey light coming from the window behind him.

The photo had a grainy quality, as if it had been taken with very fast film, or enlarged to the point where the quality of the image was compromised.

Bradley was even more certain Chantal hadn't known she was being photographed, and he was fairly sure the picture had been retouched so it would be impossible to determine where or when it had been taken. He put the paper aside, picked up the phone and dialled Mel Dutton's extension.

Dutton answered on the fifth ring. Bradley identified himself and told Dutton why he was calling.

Dutton wasn't surprised. Bradley asked why not, and Dutton said, "That picture bothers me, too, Inspector."

"Why is that?"

"I think . . ." Dutton rattled his copy of the paper. "What's the night clerk's name?"

"Pinky Koblansky."

"Check the angle of the shot. I think he had a camera placed high up on the wall, tight against the ceiling, close to a corner. If he used a wide-angle lens, he could get everything in the room."

"How would he mount a camera so it couldn't be seen?"

"I bet if you check the hotel records, you'll find he never rented one of the adjoining rooms."

"Why is the picture so grainy, Mel? Because he used fast film under low light levels?"

"The picture's a still from videotape. It's grainy because whoever transposed the still from the tape didn't know what he was doing. My advice? Drop in on Koblansky when he's home – I'd bet an ice-cream cone against a rat's ass he's got his own darkroom."

Bradley made a few notes. He'd send somebody to the hotel to check the rooms on either side of the room Partridge and Chantal had stayed in. If he found evidence that Pinky had taken surreptitious photographs of the room, he'd get a warrant to search his home. Had Pinky become voyeuristically involved in Chantal's life and murdered the Partridge kid?

Shadows moved outside his door. He thanked Dutton for his help, hung up, and wriggled his feet into his shoes.

Knuckles tapped the pebbled glass. Nobody he recognized. Funny how all his detectives and even the civilian support staff knocked in a unique and easily distinguishable way. He sat up a little straighter. "Come in."

The door swung open and a patrol sergeant named Peter Broadhead eased into the office, closely followed by a uniformed constable Bradley had never met, but knew must be Broadhead's son, the rookie who'd given Chantal a ride across the Granville Street bridge. Bradley and the sergeant had wasted more than a few long nights in the city's downtown bars, bitching about the injustice of it all, but had eventually tired of each other's whining, and had drifted apart.

Bradley said, "Peter, good to see you. He shifted his glance to the constable, who was looking sheepish and contrite by turns. There was no need to ask why Broadhead had dropped by. He wanted a favour, and Bradley was happy to oblige. Broadhead's son had made a crucial mistake, but the damage had been done and there was no point in crucifying him. A word from Bradley would go a long way, and a favour given was a favour owed.

37

Hector and Carlos worked the streets until past three in the morning. As the night wore on they gradually wore out, so they were forced to stop more and more often to fuel up on hot coffee, or to empty their overworked bladders.

Hector drifted off at five minutes to three. Ten minutes later, despite all the caffeine he'd poured down his throat, Carlos joined him in dreamland.

The van continued on for the better part of a block without them, and then sideswiped a sparkling white Mercedes-Benz parked under a streetlight directly in front of a high-rise apartment. The impact jolted both men awake. Carlos slammed on the brakes, and the van skidded to a stop. He lit a cigarette and got out to assess the damage. The van and the Mercedes had exchanged a little white paint, and the Mercedes' side mirror had been amputated from the body of the car. Otherwise, no serious damage had been done. Still, Carlos resented the inconvenience.

He yanked open Hector's door. "Pass me the bolt-cutters."

"What for?"

Carlos dug deep into his repertoire of hard looks, and gave Hector the hardest he had.

Hector wordlessly unbuckled his seatbelt. He made his way into the back of the van, petulantly kicked aside boxes of bogus foreign currency, and stubbed his toe on the spare tire. What he had to say about that turned the air a rich, smoky blue. Where were the goddam bolt-cutters, for Christ's sake? He snatched them up, pushed his way back to his seat, and tossed them under-handed to Carlos.

Carlos took out the Mercedes' side windows first, and then tore into the windshield, roof, side panels and glossy hood. A blizzard of white paint chips flew through the air. His powerhouse swings sent the prestigious Mercedes hood ornament cartwheeling fifty yards down the street. Exhausted by his labours, he drew his pistol and took aim at a tire. But the Mercedes' strident alarm had roused the neighbourhood. Lights snapped on in apartments on both sides of the street.

Carlos scampered around the van's blunt nose and climbed behind the wheel. "Let's get out of here."

Hector said, "Good thinking, boss."

Carlos gave him another hard look. Well, no. It was the same look, really. He stomped on the gas. The van's spinning tires lay clots of scorched rubber on the asphalt, and buried them in a cloud of black smoke.

Carlos drove to Denny's on Broadway, where they stayed long enough to gobble an early breakfast and undertip the waitress. Revitalized, his mood upgraded to just short of dour, Carlos suggested they head back downtown and pick up a couple of hookers and have a whole lot of fun. Hector exercised his veto. He was tired. No, exhausted. Besides, wouldn't it be a good idea to park the van until the sun came up and they could more easily catalogue the damage? It was a sensible suggestion, so Carlos was inclined to disagree with it for the sake of form. But Hector was so worn out he was barely semiconscious, and Carlos knew there was less pleasure in flaying a dead dog than a dog who could still feel pain.

Reluctantly, he agreed to call it a night.

The following morning passed without incident, primarily because both men slept well past noon.

Carlos was up first. He wriggled into his jeans, used the bathroom, stole Hector's last clean T-shirt out of his lowboy, and went into the kitchen to put on a pot of coffee. While the coffee brewed he prowled the building's narrow hallways, hunting in vain for a complimentary newspaper. Amazing, wasn't it, how goddam thoughtless people could be? He put on his boots, and went outside and cased the row of newspaper boxes on the corner. There were only a few people around, nobody he recognized. He had his choice of the *Vancouver Sun*, the *Globe and Mail*, the *National Post*, or the *Georgia Strait*. The *Strait* was a giveaway, but he decided to take one anyway, for the telephone-sex ads. It took him only a few seconds to kick in the plastic windows of all four boxes. On the spur of the moment, he took all ten copies of the *Globe and Mail*.

On the way back to his apartment he played paperboy for a day, dropping copies of the newspaper on his neighbours' hypocritical welcome mats. Hector was in the shower, murdering "My Way." Carlos stuck his fingers in his ears and hurried past the bathroom to the kitchen, where he poured himself a mug of coffee and dropped a couple of Pop Tarts into the toaster. He peered into the toaster's fiery depths. The smell of the Pop Tarts made his mouth water. Maybe hell was a bunch of gigantic toasters, but loaded with unrepentant sinners instead of Pop Tarts. He imagined the tortured screams of the doomed as they burned for eternity, the endless bouncy *sproings* as toasters launched billions of overcooked penitents into the smoky air, then caught them up and toasted them all over again. Not that Carlos necessarily believed in hell. How could he, and enjoy the rewards of his violent lifestyle? By not thinking about it.

The toaster went *sproing* and the Pop Tarts were flung high into the air, came down hard and hit the toaster and skittered across the yellow Formica in opposite directions. Carlos snatched at the one on the left, but he was too slow. The Pop Tart overshot the counter and splashed into the fetid sink.

Carlos hardly noticed, because his eye had been caught by a lurid headline, POLICE SEEK MURDER WITNESS, and Pinky

Koblansky's unartistic but eminently recognizable, sweetly candid, over-the-shoulder pic of the working girl Carlos had pleasured only a night ago.

As he read the article aloud, Carlos' meaty lips moved like an inchworm laboriously working its way across a mirror. The article was almost three hundred words long. A magnum opus, by the paper's taut standards, which were predicated on the average elapsed time between inner-city bus stops.

Carlos learned nothing he didn't already know about Chantal, other than the fact that the cops seemed to know even less about her than he did. He moved on to the Pinky Koblansky interview. The Lux Hotel was mentioned. Carlos was particularly interested to learn that the night clerk had been alerted to Nicholas Partridge's death by a shower of coins that had rattled on the lobby's marble floor scant seconds before Nicholas himself had taken his "fatal plunge."

Carlos reread the article, top to bottom. A dollar coin falling from a height of fifty feet would hurt like hell, maybe even put a dent in a person's skull. If it hit him in the eye it could blind him. He remembered reading about a tourist who was killed instantly when he was struck by a handful of pennies tossed off the top of the Empire State Building.

Hector padded barefoot into the kitchen with a green towel around his waist and a red towel wrapped around his head.

Carlos said, "You look like a traffic light."

Hector pointed. "That's my last clean T-shirt."

"Not any more."

Hector scooped the Pop Tart off the counter. He took a big bite, and chewed thoughtfully. "That's her!" he said, pointing at the newspaper.

"No kidding, you really think so?" Carlos read the article aloud. It took him only about ten minutes. When he'd finished he said, "I can't help wondering if this guy Pinky got hit by a shower of twenty-dollar bills instead of coins."

"Then why mention any money at all?" said Hector. He

poured himself a coffee. "I mean, why not just keep his mouth shut?"

Carlos shrugged. "How should I know?" He tossed the paper on the counter. "If a bunch of twenties fell into his greasy little mitts, he sure as hell wouldn't tell the cops about it. But at the same time, he might think he had to tell them something . . ."

Hector rummaged through the cupboard until he found the Aunt Jemima. He poured syrup onto the remains of the Pop Tart, munched thoughtfully as he read the lead article. He looked up. "It says here that the hooker we're lookin' for, Chantal, robbed a grocer on Granville Island."

"So what?"

"So the dead kid, Partridge, if he'd had a wad of American twenties on him, it would've said so. And we know Chantal's broke, so she doesn't have the money either, or why would she commit a robbery?"

"Force of habit?" theorized Carlos.

"Maybe, but I doubt it. She's on the run from a murder rap. If she's flush, why would she take that kind of chance?"

"Knock off the riddles, you're giving me a fuckin' headache. Jeez, Hector, call a time-out and take a listen to yourself, you sound like a goddam 'Columbo' rerun."

Hector said, "I wasn't there, so I don't know what happened, but what if Chantal and her pimp boyfriend fought over her big windfall, he gave her a push, and she pushed back?"

"What pimp boyfriend?"

"The Partridge kid, Nicholas. He's been hanging around the room all night, she finally comes home, so naturally he wants to party a little, spend some of her hard-earned money. But she's tired, she ain't interested. He grabs the money and takes off, but she catches up to him in the hallway."

Carlos had seen a million violent deaths on television and at the movies. Guys were always taking the big drop, and it was always the same. A hazy image formed in his brain of the two lovers fighting.

Chantal waved the handful of money in her lazy-ass pimp's face, taunting him with what she'd done to earn it.

The pimp lunges at her, misses, and tumbles over the railing. She's horrified. Or gives him the finger.

Either way, down he goes, getting smaller and smaller. His body hits the floor, ka-thump. Suddenly he's dead. A pool of blood forms around his head. His blank eyes stare up at nothing. Maybe his fingers twitch for a second, to emphasize the perfect stillness that follows.

Chantal peers over the railing. She screams, and drops the money. Or the dead kid already dropped the money when he took a header over the railing . . .

Carlos opened his eyes, curious about the slurpy sound that wouldn't go away. Hector was busily licking Aunt Jemima from his fingers. He dried his hands on the green towel, looked at Carlos and said, "Maybe we should talk to Pinky."

Carlos nodded. Talking to Pinky seemed like a real good idea.

38

Mabel Mah saw them coming. She turned her work-stooped back on them and got busy rearranging a box of turnips. Turnips had a long shelf life, and were twice as profitable as potatoes, so she always kept some on hand.

"Mrs. Mah?"

"Yeah, what you want?" She had no use for the police but didn't want any trouble because she had a cousin living in her basement who had overstayed his tourist visa. He was a free thinker, a student and writer. He dreaded returning to China because the forces of repression would arrest him the moment he stepped off the plane. If he was lucky he would spend ten years in a camp. If he was unlucky, he would be tried and summarily executed. Mrs. Mah had been born in Guangdong province. She made it a point of honour never to buy anything that had been made in China.

Mrs. Mah glanced up. How surprised and pleased she was to see two new customers.

"How may I help you – turnips, yes? Fresh this morning, and you will not find better prices!"

Parker flipped open her badge case. Mrs. Mah's delicate oval face was heavily lined. Her eyes were black, but warm. Callused hands fluttered against her small breasts. Her fingernails were cut very short, like a man's, to make it easier for her to keep them spotlessly clean.

"Police! Is my vendor's permit expired? I will renew it immediately, I promise!"

Parker showed her a four-by-six copy of Pinky Koblansky's
candid photograph of Chantal.

"Ah, yes. The thief." Mrs. Mah glared at Willows. "She emptied
my cash register, more than one hundred dollars, and she stole
every penny! A common thief! I dial 911 and the policeman comes
three hours later, during the busy time. He writes down my name
and off he goes. I run after him, in my apron. Will he catch this
pretty girl who is a thief? He laughs and tells me maybe so, but I
can see he has no interest, and no hope. But now this girl is in the
newspaper, a big star, and everybody runs around like in a Jackie
Chan movie. But still nobody cares about my money. Is it because
I am a poor Chinese greengrocer, and not some pretty white girl?"

"We understand your frustration," said Parker.

"Why don't the police send a Chinese detective to speak to me?
Because there are no Chinese detectives, yes?"

"No," said Parker firmly. "Our Chinese-language officers are all
assigned to the Asian-crimes squad. Detective Willows and I are
here because we're investigating a homicide, a possible murder."
She smiled. "Besides, we don't need a Chinese constable, because
you speak such good English."

"How many Chinese constables you got?"

"I'm not sure, offhand."

"Any murder detectives? No!"

Willows noticed a Chinese boy in his late teens working his way
through the crowd towards them. "Is that your son?"

"Yes, Alvin. He is a good boy, but the pretty girl spoiled his judge-
ment, and made a fool of him." Mrs. Mah deftly rearranged a stack
of radishes. She said, "He knows nothing, he cannot help you."

Parker smiled. "Even so, we'd like to talk to him." As Alvin drew
near, she turned towards him and offered her hand. "Alvin, I'm
Claire Parker. This is my partner, Detective Jack Willows."

Alvin nodded, acutely aware that his mother was watching
him closely.

Parker said, "You know why we're here, Alvin. What can you tell us about the woman we're looking for?"

"Not much. I've already talked to the police. I told them everything I could think of."

"We'd like you to go over it again," said Parker. "The other officer was responding to a robbery call. We're investigating a possible murder."

"I understand, but . . ."

"We can't figure out why Chantal came here, of all places."

"Maybe you should ask the officer who drove her."

"We did," said Parker. "She told him she had a job here, working for you and your mother."

Mrs. Mah said, "If that's what she said, she lied! My son is a good boy, a student and hard worker!"

"I'm sure that's true," said Parker. She took Alvin by the arm and led him a little farther down the crowded aisle.

"Where you going?" cried Mrs. Mah

Willows said, "It's okay, Mrs. Mah. Watch your customers, and we'll be gone before you know it."

"I hope so!"

Fierce Mrs. Mah. Willows made his way through the milling throng of shoppers just in time to hear Parker say, "It's just between you and me, but I have to know if you and Chantal had a relationship."

"No, of course not, don't be ridiculous!" Alvin had flushed red as a tomato. No, thought Willows, not a tomato, a beet. Or possibly a radish.

Parker said, "Alvin, we're not interested in your sex life, and I promise you that anything you say . . ."

"Give me a break! What's wrong with you! I'm nineteen years old, and I've never even had a date. I go to school and I work and that's *all* I do. I don't have the time or energy or money to do anything else." He pointed at his mother. "Look at her, how hard she works. That's the family business! How could someone like me afford a prostitute? Do you think she *pays* me to work?"

Alvin had begun speaking in a barely audible whisper, but now he was shouting at the top of his voice, his cry of long-standing sexual torment ricocheting off the market's walls and cavernous roof.

Parker lamely said, "Well, thanks for your help."

"You're welcome!"

Mrs. Mah hurried towards them, burrowing determinedly through the amazed crowd. Parker stuck her card in Alvin's apron pocket. "Call me if you think of anything."

"I don't think so!" shouted Alvin bitterly, tearing the card to pieces and flinging them away.

Outside, it was raining lightly and there was a breeze off the harbour. A disorderly row of gulls perched on a wooden bench. Rats cavorted on the breakwater. A small child toddled shrieking towards the gulls, and made them fly away. If the birds were irritated, they didn't let on. How calm their faces were, how unhurried the beat of their wings. They wheeled and dipped, returning gracefully to the bench. Cheeky things. The child decided to have another go at them, but was held back by his mother. Parker was barely able to hear her cellphone over the sound of his anguished screams.

Willows fished in his pocket for his keys. Where had they parked the car? That couldn't be it, because there was a ticket on the windshield, neatly tucked under the wiper blade. He spun the keyring on his finger. Just what he needed – more paperwork. He crumpled the ticket into a ball and let it drop, unlocked his door and climbed into the car. Tripper was all over him. He pushed the dog away, unlocked Parker's door, and started the engine as she buckled her seatbelt.

"Down, Tripper!" Parker put the phone back in her purse. "That was Carolyn Budd."

Willows checked the side mirror. There was no traffic except for a kid on a motorized skateboard. The skateboard's tiny engine sounded like a mosquito on steroids. If he hadn't thrown away the ticket, he could've given it to the kid. Serendipity was fate's weak sister, and easily frustrated. He waited until the skateboard had buzzed past and then pulled onto the narrow road.

Parker said, "You remember Carolyn, don't you?"

Willows frowned. "I am trying so very hard . . ."

"Carolyn's the lawyer I met a couple of weeks ago in my aerobics class at the community centre."

"Right," said Willows.

"She's decided to take Tripper."

"As a client?"

"No, she wants to keep her."

"Fine with me."

"She and her husband split up a few months ago, and she's lonely."

"Well, of course she is."

Parker gave him a look. She said, "Carolyn's going to take Tripper for the weekend. If they get along, she'll keep her. But only if she can have her spayed."

"No wonder her marriage didn't last."

"Very funny."

But it wasn't, because Parker desperately wanted children, and he kept avoiding her attempts to discuss the subject. Why? He was *conflicted*. He loved Claire unconditionally, wanted to marry her and grow old with her. But Sean and Annie would soon be adults. They were both living at home, but either or both of them could move out in search of their own lives any day now. Willows wasn't a young man any more. If he and Claire had children, he'd probably be closing in on his mid-sixties before their children left home.

Parker said, "Carolyn's a partner in a small firm. Their offices are on Commercial, between Eleventh and Twelfth. She said we can drop Tripper off right now, if we've got the time."

Willows said, "Sure I've got the time. Have you got the time?"

"I do if you do," said Parker.

Willows made a hard left, his eye on an idling taxi that was partially blocking the road. Parker was watching him closely. Who did she see? It was entirely the wrong question. He should have asked himself how she knew exactly what he was thinking.

39

Hector made a fresh pot of coffee. While the coffee brewed he toasted and ate six more Pop Tarts. The little suckers were so addictive it was a wonder they weren't illegal. While he ate, Carlos wore out his vocabulary reading the mini-articles relating to Nicholas Partridge's sudden, unexplained death. All available info absorbed to the max, he rolled up the newspaper and poked Hector in the Pop Tarts.

"Get dressed. We got places to go and people to beat."

Hector slurped his coffee. "You're talkin' about the night clerk?"

Carlos nodded. "Our man Pinky."

"But he's a *night clerk*. He ain't gonna be on duty until, uh . . . tonight."

"No, you're wrong. I called the hotel, said I was a reporter. He works twelve on and twelve off. By the time we get down there, he should be ready for us."

Carlos was dressed in army-surplus cammies, which had been Hector's first choice for the day, but since he didn't want people thinking they were the Bobbsey Twins' older and more lethal brothers, he dressed head to toe in black, like a bad guy in a martial-arts movie. From the living room, Carlos yelled at him to get cracking. Fuck Carlos. Hector honed his switchblade and took a moment to make sure the mechanism was well oiled. Carlos was fiddling with his pistol, repeatedly racking the slide.

Hector considered suggesting that they formulate a plan of attack, take a minute to figure out what they were going to do before they rushed off to do it. But that would be asking for trouble.

Even so . . .

Carlos didn't look up from his pistol. "*Make a plan*? You're turning into a little old lady, Hector."

"Just don't try to take advantage."

Carlos sniggered, his mood improving. He eased a last bullet into his pistol's magazine, slammed the magazine into the butt of the gun and pointed the weapon at Hector's genitals. As he pulled the trigger, he yelled, "Ka-pow!"

"I wish you wouldn't do that."

"Yeah? What've you got against a little harmless fun?"

"Nothing, until you forget there's a round in the chamber and blow away my privates."

"Maybe that'd be even more fun," said Carlos recklessly. He wiggled his eyebrows. "How will I know until I try it?" Lifting the barrel to his semi-literate lips, he blew away a wreath of imaginary smoke.

Hector decided it would be a good idea to vacate the apartment without further delay. They'd been babysitting Jake's millions for almost forty-eight hours now. Carlos had a volcanic look about him. He was obviously feeling the pressure, ready to erupt at any moment.

Twenty minutes later, Carlos parallel-parked the van in the alley behind the hotel, close to a dark-blue dumpster. He activated the van's sophisticated alarm system. He and Hector walked around the corner and up a flight of narrow stairs, past a battered wooden door, and into the lobby. They could see where Partridge had died, because somebody had scrubbed the tiles clean, and some of the grout had been replaced.

Carlos rattled his keys against the chicken-wire cage. The desk clerk opened his eyes one at a time. He spread out his pale, hairy arms and yawned widely. Hector wondered how he could be so fat when he had so few teeth to eat with. The paperback that had put him to sleep dropped heavily to the floor. He bent to pick it up, overbalanced, and fell out of his chair. Reappearing, he said, "What can I do for ya, gents?"

Hector said, "We want to talk to Pinky Koblansky."

"About what?"

"Is that you?" said Carlos.

"No, I'm Myron." Who were these guys? It made Pinky's heart pucker up just looking at them. His glance skittered off the walls and ceiling. He looked everywhere but at Carlos. "Pinky's off till eight."

Hector said, "Since we gotta wait, we might as well take a room."

"Two beds?"

"Don't be a smartass!" Carlos' glare easily penetrated the chicken-wire barrier.

The clerk offered a weak smile. His clothes were supplied by the Salvation Army, but his teeth were by Gap. He said, "Oops, my mistake, we're booked solid."

Carlos clawed at the wire. "You're lyin'!" His fiery gaze took in the chipped walls and scabrous paint. "Who'd want to stay in a dump like this?"

"Well, it seems that you would."

Hector's mom had taught him that vinegar wasn't nearly as sweet as money. He banged his wallet against the wire. "We'd be glad to pay a little extra . . ."

"I told you, we got no rooms!" Well, that wasn't entirely true. The dead kid's room was vacant, but the cops had sealed it with crime-scene tape, and told him he couldn't rent it until they'd finished their investigation. Sometime before the next millennium, hopefully.

Carlos finally spotted the *Province* photograph push-pinned to the wall behind the desk.

Pointing at the photograph and Pinky in rapid succession, he said, "That's him!"

Hector drew his knife. The razor-sharp blade was so lengthy it turned Australian film stars crocodile-green with envy. "Come outta there!" He hacked at the chicken wire.

"Beat it, or I'll call the cops!" Pinky grabbed the desk phone, a heavy black rotary model dating from Elvis' happier days. He dialled 911, but neglected to pick up the handset first.

Hector thrust his scrawny arm through the ragged hole he'd made in the wire. He swung the knife in a shining arc. Pinky clutched his throat and fell back against the wall, wide-eyed and trembling.

"Leave me alone! What d'you want from me?"

Carlos smiled through the wire. He said, "So many questions, so little time."

Pinky peered down at the puddle of blood in the palm of his cupped hand. He gingerly dabbed his fingers at his throat, tracing the long, curving, extraordinarily shallow trench the knife had cut in his flesh.

Until now, Carlos hadn't realized how little chance chickens had against chicken wire. The stuff was incredibly strong. He guessed they must use it to keep out foxes. But then why didn't they call it fox wire?

He snapped his fingers. "All we want is our money. Give us back our money, and we're outta here."

"What money?" Pinky eyed the phone. It was tantalizingly close but within easy reach of the madman with the undersized machete. Pinky could easily escape through the door behind him, but the key was in the top drawer of the desk. He was trapped. Trapped! But not helpless.

Pinky's cry for help easily drowned the muted whisper of Carlos' silenced pistol, and the dull thud of bullets swarming into his body. He peered down at his chest and belly. Cripes, he had more holes in him than Bonnie and Clyde, and look what happened to them. His strength left him like rats fleeing a doomed ship. He sagged against the bloody wall. The last bit of wind sailed out of him, and he died in the precise moment he wondered if he was dying.

His knees buckled.

He fell face up on the grimy floor, bounced once, and was exceptionally still.

Hector said, "Now look what you've gone and done."

Carlos nodded. He had gone and done shot the dumb-ass night clerk in the chest, drilled him with all ten shots, as far as he could see. Pinky lay on the floor like a pile of dirty laundry. Amazingly, he was still alive. Or was he? Nope.

Carlos reloaded while Hector hacked at the chicken wire. He soon had a hole large enough to crawl through. Carlos averted his eyes as Hector's ungainly behind followed the rest of him through the hole.

Hector's busy hands danced over Pinky's rapidly cooling body. Everybody had a wallet – where was Pinky's? Hector rolled him over. The back pockets of Pinky's cheap pants contained a large quantity of lint, but no cash. Hector flipped him over again, and gave him a shake. "Where's the money!"

Pinky gurgled like beer racing out of a bottle.

Hector yanked open the hotel desk's three drawers. He pawed through Pinky's collection of top-shelf magazines, a deconstructed cellphone, more sex mags. Frustrated, he hurled the drawers away, then ducked as they hit the chicken wire and came ricocheting back.

Carlos said, "Hector . . ."

"*What?*"

"We got company."

Carlos tilted his head, in an instinctive bid to enhance the stereophonic qualities of his ears. He heard the dull rumble of approaching boots. Big men, and plenty of them, were coming down the stairs towards the main floor. They were making good time.

Pinky stared unblinkingly at the ceiling.

Seeking an outlet for his frustration, Hector leaned over Pinky and stabbed him in the chest. The blade penetrated about three inches. He jumped on the brass handle, driving the knife deeper and deeper.

Carlos said, "C'mon, let's get outta here."

Hector jumped on the knife, one last time, and felt it crunch through bone.

He grasped the handle with both hands, rested a foot on Pinky's chest, and pulled with all his strength. The corpse made a horrible gurgling sound, and then the knife came free. He wiped the blade clean on Pinky's shirt. The thunder of approaching boots was suddenly much louder.

In the alley, the van's alarm light blinked at half-second intervals, staining the interior a lurid whorehouse-red. Carlos unlocked the door and scrambled inside. He pulled away from the hotel's crumbling brick wall so there was room for Hector to get in the passenger side. But when Hector tried the door, he found it locked. He trotted alongside as Carlos cruised down the rain-swept alley. The van picked up speed. Hector broke into a shambling trot. An unseen puddle filled his boots with oily water.

Carlos was forced to brake at the mouth of the alley, to avoid hitting a passing truck.

Hector managed to catch up. He tried the door again, and it swung open in the face of his expectations. He lost his balance and nearly fell. A drunk yelled a few murky words of encouragement and comradeship. Hector climbed into the van. He slammed the door, and wrung some of the water out of his hair.

"What'd you kill him for?" Hector asked.

"He wouldn't give us his wallet, so I decided to take it. Why'd you stab him, when he was already dead?"

Hector wished he knew. Simple blood lust? Something more sophisticated than that, he hoped. He sighed heavily.

Carlos turned on him. "What're you, exasperated?"

"You murdered the guy for no good reason. Now the cops are going to come after us."

"Wrong," said Carlos. "The cops got no idea who we are. How could they?"

Hector shrugged, somewhat mollified. He said, "How many times did you shoot him?"

"Ten, and then I had to stop to reload, and lost momentum." Carlos tried to light a cigarette, but there was something wrong with the match. He tore another from the pack. It fizzled and died. He tried a third, and accidently lit the pack on fire. He burnt his fingers and dropped the matches in his lap. The van careened across the road. Carlos brushed the burning matches off his pants. He stomped out the fire. Hopefully the warranty would cover his ruined carpet. He said, "You're wrong about Pinky dying for no reason. Know why I killed him?"

"Not really."

"For practice," said Carlos.

40

A burst of thunder directly overhead yanked Chantal from a dream that exploded into a million fragments of light. She rolled over on her back. The people upstairs were awake. A chair scraped like a giant piece of chalk dragged across a giant blackboard. Footsteps thumped across the ceiling from left to right, like a stereo effect. She heard childish singing, and then a scream of delight cut short by a heavy crash. A brief, riveting silence was shattered by shouts of anger and the unmistakable sound of a blow, a child's terrified howl.

Chantal went into the bathroom and turned on the shower, ran the water until it reached its maximum temperature of barely tepid. She shivered as she soaped herself down under the unsteady trickle leaking from the shower's rusty, pitted nozzle. How much rent was Tim paying? Christ, this was worse than the Lux. Tim's shampoo was an obscure brand she'd never heard of. She washed her hair and then unhooked the shower hose and wandered the drizzle of lukewarm water over her body, until the suds were finally rinsed away. She dried her hair, wrapped the damp towel around her body, and went back into the bedroom to get dressed. Other than the bowl of tomato soup, she hadn't eaten anything for almost twenty-four hours, and she was starving.

Outside, the sky was pale grey and it was raining lightly. She found the mall without any trouble, got a basket from the stack

by the grocery store's door, and hunted up and down the unfamiliar aisles. Because she had no list or any concrete idea of
what she wanted, she snatched items off the shelves spontaneously, and more often than not abandoned them shortly
afterwards. She put a half-pound of butter in the basket, a loaf of
white sliced bread, a small jar of peanut butter, and a few tins
of tomato soup.

She studied the meat counter. Nothing appealed to her. Her eye
was attracted to the scrawled pink neon sign of the in-store deli.
She decided to get what she needed there, to save cooking and
washing up.

There was a lineup at the deli counter. An elderly woman
wearing tinted glasses and a black ankle-length coat scrutinized
Chantal for the better part of a minute and then said, "You'd better
get a number, young lady."

"What?"

"A number, you have to get a number." The woman pointed at
a red plastic dispenser, and then at the large digital display on the
wall behind a meat slicer.

Chantal plucked a slip of paper from the dispenser. She was
number 68 and they were now serving number 54. How long
would that take? Not that she was in a hurry. She browsed the
glass counter, checking out the food. It had been a long time
since she'd eaten a full meal anywhere other than at a restaurant.
There was Chinese food, and a wide choice of salads. Barbecued
spareribs. Her mouth watered. Finally, she decided on a whole
roast chicken and a large plastic container of Greek salad.

The clerk called out a number, and the woman in the black
coat stepped forward. Chantal noticed she was wearing gloves.
Maybe she had a disease. Or wore an enormous diamond
ring and was afraid somebody might steal it. Nick had promised to buy her a diamond ring, someday. Chantal drifted
into warm memories of Nick, their days and weeks dis-
tilled into the good times, the fleeting but here-forever, happier
moments.

She flinched as someone touched her arm. The woman in the black coat said something to her. Chantal realized her number had finally come up.

A few minutes later she joined a short line at the fifteen-item checkout. The man standing in front of her eyed her covertly and then turned to her and said, "You probably don't remember me, am I right?"

He was old enough to be her father, wearing mud-brown pants and a cheap jacket made of about sixty different pieces of leather. She said, "No, I don't remember you." The cold look she gave him was as clear as if she'd held up a big red balloon with FUCK OFF! printed on it in big black letters.

The man kept smiling. Didn't he know the difference between a supermarket and the back seat of his car? Moron.

In a sickly sweet tone of voice he said, "I bet you remember my darling little Jeremy, though."

It was amazing, the names some guys gave their dick. She remembered a redhead who'd called himself Mr. Happy.

He kept at her. "I'm David. Dave. You took care of little Jeremy about, oh, I don't know, two or three years ago? Time sure zips by, doesn't it? You've grown a lot since then." His hand hovered just above his belt buckle. He said, "I remember you only came up to about here."

"You must be thinking of somebody else."

He snapped his fingers. "Steffi, right?"

She smiled, leaned into him, put her hand on his shoulder, and whispered a few small truths into his ear.

He pulled violently away from her, his face white, and bulled his way down the narrow aisle, his groceries abandoned on the moving belt. He wasn't quite running, but it was a near thing.

The checkout clerk was a skinny blond kid of about her own age. A gold hoop dangled from his left ear. His name tag said "Kurt." He was staring at the abandoned groceries as if he weren't quite sure what to do about them.

Chantal said, "I think he forgot his wallet. Maybe we should move on. What d'you say?"

Kurt nodded uncertainly, and then shifted back into automaton mode. He put the abandoned groceries aside. Another clerk, one of the girls who'd been at the restaurant when she'd met Tim, hurried over to help out. Smiling brightly, she said, "And how are things with you?"

"Fine," said Chantal, her face expressionless, not putting anything into it.

The girl offered to double-bag her groceries. She asked Chantal if she was on foot. Chantal saw that she was being nice, not nosy. She said she lived only a couple of blocks away.

Kurt had almost finished ringing up her groceries. He said, "Kind of wet out for a picnic."

"Life's a picnic, Kurt."

Kurt's mouth closed in on itself, anemone-like. He wasn't going to argue with her. He'd only been working a few months, and was still on probation. For all he knew, she was a plant. The cash register spewed a tongue of thermal paper. He glanced at the electronic readout. "That'll be thirty-eight-seventy."

Chantal tossed a couple of twenties on the counter.

Kurt said, "Thank you very much."

Was he trying to be ironic? Or just being Kurt? She hooked her fingers under the bag's built-in handles, and waved away the change.

"Keep it."

"I'm sorry, but I'm not allowed to do that, ma'am."

"Then I guess you're in big trouble, aren't you?"

The lineup had doubled in size. A man who looked like a retired jockey held up a copy of the *Province*. He said, "That's you, isn't it?"

Chantal stared at the photograph. It was like looking into a weird kind of mirror that could drag you backwards in time. How could she look so young when she felt so old?

"No, that's not me. It never was."

Chantal snatched her change out of the clerk's hand and hurried through the slow-moving crowd. A pregnant woman stepped in front of her, blocking her way. She pushed aside a shopping cart, sent it clattering against a row of carts. An elderly couple stood in her path, oblivious to her. She pushed between them, forcing the man to step back. The glass door swung open, and she hurried outside.

She was halfway across the parking lot when Kurt grabbed her arm, squeezing it so hard she gasped with pain.

"Gotcha!"

Chantal swung the bag of groceries. The tin of soup caught Kurt just below the eye. His head snapped back. A half-circle of blood welled up on his cheek. He toppled backwards, staggered, and lurched forward. Chantal hit him again. He dropped soundlessly onto the wet, oil-streaked, unforgiving pavement.

A dozen gaping onlookers reached for their cellphones and speed-dialled 911. Three patrol cars were diverted to the scene. A dispatcher radioed Willows about the Chantal sighting just as the traffic light he was waiting on turned green. The unmarked Crown Vic's tires chirped, and the kid in the next lane grinned at Parker as he popped the clutch on his black Acura. The Acura shot past as Willows lit up the dashboard-mounted fireball. The Acura's brake lights flashed. Willows hit the siren, and the Acura obediently pulled over to the curb. Parker blew the chastened driver a kiss as they roared by.

Willows' tattered inner child exulted as they raced through the city's undulating, momentarily paralysed streets, siren wailing feverishly, dashboard fireball pulsing like a monstrous overworked heart.

41

Carlos pulled over to the curb and told Hector to drive. A first, for sure. He said he was tired, but Hector knew something else must be bothering him. He eased behind the wheel, waited until Carlos had settled in the passenger seat, and goosed it. The van squirted noisily away from the curb. He scooted through an intersection as the light turned red.

Nobody bothered to honk or yell at him. The city's streets constantly glittered with pebbles of glass and bright shards of metal. The gutters ran red with the mingled blood of drivers and pedestrians. Rush hour lasted through most of the day, and the downtown core was one vast bumper-car pavilion. Blaring horns, sirens, and shouted oaths drowned out the cries of the wounded. The carnage was inevitable and horrendous, but nobody seemed to care.

Carlos firmly believed that about 80 per cent of drivers inhabited such stressful lives that they were subconsciously suicidal. Most so-called accidents weren't accidents at all. People wanted out. Crashing the family car was a universally accepted way of getting there. Two tons of steel wrapped around twenty or thirty gallons of premium gasoline blew up real good.

On the other hand, though life might be unendurable, suicide was a one-time stunt. Carlos believed this explained the public appetite for ludicrously bloated SUVs. Some of those vehicles were the size of a tank, and equipped with enough airbags to refloat the

Titanic. You could drive one of those babies into a concrete wall at triple digits and walk away unscathed.

Naturally, there was a kicker. Those cowardly SUV drivers could rest easy, knowing that their enormous, pollution-venting vehicles were killing everyone on the whole damn planet.

Closer to home, why was Hector driving so recklessly? Was he caving in under the pressure of Jake's money?

It occurred to Carlos that he wasn't doing an awful lot of crystal-clear thinking his own self. He was scooting blithely from the horrendous scene of what was essentially a gratuitous murder, and it hadn't dawned on him until now that it might be a good idea to turn on the scanner, see what the cops were up to.

He popped open the glove compartment, grabbed the scanner and turned it on.

He'd expected the police band to be crammed with references to Pinky, but apparently the body hadn't been discovered yet. In retrospect, that was no great surprise, since the hotel's clientele weren't the type of people who liked to mix it up with the cops.

Hector said, "Turn it up."

Carlos compromised by turning down the car radio. He cocked an ear. Something was going down at a mini-mall on the far side of town. The dispatcher was diverting a large number of cars to the scene, apparently in search of a female customer who'd cold-cocked a grocery-store employee. Hit him with a can of tomato soup? Hector thought that was pretty funny.

Carlos yelled at him to shut up, because the dispatcher had just mentioned Chantal's name, and now she was broadcasting her description to the multitude of cops converging on the scene.

Hector hit the brakes and spun the wheel. The van described a tight half-circle, tires smoking. Hector stomped on the gas with both feet. A rooster tail of black smoke chased them for the better part of a block. The dispatcher was still directing traffic towards the mall when Hector turned in to the parking lot.

There were a few police vehicles in the lot, but nowhere near the hundreds Hector had expected. The other cars must be scouring the neighbourhood. He parked in a handicapped spot directly in front of the Safeway. Carlos fished the blue-and-white handi-capped tag out of the glove compartment. He checked his pistol and shoved it into the waistband of his camouflage pants.

Inside the store, things were more or less back to normal. A handful of shoppers formed a semicircle around the store's manager, who was relating his version of events to a TV news team.

A few aisles away, a kid in a white smock was stacking cans of peaches. Carlos drifted towards him. Hector followed close behind.

The clerk was intent on his work. Carlos tapped him on the shoulder and showed his teeth. "What's your name, kid?"

The clerk glanced down at his plastic name tag. He said, "Toby."

"Toby, what's the name of the guy got whacked with the can of soup?"

"Kurt."

"What's Kurt's last name?"

"Uh . . ." Toby glanced around. "I'm not sure I can tell you that."

"Why not?" Hector took a can of peaches from Toby's hand. He drove the blade of his knife deep into the can, and began to cut it open with a vigorous sawing motion.

"Uh . . . the manager said we shouldn't talk to anybody from the media."

Hector pried up the lid with the flat of the blade. He tilted the can and poured the syrupy juice onto the floor, fished out a wedge of peach and ate it. He leaned the point of the knife into the boy's chest. "Toby, have you got any idea how fast something lethal can happen to a person?"

Toby didn't, but he could guess. "Kurt's last name is Butler. Like the dental floss." He spelled out Kurt's name as slowly as he knew how. His legs felt weak and his mouth was dry. He couldn't stop thinking about the knife in his apron pocket, a short-bladed, razor-sharp tool that he'd been given to slice open cardboard boxes. He could take one of them, for sure, but not both. He was almost nineteen. Marginally too young to die.

Carlos said, "What'd Kurt say to the broad that smacked him upside his candy-ass head?"

"Huh?" Toby was clearly bewildered.

"Woman," said Hector. "What did Kurt say that pissed the woman off so bad she popped him one?"

"How should I know?"

"Kurt must've said *something* to the cops."

"No, he was unconscious. He got hit right here." Kurt touched his hairline just by his ear, which stuck straight out from his head. No wonder his parents had named him Toby.

"What hospital they take him to?"

Toby hesitated.

The knife impaled another can. Peach juice thick as blood splattered heavily on the linoleum.

"General," whispered Toby.

Carlos sucked noisily at the wounded can. He swallowed and burped. "Toby, gimme your wallet."

Toby reached for his back pocket.

Carlos flipped the wallet open and extracted Toby's driver's licence. He put the licence in his own wallet. "Now I know who you are, and where you live."

Toby swallowed hard.

Carlos said, "If you're stupid enough to tell anybody about us, I'll come after you."

"I won't say anything – promise!"

The knife flashed. A line of blood rose up across the back of Toby's hand.

Hector gave him his undertaker's stare. He said, "Now you know how soft you are."

Outside, the parking lot was swarming with cops. Both Carlos and Hector were alert to the possibility that Toby might summon up his courage and come running after them. It was pretty much impossible to intimidate people nowadays, because the mayhem they saw on television blurred the line between art and reality.

Carlos was so tense he skipped a step when his cellphone started ringing.

It was Marty, keeping tabs. Jake had miraculously turned the corner. Unless he suffered a relapse, he was going home in the next day or two. Marty said Jake intended to take the reins the minute they lowered him into his beloved wheelchair.

Carlos said, "That's good news!"

Marty told him to sit on the money, but be ready to move at a moment's notice. He mentioned in an overly casual sort of way that he could expect a fat bonus.

"Terrific," said Carlos.

Marty warned Carlos that Jake expected him to count the money when they handed it over.

"Count it?" said Carlos, aghast. He compounded his error by adding, "All of it?"

Marty said, "Let's hope so."

42

There were lots of witnesses. Typically, no two of them agreed about what they'd seen. Sorting through the conflicting statements was a time-consuming chore, and neither Willows nor Parker wanted any part of it. Despite this, a pushy rookie cop named Herb Montague insisted on introducing them to the Safeway employee who'd bagged Chantal's groceries.

Cheryl Hogg was in her early twenties, confident and smart. She was an ideal witness: observant, thoughtful in her responses, and unflappable in the face of rigorous cross-examination.

Parker said, "Okay, I appreciate that you've already gone through all this with Constable Montague, but let's just make sure we got it right the first time."

Cheryl nodded agreeably.

"Can you describe the woman who hit Kurt?"

"She was seventeen or eighteen, about five-four, on the thin side. Not emaciated, but definitely thin. Small-boned. Blond hair, cut short. Dyed, because her roots were showing. She looked just like the picture in the paper, except really tired."

"What was she wearing?"

"Uh, black boots, jeans, and a man's jacket."

"How do you know it was a man's jacket?"

"It was way too big for her, and the buttons were on the wrong side."

"Okay, good. Was she alone?"

"I think so. She behaved like she was alone. I didn't see anybody with her."

Parker scribbled it all down in her notebook. "What else can you tell us?"

"Well, I noticed she didn't have an umbrella, and her hair and jacket were damp, but not wet. I offered to double-bag the groceries, because she was on foot, but she said it was okay, she only had to go a couple of blocks."

"Did you follow Kurt when he went after her?"

"No, I was bagging for two checkouts. We were fairly busy, so I had to stay where I was, keep working. I'd seen her pay for her groceries, so I knew she wasn't a thief. Kurt didn't seem angry. To tell you the truth, I didn't know what he was so excited about. He certainly didn't act like somebody in hot pursuit of a murder suspect."

"What *was* his attitude?"

"I'm not sure . . . he seemed to be enjoying himself, having a little fun." She thought about it for a moment and then added, "I've got a cat, and the people next door own one of those fuzzy little yappy dogs, a cockapoo. Sometimes their dog chases my cat. He never catches her. I doubt if he really wants to. But he sure gets a kick out of the chase. That's what Kurt looked like, as if he was enjoying the chase."

"Anything else you can think of, Cheryl?"

"Not really. Well, I guess I should mention that . . . what's the girl's name?"

"Chantal."

"Some guy in the lineup was hitting on her. An old guy. I mean, old enough to be her father. She got rid of him without any problem, but I could see that she was really angry. Then her face changed, and she looked sad. Really sad." Cheryl looked directly at Parker. "Sometimes you're so unhappy in your own life that you wish you were somebody else?"

Parker nodded.

"That's what Chantal looked like, the saddest person in the world."

Parker thanked Cheryl for her help. She gave her a card and Cheryl promised to call if she thought of anything else, anything at all.

Twenty-odd witnesses had seen Chantal run diagonally across the parking lot, and down the street. It would be hours before they determined ownership of the dozens of cars in the lot, but at this point it seemed likely that Chantal had been telling the truth when she'd said she was on foot.

Had she really gone to ground within a few square blocks of the mall? Parker hoped so. Maybe she'd grown up in the area, or had friends or relatives who lived nearby.

Parker said, "Jack . . ."

Willows glanced up as Homer Bradley stepped from his dark-blue Lincoln Town Car. Bradley waved him over. The inspector wore a black fedora and long black raincoat. He carried a tightly furled black umbrella with a gleaming silver tip. Rain speckled his shiny black shoes. He stood perfectly still, with his black-gloved hands at his sides. Parker thought he looked like a character from a thirties-era film, somebody Ted Turner would love to colourize.

Willows brought Bradley up to speed. He wanted to canvass the homes and apartments within an expanding radius, as many as twelve to sixteen blocks in total. Bradley pointed out that canvassing such a wide area would require more manpower than was readily available. Willows said he didn't see any other way to handle the situation. Bradley appeared not to have heard him. He worked his fingers more deeply into his black gloves, touched the handle of his umbrella to the brim of his fedora, turned his back on Willows and Parker and walked slowly back through the rain to his idling car.

Half an hour later, cops started pounding on doors.

43

Bobby Dundas waited until Dutton had stopped taking pictures, then crouched down beside Pinky Koblansky. He was careful not to get any blood on his clothes as he reached out and took Pinky's limp hand.

"Pinky, you okay?" He made a show of taking Pinky's pulse, and then looked up at Eddy Orwell. "Eddy, I got some bad . . ." His voice broke. "I got some real bad news, Eddy . . ."

Orwell rolled his eyes.

Bobby tried to roll Pinky over on his stomach. Pinky was even heavier than he looked. Bobby motioned to Orwell. "Gimme a hand."

"Forget that. No way we should move him."

Bobby sneered up at his partner. "What're you afraid of, a hernia? I bet the heaviest thing you've lifted in the past six months is a six-pack."

Not quite true. Judith's sudden departure had depressed Orwell something awful. The heaviest thing he'd lifted wasn't a case of beer, it was his heart.

Bobby snapped his fingers. "Gimme a hand, you wimp!"

Orwell knelt down beside Bobby.

"All set? On the count of three . . ."

But when they tried to roll Pinky Koblansky over, he wouldn't move an inch.

Bobby said, "What the hell! Jeez, we're gonna need a fucking forklift."

Orwell stared at the bloody, overlapping bootprints on Pinky's chest. He said, "The way I see it, the killer must've shot him, then cut a hole in the mesh . . ."

"Chicken wire."

". . . and crawled in here after him. Pinky's lying on the floor. Mortally wounded, too weak to move . . ."

Bobby got a two-handed grip on Pinky's belt, and yanked hard. Pinky flipped over, quick as a pancake. Bobby lost his balance and sat down hard on the bloody floor. Cursing, he scrambled to his feet.

"Look at my goddam coat!"

"Ruined," said Orwell cheerfully. "Blood's a bitch. Those damn spots will never come out. The harder you scrub them, the bigger they'll get."

Bobby eyed him suspiciously.

Orwell delicately patted Pinky's butt. Pinky was not packing a wallet. Where was it? Orwell assumed the killer had stolen it. Money was always a popular motive, because murderers were just like everybody else, obsessed with getting and spending. Orwell patted Pinky down again.

Bobby said, "Watch it, Eddy. Once is business, but twice is asking for a bum rep."

"Very funny." Orwell pawed through a stack of sex magazines that had spilled across the floor. It seemed that Pinky was fond of close-ups. Why leave anything to the imagination when your readers probably didn't have an imagination? But could this be love? Bobby reached past him and snatched up a magazine. He tried to flip through the pages, but many of them were stuck together.

Pinky's wallet lay under a particularly revolting magazine. He had no credit or ATM cards, or plastic of any kind. No pictures of loved ones, or relatives, or even people he didn't like. His driver's licence had expired prior to the rollover of the millennium. A coin pouch contained a dime-sized medallion of St. Christopher, the patron saint of Catholic travellers. Eddy slipped the medallion back into the pouch. Pinky was a traveller, all right. Flush, too. Orwell's thumb catalogued a fat wad of crisp new American twenties. Five, six hundred bucks. Had unadorned robbery been the motive? It seemed likely.

Orwell fanned the bills out on the desk. "Bobby?"

"Yeah, what?" Bobby stared blankly at the money.

Finally, Orwell pointed out that all the serial numbers were identical. The bills were counterfeit. He turned on the gooseneck desk lamp and held a bill to the glare. "This is nice work."

Bobby shrugged, unimpressed.

Orwell glanced down at Pinky. If the deceased night clerk had been involved in the highly lucrative bogus-currency racket, maybe he wasn't such a total loser after all.

Orwell said, "We better call Jack."

"Why?"

"Because if Chantal killed her boyfriend, that Partridge kid, she probably bumped Pinky, too." Orwell triumphantly snapped his latex gloves. For the first time since Judith had bugged out on him, he felt like a genuine, fully-functioning detective.

44

You couldn't assault a person, knock them cold or maybe even kill them, and expect to stroll off whistling your favourite tune and not be noticed.

Chantal was already on the run, described by the VPD as a "person of interest," a twitchy phrase she and everybody else in the world translated to "murder suspect." She waited until the mall parking lot was out of sight, then ducked into an alley and ran like hell.

The people who lived in this modest working-class area had apparently developed such a strong emotional attachment to their cars and major appliances that they couldn't bring themselves to get rid of them after they'd died. Most of the backyards served as ersatz graveyards. Many of the crumbling, swayback garages had been converted into automotive crypts.

She'd made it about halfway to Tim Shepherd's apartment when she heard the first police siren. A shot of adrenalin fuelled a short burst of speed, but she was soon winded. Doubled over and gasping for breath, she stumbled into an open garage and dropped to her knees. She soon recovered her breath, but the pain in her side wouldn't go away. She was about to leave the protection of the garage when she heard a splash that her brain automatically registered as a car tire hitting a puddle. She retreated into the shadows as a patrol car cruised slowly past, the driver and the cop in the shotgun seat swivelling their heads from side to side in asymmetrical rhythm.

Chantal's heart rose up into her throat. How could they have missed seeing her? She made herself count to ten, very slowly, and then risked a quick peek outside. The patrol car had vanished.

The circuitous route she took back to Tim's apartment was designed to minimize her exposure to the long view. It took her almost half an hour of bobbing and weaving to gain a single block.

Once – and one time only – she made the neophyte escapee's error of cutting through a yard surrounded by a high wooden fence.

The enormous mixed-breed dog idly snoozing on his owner's back porch was not amused to see her. The animal lifted a head the size and weight and approximate density of an anvil. He tested the breeze, stared myopically down at her with eyes black as the wrought-iron gates of hell.

Chantal tried to make herself just as small as small could be. The dog laboriously stood up. His threatening growl was a near-subsonic rumble that came from somewhere deep inside his carnivorous bowels. Chantal was so terrified that it felt as if her soul had been pinched out like a match. She broke eye contact, and backed slowly away from the dog, angling across tall weeds and clumps of clinging wet grass that had long since gone to seed.

The animal tracked her, growling and snarling. It drew back its heavy flews, baring two large horseshoes of sharp white teeth. A stringy rope of drool lowered itself from its jaws.

Chantal said, "Good dog!"

Both of them knew it was a lie.

The huge creature was like a train. It's enormous mass didn't encourage a quick start, but once it got under way the die was cast. It's chunky hind end waggled comically as it hustled down the porch steps, but nobody was laughing.

Chantal hurled a loaf of white sliced. The dog kept coming, slowly but surely picking up speed. She threw a can of soup at it, missed by a mile, and turned and ran.

The beast lunged after her, huffing and puffing, one hundred and thirty pounds of meat and bone and pure bad attitude. The gate was about twenty feet away. She lost her footing and fell heavily and face down into the grass. She struggled to her knees. She'd tripped over a child's tricycle. The bike was red, with white fenders, and was spotted everywhere with rust. Red-painted wooden blocks had been bolted to the pedals. She grabbed the handlebars and pulled hard. The spoked wheels were entangled in grass and weeds. She pulled with all her strength, and the bike suddenly broke free. She lifted it high above her head. Christ, it weighed about fifty pounds!

The dog was not fast but he had oodles of torque. His claws tossed up a roostertail of grass and dirt and weeds. As the space between them slowly shrank to nothing, Chantal tried to keep in mind the vital fact that timing was everything.

In the sport and pastime of baseball, the elite hitters have the vision of a peregrine falcon, the timing of a Rolex, the discipline of a Gandhi. Of the three vital elements, discipline, or *control of self*, was the most difficult skill to attain.

Chantal struggled not to swing too soon. But the charging dog was all jaws and teeth and he was so close, and gaining speed . . .

Wait.

Wait.

Wait.

Now!

45

The world was your oyster if you owned one of those little blue-and-white handicapped parking tags. Carlos' had cost him thirty-five bucks, but it was worth every penny, because it had saved him a fortune in shoe leather and Band-Aids. The same feisty pensioners who'd been so eager to punch his lights out now gravely offered to help carry his groceries.

He parked the van and killed the engine. He and Hector got out and hurried across the sidewalk and into the hospital.

Hector slowed his pace to a crawl. He glanced around with an awestruck look on his face, enchanted as a serial killer enjoying a guided tour of Hitler's bunker. "So this is where it all comes together."

"If you're lucky. But first, they gotta take you apart."

Hector's hairline dipped into his eyebrows. "What're you talking about?"

"Surgery." Carlos gave him a quizzical look. "What in hell are *you* talking about?"

"The TV series."

Hector's boots echoed on the tile floor of the hospital's cavernous foyer. He turned left, following a large green arrow directing them to "Information," which they badly needed.

He added, "It's on in the middle of the afternoon, five days a week. 'General Hospital.' It's a soap. A quality soap. The best. I can't believe you never heard of it."

Carlos' low chuckle contained zero mirth quotient. He said, "This ain't the hospital where they film the TV series, you dope." He adopted a gratingly patronizing tone. "See, there's general hospitals all over the world. It's a popular name, like Tyler for little boys."

"No kidding," said Hector sarcastically.

Carlos glared at him. Nobody liked being made fun of. Especially him. He silently drove another nail in Hector's coffin.

They continued to plod down the wide, overly bright hallway. Carlos was in a hurry, but he was no athlete. The criminal lifestyle encouraged a high cholesterol level, and a lazy heart. Maybe *he* should think about joining a club . . .

They passed dozens of doors, all of them shut. Drugs in there, probably. Hector hadn't seen any security guards, but he knew they were out there, on the bloodthirsty hunt for desperate junkies hoping to make a quick score.

A passing nurse eyed them warily. Hector returned the favour, in spades, glaring at her with such unrestrained hostility that she ducked her head and looked away. His mother had drummed into him the necessity to be courteous to the weaker sex. It was a rule he had memorized but broke constantly. The information kiosk was just ahead. Carlos surprised Hector by suggesting it might be better if he approached the booth alone.

"Me?" Hector was instantly suspicious.

"Look at me." Carlos was dressed in his two-piece mottled grey-and-brown Desert Storm suit, and sturdy paratrooper boots fit for stomping a grizzly. "I walk up to her, she's gonna think she's being invaded."

The woman in the kiosk was on the phone, smiling and giggling. She swung one of her long, crossed legs in a steadily accelerating rhythm. Hector was no more perceptive than a mirror, but couldn't help wondering about the topic under discussion. He pressed his mouth against the circular hole in the thick sheet of polycarbonate intended to protect her from dudes one quarter as bad as him.

"Excuse me? Ma'am? Miss? Excuse me, could I ask you a question?"

She glanced up, gave him an irritated look.

Hector smiled. "Sorry to interrupt. Kurt Butler's room, please."

The phone snugged between her chin and shoulder, her leg still pumping away, she jabbed furiously at her keyboard with both index fingers. Without bothering to look at him, she said, "Are you a relative?"

"His older brother, Heinz." Now she did look up, and he saw the doubt in her sex-clouded eyes. But she was too wrapped up in her phone call to bother doing her job. Pointing, she said, "He's in emergency. Follow the red line."

Hector thanked her, but she was already back on the phone, whispering dirty and having a wonderful time. He warmed at his own sweet memories of several long, shockingly intimate and wildly pornographic conversations he'd had with an ex-girlfriend named Melba.

Three-ninety-five a minute, and worth every nickel.

In the chaotic emergency ward, Hector and Carlos learned that Kurt Butler had been treated and released only moments ago. Carlos said, "I missed him? Where'd he go?"

"How would I know?" The woman made a shooing motion with her hand, treating him like a bothersome insect.

Well, fine. Carlos stared down at her, memorizing her face. Hector tugged at his sleeve.

"C'mon, we're wasting time." The two thugs strode hurriedly out of the emergency room, the automatic glass doors skedaddling aside barely in time to avoid certain destruction.

Kurt Butler loitered on the sidewalk just outside the door, so unexpectedly close they might have overrun him if Carlos hadn't spotted the pale glimmer of gauze peeking out from beneath Kurt's tuque.

"Kurt Butler?"

"Not me, buddy." The battered clerk was anxiously waiting for his mother to come and pick him up. In the meantime, he meant to keep a low profile, because his experience with Chantal had taught him that bad things could happen to mediocre people.

Carlos knew a lie when he heard it. He asked Kurt for the time and, when he glanced down at his watch, drove a hard left hook into his belly, knocking the wind out of him. Moments later, Kurt was curled up in a defensive ball in the back of the van, wheezing helplessly.

Carlos said, "Punch or drive?"

"Punch," said Hector.

Carlos grumpily climbed behind the wheel. He backed the van out of the parking lot, and gunned it.

From the back, Hector yelled, "Find an alley!"

Carlos sighed heavily. Well, duh.

Hector crouched beside Kurt. First things first. He banged his knuckles off Kurt's forehead. "Gimme your wallet."

Kurt's wallet had a liquid-silver finish, like a survival blanket. In the world of fabrics, it was the age of miracles. The wallet was fat as a piglet. Hector pried it open. Cash, and plenty of it. Either it was payday, or the kid was dipping into the till. He said, "You dipping into the till?"

Kurt nodded. "Just on weekends, mostly."

No credit cards, but he had an ATM card.

"What's the secret code, Kurt?"

Kurt was struck mute by terror. He might have been auditioning for a bit part in a silent film.

Hector took a swipe at him with the card. "The secret code, Kurt. Don't make me pull out your fingernails, 'kay?"

"Four one seven eight."

Hector checked Kurt's driver's licence. Sure enough, he'd used his street address for his ATM code. He angled the licence towards him. "Is this you?"

Kurt nodded. His head throbbed. He grimaced, but in a manful way, hoping for a smidgen of sympathy.

Hector smiled. "Man, you're the first guy I've ever seen was uglier than the picture on his driver's licence." He reared back and bounced Kurt's head off the steel floor. "Pretty good acoustics, huh? So tell me, how long have you and Chantal been an item?"

"What're you . . . ?"

Hector raised his fist.

"I don't know her, honest!"

"Then how come she hit you, if it wasn't a lover's quarrel?"

"I'd seen her picture in the paper. I knew the cops were after her and I thought I'd make a citizen's arrest."

"Be a hero, except you flopped. That's it, end of story? I don't think so. C'mon, Kurt. Gimme something. Make me happy."

"I, uh . . . I let the cops think she knocked me out when she hit me with that bag of groceries. But she didn't. I was a little dizzy, that's all."

"That must've been a novel experience. You lied to the cops? Maybe there's some hope for you after all."

"Have you ever been hit with a can of soup? It really hurts. I didn't want to get hit again, so I stayed down. But I watched her, and I saw her cross the parking lot and then double back, past the paint store at the far end of the parking lot."

"Heading where?"

Kurt had to think about it. Finally he said, "East, in the opposite direction the cops think she went."

"And you didn't tell anybody?"

"No, because if I had, everybody would've known I wasn't as badly hurt as I said I was. They'd have thought I was afraid of her."

They dropped Kurt off a few blocks from the hospital, in the narrow space between a dumpster and a concrete wall, where he was out of the weather. Carlos wanted to squib him, but Hector pointed out that they'd already murdered Pinky. If they did Kurt, somebody might label them serial killers. Jake didn't appreciate that kind of notoriety in his employees. Neither did Marty.

Carlos twirled his pistol on his finger and took aim at a coyote scuttling down the alley. He could easily have nailed him, at the cost of a hole in the windshield. This urban wildlife thing was getting out of hand. If all the squirrels, skunks, coyotes and raccoons who lived in the city ever got organized, no one would be safe. The coyote turned a corner. Carlos shoved his pistol inside the elasticized waistband of his Desert Storm pants.

Not that anybody was safe now.

Especially Chantal.

46

A dozen officers were assigned to canvass the neighbourhood. A corner of the mall's rain-spattered parking lot was taped off and used as an assembly area. Despite Willows' vigorous entreaties, Bradley refused to commit more men or say how long he'd keep them on the assignment.

The canvass did not proceed at a rapid pace. This was a high-density neighbourhood of duplexes, illegal basement units and big old houses that had been converted into warrens of self-contained suites.

Many of the people who were questioned knew Chantal's name, but only a very few recognized her photo from the newspapers or TV. No one had seen her in the flesh. A surprising number of people asked after her dog, Tripper.

Bradley sat in the back seat of his midnight-blue Lincoln, busy with his pushpins and large-scale maps. An hour had passed without incident. His men were working hard, but all they were getting was wet.

Willows' knuckles were raw and chafed. Next time somebody knocked on his door and tried to sell him something he didn't want, he'd try to be a little less short-tempered. He and Parker climbed yet another steep flight of wooden stairs, and he knocked firmly on the door. There were lights on inside, but the house felt empty. A shadow drifted across the door's bevelled glass panels, and then the porch light snapped on. The door swung open on a dimly lit hallway. An elderly woman balanced a screaming child on her hip. Willows briefly explained the situation. The woman told him she had no English. Her voice was low and guttural, impatient. Parker showed her Chantal's photo. The child snatched at it, but the woman paid no attention at all.

Parker said, "Have you seen this woman?"

The woman eased the door shut. The lock clicked.

Carlos pulled into the self-serve area of a Petro-Can gas station. He killed the van's engine, lit a cigarette, and leaned back in his seat.

Hector saw what Carlos was up to. He put his feet up on the dashboard.

Carlos flicked ash onto the van's carpeted floor. He glared at Hector. "What're you waiting for?"

"Hell to freeze over."

"It's your fuckin' turn, Hector."

"No way! I filled up last time. You cut in front of a guy in a silver Mercedes, remember? And then I had to get out and fill the goddam tank, spend the whole time listening to his wife chew me out for being such a jerk."

"That wasn't the word she used."

"Whatever."

Carlos took a long pull on his cigarette. Come to think of it, he did remember the Mercedes. Against all the odds, Hector was right. It *was* his turn to fill the van's tank. But that didn't mean he was gonna do it . . .

His cellphone rang. He turned down the volume on his Radio Shack police scanner and picked up.

"Yeah?"

"Where we said before, exactly two hours from right this minute. Got it?"

"Yeah," said Carlos, but not before Marty had disconnected. Hector was watching him. He said, "That was Marty. He said it's definitely your turn to pump gas. He also mentioned we gotta deliver the money to Jake's in exactly two hours from right this minute." He grabbed Hector's arm, pushed up the sleeve of his jacket and twisted his wrist so he could more easily read his watch.

Hector yanked his arm free. "Whyn't you look at your own damn watch?"

"Don't want to wear it out." Carlos leaned across him, pushed open his door. "We got two hours to find the bitch and get Jake's money back. We're a dime short, I already told you what he's gonna do about it. Feed you to his dogs. Cut slices off you and . . ."

"Yeah, yeah, yeah. I got the picture." Hector unbuckled and climbed down out of the van. As he filled the tank, he mulled over his unfair predicament. If they didn't find the hooker, Carlos would kill him to save his own skin, and to prove to Jake that he was a serious fellow who took his responsibilities seriously.

Carlos was a fool to think Jake would let him off the hook, because Jake would use that hook to hang Carlos by his balls. If they didn't find Chantal in the next couple of hours, they were both dead men. Unless he delivered Carlos' corpse to Jake, and told him that *Carlos* had paid the hooker . . . No, that wouldn't work. They had to find the hooker *and* get the money back.

Half an hour later, cruising the neighbourhood to the east of the Safeway, Carlos failed to see the pedestrian strolling across the street in a well-lit, clearly marked crosswalk.

"Fuck!"

The van's tires skidded on the wet asphalt. They fishtailed gracefully through the intersection. Seen through the rain-specked windshield, the pedestrian in the marked crosswalk loomed larger and larger, until he was damn near the size of the Goodyear blimp. He had a backpack, so Hector assumed he was a student. The stuff they didn't teach you in school! The kid's face was bleached white by the headlights, and then there was a sickening thump, and the backpack flew away into the darkness. The van's momentum had been slowed by the impact, but even so, they'd slithered right through the intersection before finally stopping. Carlos glanced around. Several cars had stopped behind him, and another had pulled up to a stop sign on his left. There was a good chance somebody had already written down his plate number, a better chance somebody else had a cellphone. The kid he'd hit was sitting up, looking dazed. But maybe that was his normal expression. He seemed to be okay. If he had serious injuries, they were internal, which hardly mattered. Out of sight, out of mind.

Carlos jumped out and hurried around to the front of the van. Glass crunched underfoot. The kid had smashed a headlight. Carlos walked right up to him, working hard to keep his face blank. He helped the kid stand up.

"You okay?"

The kid mumbled something about feeling dizzy. Carlos showed his teeth. He said, "That's great. Stand up, you little fuck! You fall over, I'll fuckin' kill you!" He gave his fellow drivers a big thumbs-up, but one of them was already out of his car. Narrow shoulders hunched against the rain, he trotted over and said, "How is he?"

"Never better!" Carlos added, "He's my neighbour's son, lives right across the street from me." He waved his arm, brushing the guy back. "We're just a couple of blocks away, I'm gonna drive him home, see if his mom wants to take him to the hospital."

The other vehicles were already moving away, lights flashing, a horn beeping, potential witnesses anxious to be gone.

Carlos bundled the kid into the van.

"Thanks for your help, I appreciate it!"

Hector stomped on it, and they were gone, two gorillas and their inadvertent victim vanished into the mist. Hector drove erratically, just in case they were being tailed. He made a hard left, and then a right, another left.

Carlos yelled, "Stop right there!" He pointed at a house under construction. Hector pulled over. The yard was a sea of mud. The building's plywood skin gleamed pale yellow. Carlos said, "Dump him."

Carlos' new lighter was shaped like a skull, the jaws hinged, bone and teeth in white enamel. He touched the lighter's flame to his cigarette. Fire danced in his eyes. He snapped the lighter shut. "Hold it a minute." He turned on the dome light.

"What's your name, kid?"

"Tim Shepherd."

"You live around here, Tim?"

Tim nodded. His head felt as if it was about to split wide open. He had no idea where he was or how he had got there, and somehow he didn't care. Alarm bells rang, but they were a long way off, and very faint. Hector patted himself down, found what he was looking for. The front page of yesterday's *Province*. He unfolded the page and held it up in front of Tim's face. "Have you seen this girl around here in the past couple of days?"

Tim peered at the much-folded picture. Rolling thunder shot through with jagged lightning bolts of pain echoed off the walls of his skull.

Hector, staring at him, saw something move in his eyes: a dull spark of recognition. He said, "Her name's Chantal. You know who she is, don't you?"

"Uh . . ." Tim was reluctant to admit that Chantal was staying at his apartment, but he wasn't at all sure why.

Carlos, losing patience, grabbed him by the throat and shook him like a mortally wounded rat.

Tim moaned. He muttered an incomprehensible complaint, and clawed feebly at the door handle. Carlos slapped his hand away. Tim's face was pale as the moon. His mouth gaped open. He made a horrible retching sound, and vomited copiously onto Hector's lap.

Chantal used Tim's rusty can opener to open a badly dented can of tomato soup. When that idiot checkout clerk grabbed her arm, she'd instinctively swung the bag of groceries at him. It happened so fast she never gave a moment's thought to the bag's contents. She could honestly say that the semi-lethal can of soup was the last thing on her mind. The shock of the blow had travelled all the way up her arm and into her neck.

She had been *so* scared!

But not as scared as when she got trapped in that yard with that huge dog. She'd tried to brain the animal with the tricycle, but the rusty metal tubing had been wet and the bike had slid out of her hands and sailed high into the air. The snarling dog had whirled around, caught the bike in its powerful jaws and tried to shake it to death.

She shivered as she recalled the brittle crunch of teeth on metal, bits of red paint spraying off the trike in all directions, like bright droplets of blood.

She'd turned and run for the gate. The dog had chased after her, huffing and puffing like a steam engine. It had been a close thing, but she'd made it.

On her way back to Tim's she'd been caught out in the open when a police car turned the corner. She'd crouched behind a parked truck until the car was gone. An elderly man had peered curiously at her from his window, but when she looked at him, he let the curtain fall.

She turned on the electric stove, dumped the soup into an aluminum pot, added milk and stirred vigorously. The apartment was dead quiet. Upstairs, nothing moved. She suddenly felt overwhelmingly lonely. She turned on the TV, and channel-surfed until she came across a debate about motherhood. Was spanking ever an appropriate punishment? It wasn't a question Chantal's father had bothered to think about. He'd beaten her at every opportunity, with a yard-long piece of wood drilled through with a pattern of holes and painted glossy black.

The soup was steaming hot. She found a bowl in the cupboard, crumbled a handful of crackers into the soup, and sat down in front of the TV.

She flicked through the channels until she found an old movie about a beautiful woman and a greasy-looking guy in need of a shave who were working their way down a jungle river in an old boat. She finished her soup, got blankets and a pillow from the bedroom, and curled up on the sofa. She could tell the actors really liked each other, and weren't just acting. She closed her eyes. The tussles with Kurt and the dog had taken an awful lot out of her. Being a fugitive was hard work.

She woke briefly when somebody knocked on the door, and then again when the upstairs children came home. The next time she woke, the apartment was dark, and hot and stuffy. Her skin prickled with sweat, and she had a headache. Upstairs, it was quiet except for the drone of a radio or TV. She stretched her arms wide, and tossed aside the blankets. Her leg and shoulder muscles ached. She decided to take a shower.

This time, there was plenty of hot water. Tim's shampoo was an unfamiliar brand. If the label could be believed, the stuff was full of beneficial minerals and vitamins that would turn her whole life around. Not a bad idea, really. She squirted a translucent pale-yellow slug of shampoo into her palm, and vigorously worked it into her scalp.

She spent a long time in the shower, holding the flexible extension hose so the water sprayed across her back and shoulders. She couldn't remember when she'd last felt really clean. Clean in a way that you can only feel when your whole life is spread out in front of you and you believe that anything and everything is possible.

Nick had never loved her. He'd turned her into a slut and a whore. Not that it was all his fault. She was partly to blame. Okay, mostly to blame. She vowed never to let anything like that happen to her again. How could she expect anybody to care about her if she acted like she didn't care about herself?

Somebody upstairs stamped heavily on the floor. Did Tim's landlord time his showers? She didn't want to get Tim in trouble, or attract attention to herself, so she turned off the water. She dried herself with the same threadbare towel she'd used earlier, and then slipped into Tim's white terrycloth robe.

Someone was knocking furtively on her door.

The landlord, come to bitch about the cost of hot water? She didn't know what she should do. She moved hesitantly towards the door. The knocking stopped, and in the jolting quiet all she could hear was the ragged sound of her own breath. Then the knocking started again, knuckles beating rapid and soft as a hummingbird's heartbeat, swiftly rising in urgency and volume to what seemed like a thunderous, deafening roar.

Chantal hurried to the door. There was no safety chain. She said, "Who is it?"

"Tim." His voice was strained. "Let me in, it's cold and I'm soaked, and freezing . . ."

Hesitantly, with a strange sense of foreboding, she turned the deadbolt's butterfly handle, and opened the door just enough so she could see. Tim stood there in the rain, looking cold and wet and very sick. She said, "What are you doing here?" Stupid question. She opened the door, and as she stepped back to let him in, he fell face down across the threshold.

Hector said, "Remember me?" He backed her into the apartment with his knife, and graphically reminded her of the nature of their last encounter.

Chantal said, "I don't do that any more!"

"Too bad," said Carlos, "because nobody likes a quitter."

Chantal retreated from Hector and Carlos until her back was to the wall. Tim lay on the floor, groaning. She glanced down at him and then back to Carlos. "What d'you want?"

Carlos shut and locked the door. He picked Tim up by his hair and belt and threw him a little further into the room, knocking the TV off its stand. Bogart and Hepburn stared up at the ceiling, bemused. Chantal turned and ran. In hot pursuit, Carlos tripped over the lone kitchen chair, lost his balance, and head-butted the refrigerator. Chantal ran into the bathroom, slammed the door and shot the ridiculous little deadbolt. She stepped into the shower and yanked on the plastic curtain. Now she was safe, protected by an army of cheerful yellow ducks cavorting in a rainstorm. She opened her mouth and screamed and screamed.

Carlos gave the door a hard kick. His boot punched a ragged hole in the flimsy fibreboard, and his camouflaged leg vanished all the way to mid-thigh. He experienced a moment of panic, thinking he might be stuck. Jagged pieces of door pattered on the floor as he extracted his leg. His paratrooper boot had come off. Fuck. He kicked the door again, and it crashed open. There was nowhere to hide but the shower stall. He tore away the curtain.

Chantal pointed the hand-held nozzle at him. She'd turned the hot water tap on full. Carlos was hit in the face, at point-blank range, with an impotent drizzle of lukewarm water. He batted the nozzle aside, grabbed a handful of bathrobe and spun Chantal out of the bathroom, slapped her a few times to calm her down, and pushed her down the narrow hallway into the kitchen. Chantal's wet feet went out from under her. She fell heavily. Carlos clutched at her but she was already up and sprinting towards the door. No problem, since Hector was waiting for her.

Carlos lifted his jacket and let her see his pistol. She turned back towards Hector and he flashed his knife. He said, "Settle down, or I'll cut you to pieces."

"Fondue-size," offered Carlos. He closed in on her, backing her into the corner between the kitchen table and the fridge. He said, "Where's our money?"

The terrycloth robe fell open. Chantal smiled tremulously. She said, "Isn't this what you really want?"

Smirking, Carlos grabbed at her with both hands.

The stainless-steel fork struck him in the side of the throat, penetrating his carotid artery to the full depth of the tines.

Bellowing in pain, Carlos yanked the fork out of his neck and flung it clattering into the sink. Blood spouted forcefully from an evenly spaced quartet of puncture wounds. He spat more blood as he roared his dismay. Chantal edged away from him, but there was nowhere to go. He fumbled for his pistol. She reached into the sink and scooped up the bloody fork and stabbed him again, in his cheek and throat, his flailing arms. The pistol skittered across the linoleum. Carlos dropped to his knees. Chantal kept at him, stabbing and stabbing.

The pistol bumped against Tim's wrist. His hand closed on the grip. Hector was inches away, crouched on all fours. Tim lifted the pistol. The blade front sight obscured much of Hector's sweat-blistered face.

Tim had suffered a concussion, and several fractured ribs. He had a migraine-quality headache, blurred vision, a rising fever. The pistol was very heavy. He held it with both hands but it was still too much for him. The black muzzle drifted down and down until it was pointed directly at Hector's genitalia.

Due to the nature of Tim's injuries, and his confused state of mind, not even he could say whether the gun discharged accidently, or was fired with lethal intent.

47

Tim Shepherd's neighbourhood was thick with cops. Every last one of them was bored, frustrated, achingly hungry, and soaked to the bone.

The police dispatcher who took Chantal's garbled call had lost no time broadcasting a "shots fired" call, and Tim's address. The response was immediate, and overwhelming. Within minutes, a small army of uniformed officers descended on the house. There was no time or inclination to call in the department's highly trained emergency response team. Uniformed patrol officers jostled on the home's front and back porches for the privilege of kicking in the door.

The door to the basement suite was already wide open when the first wave arrived. Soon the tiny apartment was crammed with cops. Willows and Parker shouldered their way through the mob. A circle of cops stood solemnly over Carlos' sprawled-out corpse. He'd bled out, and his vital fluids had followed the floor's slight decline, flowing over the linoleum to the kitchen cupboard, and then running along the baseboard as far as the shattered bathroom door.

A sergeant named Morris handed Willows a plastic evidence bag containing Carlos' silenced pistol. Morris had removed the gun's magazine, and racked the slide, ejecting the round in the chamber.

He told Willows he'd pried the cocked pistol from Tim Shepherd's unconscious fingers. He pointed down at Carlos and said, "Charles David Cunningham. I busted him about five years ago, on an assault charge. He's got a sheet a backyard long. I heard a rumour he's been working for Jake Cappalletti."

Willows nodded. Carlos and his partner, Hector, had both been working for Jake for several months. Low-level stuff, the way he heard it.

Somebody had covered Tim Shepherd with a blanket, from his feet to his chin. Parker said, "What happened to him?"

"Cunningham ran him down with his van. He used him to get into the apartment, so he could get at our murder suspect."

Willows said, "What murder suspect?"

"The kid, Chantal. From that homicide at the Lux." Morris smiled. "The mysterious girl with but a single name, like Cher."

Willows crouched down beside Tim Shepherd. He rested two gentle fingers on Shepherd's carotid artery.

Morris said, "I think he's got a busted rib. His breathing's okay." He glanced at his watch. "The paramedics should've been here by now." He jerked his thumb towards the open bedroom door. "Your suspect's in there, cooling her heels. She's okay, but she's in shock. Said she killed Cunningham. Told me before and after I'd warned her. Cunningham's partner beat it after Shepherd shot him."

"Shot him?"

"That's what the girl said. We found a few drops of blood by the curb. The guy's driving a white Econoline with a smashed left-side headlight. We'll find him." Morris saw the look in Willows' eye. He said, "Yeah, it's a mess, but what was I supposed to do? I got here, I found a corpse, a coma, a juvie murder suspect in serious need of a sedative, and ten thousand cops stampeding all over the crime scene."

Parker said, "Did she say why she stabbed him?"

"He broke into the apartment, assaulted her, threatened her with the gun."

"Does she know him?"

The cop nodded. "Yeah, but she wouldn't say how."

The paramedics arrived. Willows hadn't heard the siren. He thanked Morris for his help, and told the paramedics there was a second victim in the bedroom, but to attend to Shepherd first. He and Parker went into the bedroom.

Chantal lay on the bed, facing away from them.

Parker said, "Chantal . . ."

"Leave me alone!"

"I'm a police officer. My name's Claire." Parker sat down on the edge of the bed. She touched Chantal's shoulder, very lightly. "Are you all right?"

Chantal burst into tears. Always a good sign. Parker stroked her hair and murmured words of encouragement. Chantal wiped away her tears with the corner of a sheet. She said, "The people who live upstairs beat their kids."

Parker thought about that for a moment. She said, "I'll look into it, promise."

A team of paramedics squeezed into the room. Willows and Parker pushed their way into the living room to help Sergeant Morris with crowd control.

A few minutes later one of the paramedics tapped Parker on the shoulder. "The girl's in shock; we sedated her." To make it clear, he added, "You're not going to get anything out of her until the morning."

"No problem," said Parker.

At two-twenty that morning, Fire & Rescue No. 19 responded to a "fire on the beach" call from a woman who spotted the blaze from her bathroom window.

No. 19 found a fully engulfed Econoline van parked just above the high-tide line. The burning vehicle's gas tank had exploded a few minutes before they arrived on the scene. A spiralling funnel of greasy black smoke rose out of the shattered driver's-side window, but by the time hoses were run across the beach, there wasn't much left of the van but white-hot metal.

Willows stood upwind of the Econoline's charred remains. Behind him, the city's glow was reflected in the harbour's black calm. High up on the hill above the beach, the bright lights of Jake Cappalletti's Point Grey mini-mansion shone through the rain. The house was about a mile or so away. Much too far for sound to travel. A traffic cop lent him a pair of binoculars. Blue and red and yellow and green lanterns had been strung around the sundeck.

Jake was seriously ill, but there seemed to be a party going on.

Or it might've been a wake.

The Econoline was cherry red, as if it had just been tonged out of a gigantic kiln. The firemen ruthlessly hosed it down, until finally the twisted metal body turned black, and the last wisp of steam was pounded by the rain.

A tangled heap of bones lay on the front seat's coiled steel springs. The skull had rolled onto the floor. Handcuffs dangled from the steering wheel.

Parker let Willows sleep until noon, and then woke him with a kiss. She'd made breakfast – scrambled eggs and bacon, whole-wheat toast smeared with homemade blackberry jam, fresh-squeezed orange juice, and coffee. She set the tray down on the night table beside the bed. Willows blinked the sleep out of his eyes. He spread his arms, and yawned widely. He had a cop's knack for waking up in a hurry. Parker handed him the *Sun*, keeping the *National Post* for herself, because the paper had a vastly superior books and arts section.

Willows thanked her for breakfast. "The kids home?" Parker gave him a look. He smiled. "Just asking."

"Annie and Cindy Palmer went downtown to stroll the malls. Sean took Tripper for a walk around the block; he should be back any minute."

Carolyn Budd had returned Tripper the previous evening. The dog had destroyed a leather jacket and three pairs of expensive Italian shoes Carolyn had bought during a recent vacation in Rome. Worse, Tripper had intimidated her chartered-accountant fiancé. Willows sipped his coffee. It had been years since he'd slept in this late, and he was enjoying himself immensely. Of course, next time he and Parker slept in, it'd be his turn to cook.

He was reading the sports section when the front door banged open. Sean yelled a cheerful hello, and then Tripper came racing up the stairs and down the hall. The dog jumped up on the bed and gave herself a shake.

Willows defended himself with the raised paper. He looked out the bedroom window. Sure enough, it was raining.

"Bad dog!" said Parker sternly, and fed Tripper a rasher of bacon to prove she meant it.

Willows smiled at her, and she smiled nervously back. What now? Something was on her mind. He realized that she wasn't having any coffee, just juice.

She'd stopped drinking coffee quite a while ago, come to think of it.

Alcohol, too.

He said, "Is anything wrong?" He put his cup down and stared levelly at her, waiting.

The seconds ticked past. Finally, Parker blurted out the words that were ceaselessly on her mind. "Jack, I'm pregnant."

"Lucky us," said Willows, enfolding her in his arms.